# A Wartime Wish

*Also by Kitty Danton*

Evie's War
Evie's Allies
Evie's Victory

A Wartime Christmas

# A Wartime Wish

KITTY DANTON

ORION

First published in Great Britain in 2020
by Orion Books,
an imprint of The Orion Publishing Group Ltd
Carmelite House, 50 Victoria Embankment,
London EC4Y 0DZ

An Hachette UK Company

1 3 5 7 9 10 8 6 4 2

A CIP catalogue record for this book
is available from the British Library.

ISBN (Hardback) 978 1 4091 7851 4
ISBN (eBook) 978 1 4091 7853 8

Typeset at The Spartan Press Ltd,
Lymington, Hants

Printed and bound in Great Britain by Clays Ltd,
Elcograf S.p.A.

MIX
Paper from
responsible sources
FSC
www.fsc.org   FSC® C104740

www.orionbooks.co.uk

For Josie and Louis

# Chapter One

The second of January was probably the worst day of the year, thought Sukie Scott as she shook out a slightly frayed duster and then glumly refolded it so that she had a clean bit ready for her next assault against the London dust.

The Christmas and New Year kerfuffle was well and truly over now, and there was nothing to look forward to for a few months other than short and chilly days and little excitement, as nobody had spare cash and there was hardly any tasty food or frivolity in the offing. All the Christmas decorations had been taken down first thing that morning and carefully packed into an array of tea chests. The normally welcoming bar at the hotel seemed depressingly empty and gloomy without the cheery twists of red and green crepe paper, or gaily coloured tinsel.

There was a sharp splatter of wintry rain against the windows. The weather was still bitingly cold, but the festive snow – so pretty as it had blanketed the Covent Garden street outside the Edwardes Hotel in pillowy whiteness over a week ago – was now nothing more than the odd grimy patch of sludgy grey grit.

Sukie smiled as she thought of the fun of the Christmas party. There'd been more than a few hiccups along the way, but the end result had been a triumph, with dancing galore and some happy but very squiffy guests. Sukie had been hoisted on to the stage by her fellow Eddies – as the staff members of the Edwardes Hotel called themselves – to take a bow, as everyone had been so impressed with what she'd been able to do in a short time and on a shoestring budget.

As the memories of the party faded, Sukie felt stiff and distinctly cheerless too. She stretched her neck from side to side and relaxed her shoulders. The ancient central heating clunked from somewhere deep in the basement, and she fancied there was an answering miserable wheeze from the heavy metal radiators ranged underneath the windows. It was as if her blue mood was being echoed by the old hotel.

Sukie glanced into the patterned mirror behind the spirits lined up at the rear of the bar and ran her hand over her hair to settle any strays. She must have been using the duster quite vigorously as her blonde curls had gone skew-whiff. But she had to admit that mirror-Sukie appeared decidedly better than she had six months ago, although she knew she still lacked the sparkle of this time the previous year. Back when Wesley had been a regular visitor to Sukie's reception desk, that was.

Sukie caught her breath as the unbidden memory of Wesley caused a tiny punching sensation just beneath her ribcage. But before she could think of all the what-might-have-beens, there was a dragging sound from the black and white marble tiles out in the corridor. Mr Bright, the manager of the Edwardes Hotel, slowly shuffled his way past the entrance to the bar, tipping a slightly shaky finger to his forehead and then cocking it in her direction by way of greeting, and she smiled warmly back at him.

Mr Bright was more sure-footed than even a week ago, but he still needed his stick. He wasn't well enough to return to work yet, but Sukie didn't think it would be long. She had taken over his duties, and was now temporary manager until Mr Bright was ready to resume his duties.

With a frown, Sukie remembered how gracefully Mr Bright had slid to the ground right at her feet, and the skittering sound his metal-rimmed spectacles made as they scooted across the floor almost to the other side of the foyer.

When Mr Bright demanded his office and his manager's badge

back, as he surely would, Sukie knew that it would mean that she would have to return to her old post on the hotel's reception desk. There were many worse jobs to be had – and of course nobody could complain in these days when everyone knew they must all pull together – but undoubtedly her old duties would feel very tame, for a time at least.

When she first stepped into Mr Bright's office to sit at his desk as emergency cover, it had been with an understandable tremor of trepidation. But Sukie had been determined to rise to the challenge, even though the step-up from receptionist to hotel manager was a big one.

It hadn't been easy, either, as the ledgers revealed the Eddy was hardly breaking even and in fact was in real danger of going to the wall, as so many other mid-range London hotels had already.

The problem, Sukie could see, was that pre-war it had been events and functions designed for nothing more than pure entertainment – wedding receptions, debutante coming-out parties and the like – that had driven a hefty chunk of the Eddy's profits.

But with war had come the loss of this 'frivolous' income. And it was easy to see why so many hotels had been unable to claw back turnover from elsewhere, for the government had capped meal charges and room rates had to remain competitive.

Sukie's solution had been to throw herself into organising the lively charitable fundraiser of a Christmas party and then a smaller, select dinner-dance to see in the New Year. The events had been well supported and – best of all – nicely profitable.

Sukie knew that others in her position would be feeling very proud at what they had achieved in such a short time. She felt instead that she could – and should – have done more.

Sukie gave up on the needless dusting, and instead stared at the framed photograph of Wesley's bench that had been placed among the bottles near the mirror.

Between Christmas and New Year a commemorative wooden bench and brass plaque had been placed in a beautiful spot high on a hill-top near his hometown of Bristol to honour his life.

Sukie's new pal Tracey Benn had organised a local photographer to take a picture of the bench, and then in a private moment, on the stroke of midnight, she presented two framed copies to Sukie just as everyone in the upstairs function room belted out 'Auld Lang Syne' to mark the end of 1943.

The timing of her friend's gesture was all the more poignant for Sukie as New Year's Eve meant it was two years to the day that she had very first set eyes on Wesley.

Back then, Evie, who was Pattie's sister and Sukie's favourite person in the world, had been struck down by influenza when she was in the middle of arranging a New Year's Eve dance in the village hall in Lymbridge, high on the West Country's Dartmoor tors where they had both grown up.

Sukie had had to step in to make sure the dance would happen. She'd booked a highly recommended swing band from Bristol, never thinking for a moment the members of the band would all turn out to be *black*.

Sukie and Wesley – the singer – had fallen for each other at first glance. In her eyes Wesley was, quite simply, the cat's pyjamas. When he suggested they become engaged, she hadn't hesitated. Not long after, they celebrated their first Christmas together at Lymbridge's only public house, the Haywain, endlessly bumping into each other accidentally-on-purpose beneath the mistletoe...

A few weeks later they'd moved to London and Sukie had become an Eddy, working as a receptionist at the hotel, while Wesley eked out what he could as a singer in the West End dancehalls.

Recently Sukie had thought that if she and Wesley had known how little time they had left together, they might have used it differently, making sure every second they spent with each other was special.

But neither of them could have foreseen the freak bomb that tumbled through the sky one sunny Saturday afternoon. Wesley had been killed outright.

Tracey Benn's unexpected gift of the photographs of Wesley's commemorative bench clutched right to Sukie's very core. She felt different afterwards.

And so, that morning, the first thing Sukie did on waking was to remove the engagement ring Wesley had given her from its delicate gold chain around her neck. In his memory, Sukie made a solemn New Year's vow: to look forward, and not back.

As the dawn lightened she had carefully wrapped the chain and the engagement ring in Wesley's hanky, and then kissed the soft folds of the linen, before she slid the precious bundle into her own handkerchief case, along with all the hopes and desires she had held for her and Wesley.

Wesley wouldn't have wanted it any other way. He would have urged her to live life to the full without him, as the slipping of the ring into the folds of the embroidered case seemed to whisper to Sukie, and her heart pumped an urgent beat of love in answer.

She wished that wherever Wesley's spirit was, he knew how much she had loved him.

Since Wesley's death, Sukie had surrounded herself with a new 'family', although it was one that she hadn't recognised as such at first.

In fact, it had only been as she stood on stage at the close of the party on the Friday before Christmas, with the Eddies and Tracey Benn smiling up at her, that it dawned on her that these people cared for her and she them, and in many ways, wasn't that the very essence of the word 'family'?

This raggle-taggle group of people before her wasn't the same, naturally, as the family Sukie had been hoping to share with Wesley, and it didn't come near to the closeness she had with her best friend Evie, safe in the Devon village of Lymbridge. But it was pretty darn good nonetheless.

Sukie wasn't sure whether she wanted to smile or cry as she stood in the bar with her duster still in her hand and pondered all of this, with the photograph of Wesley's bench at her elbow and an empty spot on her chest under her blouse where the engagement ring had previously nestled.

'Give over,' Sukie muttered to herself. 'This isn't going to get the old woman her ninepence.'

Polly, the hotel's parrot, who was deep in a doze on his perch near the window, opened first one eye at the sound of her voice, and then the other, to peer at Sukie.

He fluffed his feathers with a serious expression, before enquiring in a grave manner, 'Where's the rum?'

'No rum today, Polly. It all's been drunk,' Sukie told him.

'Rum!' His claw rose as if in plea.

Sukie didn't think that Polly had ever been allowed to drink rum, but he had clearly once been owned by someone very fond of it. His past was mostly a mystery but he had spent time in a lively dockland public house, that much Sukie knew, although his swearing had proved too much even for the dockers. Fortunately, he was less potty-mouthed now, and he had quickly become a great favourite with the Eddy's patrons.

Sukie crossed to the no-smoking part of the bar (another of her ideas, and one that had proved popular), and she scratched Polly on his chin just below his beak where she knew he liked it.

'Maybe rum tomorrow,' she said quietly.

Polly closed his eyes.

Sukie kept on tickling him, as each time she went to move away he twitched his claw in a silent appeal for her to carry on.

It wasn't long before Polly's head was tipped back as far as it would go and he'd allowed his wings to fan down towards the carpet, and at the comical sight of the parrot's abandonment, Sukie began to feel more cheerful.

'You'll get that bird into bad ways.'

Sukie jumped even though she knew that it was time for John's lunchtime shift in the bar.

'It's more he who'll be getting *me* into bad ways.' Sukie grinned. 'He makes that rum sound very tempting.'

She gave Polly's feathers on top of his head, and on his chin, a smooth. Then, ignoring his raised claw, she went to sit on one of the high stools at the bar and watched as John began to count the clean glasses.

After a minute or two of companionable silence, John nodded towards a bottle of rum.

'You're still in my bad books, you know,' Sukie couldn't resist saying.

John didn't reply, and instead he made a show of checking there was ice in the bucket.

Once he was certain Sukie wasn't going to remind them both why she was peeved with him, John poured a measure of rum into a small glass, which he placed in front of her. 'Call it a perk, for polishing the bar.'

Sukie stared at the drink, and then with a 'what the devil' shrug she picked it up.

It tasted warm, strong and most definitely fortifying.

A man and a woman came in, and with a minimum of fuss John served them a Mackeson stout and a weak port and lemon, and they went and sat down close to Polly, who dipped his head to catch their attention. He knew that if he did that at just the right moment, he might get a peanut as reward.

'So,' John said, rearranging the bar equipment to get every-thing just so. 'How's Pattie?'

'Ah, now I see what the rum is in aid of,' Sukie replied with a smile.

John gave her a rueful glance. 'You're not taking sides, are you?'

'Sides? Pattie's my best friend, John, and we share a room, don't forget.' She glanced at the couple, hoping that they weren't eavesdropping on the conversation but they were entranced by Polly's antics. 'Your eye's looking better,' she observed, with a small nod towards the bruise.

John automatically raised a hand to his shiner, which was now fading to a grubby-looking yellow from the deep purple and black. He'd received it when Sukie and Pattie had come across him kissing another woman at the Christmas party. In fact, it could have been more than a kiss, given the way they

7

had hurriedly adjusted their clothes when they had been caught. Pattie had proved to have quite a punch in her right arm.

Still, morals of an alley cat or not, John was always affable and good for a word or two, and so although she prided herself on being a loyal pal to Pattie – Sukie knew that Evie would have her guts for garters if she didn't keep a weather eye on her younger sister – she decided she needed a word with a friendly face more than she wanted to let John know that he wasn't out of the doghouse just yet. John and Pattie had walked out, without ever quite making it official, on and off for a couple of years now, and until the Christmas party Sukie had thought it was slowly edging towards something more serious, at least as far as Pattie was concerned.

John lifted a sparkling clean sherry schooner up to the light, and then, although it didn't need it, he polished the glass anyway with a pristine tea towel before placing it back where he had picked it up. 'She's still not speaking to me. It's as if I've never existed.'

'I thought as much,' said Sukie. 'She's not said anything to me either, other than briefly on the morning after the Christmas party, and that was only to use a few choice Anglo-Saxon words about you and what you'd probably been up to. I keep giving her the opportunity to say something else, and she keeps changing the subject as if it doesn't matter to her, although I think it does.'

'I've apologised until I'm blue in the face,' John said. 'Or at least I would do, if Pattie would let me. I've promised too it shall never happen again, but the sneer she gave me put paid to me saying anything else. I'm hoping that if I keep my head down and behave myself, she might come around.' Then John leaned towards Sukie, and whispered, 'Between you and me, I've written her a letter, and I've just nipped up to push it under her bedroom door.'

'Well, that *might* work, I suppose,' agreed Sukie slowly, 'although it probably wasn't very sensible of you to chance Pattie finding you walking down the corridor to the women's floor, as she might think that you being so close to all those ladies could actually give you lustful ideas.'

With a little pang Sukie realised lustful thoughts felt a thing of the past for her. Since losing Wesley she hadn't experienced even the vaguest of stirrings towards the opposite sex. She had twice rather enjoyed foxtrotting in a very innocent manner with Simon, a handsome, debonair man Tracey Benn had rustled up to whisk Sukie around a dance floor, but Sukie hadn't felt even a flicker of excitement.

Still, she understood that in uncertain times, many took their comfort where they found it. In John's case, Sukie thought ruefully, he had found his comfort on a shabby old sofa – nick-named the Staff Room – by the back stairs. Pattie had been simply livid.

John and Sukie looked at each other, and then they made comedy grimaces at the other as they thought about Pattie. They said in unison, 'It's probably best not to bank on a letter working.'

All of them went back a long way, as Sukie and Pattie had grown up together in Lymbridge, where Evie had now set up home with husband Peter and baby Nellie. For quite a while John had worked in the local pub, the Haywain, after being invalided out of the Merchant Navy when his ship had been torpedoed, an incident during which he had sustained a shoulder injury that never fully seemed to heal.

These days John worked on one of the river ambulances on the Thames, and divided his time on the water with regular stints at the Eddy when he would man the bar or sometimes take over as maître d' in the hotel's restaurant.

'Have you been up to much?' she asked John. Her voice was more professional now, and so John knew she was talking about his work on the river.

'We've been restocking the ambulances,' he said in a low voice so that the couple he'd just served wouldn't hear. 'It looks as if an offensive from Jerry is coming, it's been said to us from above, and so we've been stockpiling supplies, just in case. It's under lock and key close to the docks, but clearly somebody thinks we've got another blitz coming, and likely very soon. And everybody has been warned there may be double shifts.'

If there was renewed bombing then Sukie knew the river ambulances would be very busy.

'Yes,' said Sukie, as John paused. 'I'd love to disagree but sadly I've had a similar thing told to me by one of the guests who is over at the War Office, and he suggested we check we have emergency bandages and aspirin and torches and so forth. I do hope he's wrong. What happened at the Capel was bad enough, wasn't it?'

The Capel was a hotel just a little further down the street. It had lost its roof to a bomb several months earlier, blasted beams still pointing skywards.

The pair of them shook their heads mournfully, but only a little as it was inevitable that now it was the fifth year of hostilities everyone had become quite hardened to the process of their country being at war. Everyone seemed much more pragmatic these days than they had been four and a bit years earlier when war had been declared.

Sukie pushed her empty glass towards John for him to wash. 'It's time for me to get back to work.'

Pattie chose that moment to march into the bar through a small side door the staff used. Sukie noticed her very determinedly not look towards John as she headed over to Sukie.

John plastered a welcoming look on his face as he tried to catch Pattie's eye. It was to no avail.

'Miss Scott, Housekeeping needs to see you, if you don't mind. Apparently we have a problem with vermin,' Pattie said, keeping her eyes on Sukie.

It was hotel policy that in public areas Miss, Mrs or Mr was always used with the surname of the staff member who was being talked to.

Pattie had excellent comic timing, as after exactly the right number of beats Pattie made Sukie chuckle when she added quietly but pointedly, 'I see the problem with vermin has spread from beyond the lower levels.'

Sukie slid off the high stool, hoping that John hadn't seen her smile.

Meanwhile Pattie's shoulders were proud and determined as she paraded out of the bar, her lively step purely for John's benefit, designed to remind him what he was missing.

Pattie obviously wasn't softening towards John just yet.

# Chapter Two

It was a day for personal letters, as Sukie discovered when she got back to her office. The second post had brought her a message from Dartmoor.

*Dearest Sukie,*

*Happy New Year to you from all of us in dull old Lymbridge! Peter and the baby send their love, as do Mother (she's going to write a note too that will go in with this letter, as long as I remember to put it in as my mind is like a sieve these days) and Father, and everybody else.*

*Life goes on here exactly as usual, I think, which means – as you will know – that not very much out of the ordinary is happening at all! And everything feels very flat and boring after the 'excitement' of going to the Haywain for a nip to toast the New Year in while Nellie was over at Bluebells, making sure that Ma and Pa were on their toes as she bawled her head off from the moment we dropped her off until we came to collect her. I don't think they'll be offering to babysit again any time soon.*

*So that's our news in a nutshell. Have you fainted in excitement?! Thought so!*

*And meanwhile Pattie tells us that you are quite the star Eddy at the moment, and that the Christmas party you organised was pure heaven, and very well supported, as I'm sure the New Year's shindig was also. Did you make a wish come New Year? I did, and you can probably guess what it was.*

*I know it will have been a time of both happy and sad memories for you, and so I have been thinking very often of you, and of dear Wesley too.*

*I'm going to write you a longer letter about this soon, as I've probably got about five minutes right now to get something down on paper before Nellie wants feeding again – she's hungry ALL the time, which Mother says I was too – and meanwhile the moment I don't have Nellie on my lap, Keith jumps up and purrs for England!*

*Anyway, two things: first, can you keep a special eye on Pattie at the moment? She's not gone into detail over what she and John have had a spat about, but I can't help worrying that she doesn't seem 100 per cent. She <u>seems</u> cheerful enough in her letters, but I sense that something about her is off.*

*And secondly, Mr Smith is saying that if you can get a couple of days off work, the next time that he has to drive back from London, he'd be very happy to bring you back to stay with us for a breather to freshen you up. You've been working <u>so</u> hard, it would be beyond lovely to see you, a real treat for us in fact!*

*Oh no – I must dash as Nellie is making that 'I need a clean nappy' cry, which sounds like nothing else and is absolutely NOT one of my favourites from her rather extensive collection of wails. Keith is unimpressed, as you can imagine, and so has just dug her claws into my thigh . . .*

*Sending fondest love, and please, <u>please</u> come and see us! Soon!!*

*Your friend for ever and ever, Evie xxx*

Sukie smiled as she read Evie's letter, which was without the promised note from Evie's mother Susan, and with Evie's penmanship degenerating into such a hurried habble-dabble scrawl by the end that Sukie found it almost impossible to decipher. She didn't expect that the second, longer letter Evie promised her would ever arrive, or Susan's note (which was bound to be folded in Evie's pocket or handbag, waiting to be sent) – Evie was full of good intentions, but she was very busy as well as forgetful through the demands of her new baby.

It was all so very Evie, and Sukie could vividly imagine the crying tot and the miffed tabby cat (which, despite her boyish name, was definitely a she).

Sukie realised she was missing her dear pal very badly, although she couldn't actually guess what Evie would have wished for.

On the one hand Sukie knew that Evie would love to have a little brother or sister for Nellie, and so that might have been her wish. But she knew too that Evie always tried very hard to do the right thing, and it was very possible therefore that she had wished for the war to end, or for all of her friends and family to make it through to the end unscathed.

Sukie promised herself that she would try to pay Lymbridge and Evie a visit before the summer. She felt a huge yearning just, for a few days, to be a carefree young woman in her early twenties, with all the old-fashioned simple and light-hearted thoughts of being that age, and none of the current upsetting worries that seemed to always be lurking at the back of her mind that a bomb could land on the Eddy at any moment and then it could all be over for all of them in an instant. A random bomb had led to Wesley's death, after all, and so these were far from irrational nagging fears, Sukie knew.

A few days on the stunning heather-covered tors of Dartmoor, where she could breathe in the clean country air and forget about the war for an hour or two, and have some belly laughs with her best friend, was an intoxicating thought.

Still, there were things she needed to do before she could get on to that.

Sukie sighed, and then to prevent her mood sliding further downwards, she headed to the kitchen to ask some advice from Mrs Bridge about something she couldn't make up her mind about. A chat, and often a cup of tea, with 'Housekeeping' – as most of the Eddies called her – was always cheering.

'Would you say Twelfth Night falls on the fifth or the sixth of January, Mrs Bridge?' Sukie asked a minute later.

'Whatever do you want to know that for?' said Mrs Bridge a trifle sharply. Wrestling the chambermaids' shift rota into some sort of order always put her into a bad mood, particularly as she was a couple of members of staff short.

'I've been wondering whether we could use any old customs to mark Twelfth Night as a way of generating a little extra business. There's wassailing, of course, which is popular in the West Country. But I think that us going up and down the street and knocking on people's doors isn't going to go down well in the blackout – it was fun when we did it in Devon, but here I'm not so sure,' Sukie said. 'At the Theatre Royal in Drury Lane they have a Twelfth Night cake and punch. I thought perhaps we could draw inspiration from that and in a small way kick off our own tradition, perhaps cake and punch upstairs in the bar at five o'clock, and everyone who wants to can write on a piece of paper something nasty that happened to them from the previous year that can be burned to say good riddance to bad rubbish, and then they can make a private wish for something nice they hope for. I think everyone has hopes and desires, but I wonder with all this scrimping and saving and making do – which is wearing us all down – we're not putting enough thought into thinking what we really want. I'm sure Mr Bright would say he's wishing he feels much better soon, but probably what he is really wishing for is full occupancy of the Eddy. And maybe you are wishing for another polka with Chef at the next hotel staff shindig—'

'Sukie!' Mrs Bridge's voice had more than a dash of squeal to it, and the playful nudge she gave Sukie was quite firm. Chef and the housekeeper's energetic dancing had been the talk of the Staff Room after the Christmas party.

Then, conspiratorially, they both looked around to check Chef hadn't overheard.

He was busy at the far end of the kitchen, holding a plucked chicken up in the air as, with a very serious expression on his face, he peered into its nether regions.

Neither Sukie nor Mrs Bridge knew quite what Chef was doing but he seemed puzzled and therefore decidedly comical. They looked away, and when they sneaked a second peek, he still looked confused and the epitome of someone who was never likely to enjoy a rousing quickstep or waltz, which made Sukie and Mrs Bridge laugh, as few who had seen his dance-floor antics of a few days earlier would ever forget them.

'And what about you, young lady?' said Mrs Bridge as she dabbed beneath her eye. 'What will you wish for?'

'Hmmm, I'm not sure yet,' said Sukie. 'Well, the war to end, of course. And Pattie to forgive John, or if she can't do that, to find a nice young man as she is definitely quite scratchy these days if she's tired, and I think she's the sort of woman who is happier if she has a beau in tow. I expect I'll think of something to wish for by Twelfth Night, although these days I'm not sure I wish for very much, actually. It will be easier, though, to think of all the nasty things that should be burned as bad rubbish. I expect everyone will feel a bit like that.'

'In that case we'd better have a bucket of water and some sand on standby,' said Mrs Bridge, 'just in case the bad rubbish amounts to rather a lot, and we get an inferno going. That would definitely play havoc with Mr Bright's wish for full occupancy of the Eddy.'

'You might have a point,' a poker-faced Sukie agreed.

They discussed which day they should claim for Twelfth

Night, which was actually trickier than it might seem at first glance, as Sukie had discovered that according to different traditions around the world either January the fifth or the sixth was said to be the day.

Pragmatism won – Sukie was using the date purely as a way of driving business through the bar – and after discussing the pros and cons of the different days, they decided Sukie should hold the ceremony on the sixth as that was a Thursday and therefore just a little bit nearer the weekend, and that meant if some of their patrons who were working nine-to-five had a snifter or three, it wouldn't be too long before the weekend when they could recuperate.

Sukie had been in her office just long enough for her to finish a cup of tea she had brought up from the kitchen, even though she had just had one when down in the kitchen with Housekeeping – a rare feat, as usually the moment Sukie had a hot drink before her, someone would arrive to announce she was needed elsewhere *immediately* – when Pattie came in and firmly thrust John's letter at her.

'The cheek! The damn cheek of the man,' hissed Pattie. Her eyes looked unnaturally bright and there was a flush of crimson at Pattie's neckline. 'And I suppose he ran up to the room to put it under our door himself. Probably on the way back down from one of the chambermaids' rooms, if I know him.'

'May I read his letter, Pattie, dear?' asked Sukie. She felt conflicted at prying, but only a little bit, her nosiness having won out easily over the desire to behave in a proper manner. She didn't make a habit of reading other people's private correspondence, but this time she was curious.

Pattie didn't reply, and so Sukie took that as a yes.

John's hand was surprisingly neat. Sukie had assumed that his penmanship would have been poor, but John's careful writing looked to be from a more educated man than she had given him credit for, and Sukie found she felt a bit bad about her previous casual assumption.

*My darling,*

*Words cannot express my feelings right now. You did not deserve my behaviour at the party, my dear Pattie, and if I could turn the clock back, I would. I do not quite know how it all came to be, but it was my mistake – and by that I mean it was a big mistake, in fact the BIGGEST mistake of my life if it means that I end up losing you. I hadn't realised before, and I have never told you this, but I love you, and I would like to spend the rest of my life with you. I knew that the moment you saw me at the Staff Room, and I saw your face looking down at me in fury, and the thought that maybe I had lost you was unbearable. Is there any chance you could forgive me? If so, could we get married? As I say, I am very sorry. I think it might have happened because you and me never get to spend 'alone' time together – you know what I mean, I'm sure, and if you don't, then I am happy to discuss this further with you! – and I have feelings that are strong. If we are married then we could have alone time every night of the week if we want, and each morning too if we fancied, which I am sure you would like too. Might I have another chance?*

> *Your ever loving friend,*
> *John*

Sukie and Pattie looked at each other for a long moment, and then Pattie said, 'I think his words perfectly expressed his feelings, so I don't know why he assumed they mightn't.' She bit her lip, and then with a clear twinkle in her eye, Pattie added, 'The dirty old goat.'

Sukie felt a giggle gurgling upwards. 'I've never heard it described as "alone time" before...'

They looked at each other again, and then burst out laughing.

It went on for a while, as when they would start to become serious, one or other of them would say 'alone time' again in sillier and sillier voices, or in the voices of either Mr Bright or Mrs Bridge, and then this would set the other off once more.

The situation was made worse when Mr Bright walked in as they were mid-laugh to say, 'Miss Scott, I wonder if I may get a moment alone with you.'

At this word 'alone' Sukie had to bite down on her tongue very firmly and then sniff and clear her throat more loudly than was polite, while Pattie faked a coughing fit and then managed to squeak out that she had better go to the ladies' room to sort herself out.

Mr Bright looked quickly in befuddlement from Sukie to Pattie and back again as he tried to work out if he had said something he shouldn't, and then, clearly deciding retreat was his safest option, he said, 'My mistake, ladies. I meant to go to speak to Housekeeping.'

Pattie was just on her way out of the door at the time, and she turned to mouth dramatically at Sukie, 'Mistake!' in another silent tribute to John's letter.

And at the sight of Pattie's face peering over Mr Bright's shoulder as she did this, Sukie had to employ every trick in the book not to bark out loud with merriment. It was likely to be some time before 'alone' or 'mistake' lost their power over her funny bone.

# Chapter Three

'Pattie, do you fancy seeing what's on at the pictures this afternoon?' Sukie asked the next morning. It was rare that she and Pattie had the same afternoon off, and she wanted to make the most of it, as well as ensuring that she kept an eye on Pattie, as Evie had requested.

'Hmmm, Miss Scott. Don't mind if I do,' Pattie replied quite cheerfully, and Polly, who was perched on the back of Pattie's chair in reception, echoed, 'Mind if I do'.

After a lot of toing and froing between whether to go for a 'Road to ...' film, if they could find one (Sukie's idea, in large part as she wanted to keep Pattie's current cheery mood buoyed up as she had been down in the dumps the last few weeks, although what she actually said to her chum was that she'd missed *Road to Morocco* when it had first come out, and wasn't Dorothy Lamour fabulous?), or a weepie (Pattie's preferred option in order that they could have 'a bit of a blub, and who doesn't like that?'), they ended up plumping for the comedy *Dear Octopus* as however hard they scoured the Entertainments page of the paper, they couldn't find any of the Bob Hope and Bing Crosby films, or a weepie Pattie hadn't seen.

Pattie assured Sukie that *Dear Octopus* was 'a must', as one of the cast, Michael Wilding, was set to be the next big thing, according to *Picturegoer*. Sukie rarely had time for magazines and so she had no idea who Michael Wilding was, but she was prepared to be convinced as Pattie was obviously keen on seeing him, a clue being that Pattie kept saying, 'I hear tell that he's simply the bee's knees.'

However, when they got to the Leicester Square Theatre, they discovered that *Dear Octopus* wasn't on. This was because one of the film reels had been damaged a day or two earlier by burning through under the bright light of the projector, and the cinema house was waiting for them to be replaced as too big a section had been lost for them to splice the reel together again without garnering complaints, since the burn had happened at a crucial moment, the chatty ticket seller told them.

Instead the cinema was offering a re-run of the popular romantic drama *Mrs Miniver*, and although both Pattie and Sukie had already both seen it, they decided that having walked up through Covent Garden to the picture house on a chill after-noon, then they might as well go in and watch something, and this was a very good flick that was certainly worthy of a second viewing.

They sat through what felt like an unnecessarily lengthy run of news shorts, and although she felt a bit bored, Sukie couldn't help but notice how intently nearly all of the audience watched the film reels of British offensives from all around the globe. What was being described by the male voice-overs – who were all very posh-sounding as they filled in what was happening while cameras scanned troops lined up in sunny places, or panned across various disembarkations, or showed how some troops were celebrating Christmas, even if they were in the midst of a desert – all seemed very gung-ho and as if the British forces were having it very much their own way. While of course she hoped things were going well for 'Our Brave Men' abroad, Sukie couldn't help feeling a little cynical as she watched the flickering black and white images on the screen. To her it all seemed very partisan and as if the War Office had insisted that the news companies skewed the news given to the general public to keep up morale at home. She wondered if ordinary German folk were being shown similar newsreels in their cinemas in Germany, only this time showing newsreels that suggested the German military was poised for victory.

Pattie seemed to feel similarly restless, and so soon they fell into a whispered consideration of which smoker in front of them could get the highest curl of smoke from their cigarette, as the smoke was obviously rising before the flickering screen in front of them. It was vaguely amusing for a while, but they had just become tired of watching the smoky twirls when there was a propaganda film about careless talk costing lives, and then a short drama about nothing very much at all other than a lot of women in pinnies talking about eking food rations out, Sukie and Pattie agreed, followed by an intermission.

'Thank goodness for that,' said Pattie a trifle petulantly. 'I do wonder why we go to the whole thing. At least we'll have the film we actually came to see next – when John and I last went to the flicks we had to sit through a really dreary B movie that also managed to bang on about the war. I know we need to know what our boys are doing overseas, and that we must all pull together and not eat too much, but you and I are young still, and we have been up to our ears in this sort of thing for what feels like for ever, and I don't think it's a crime to wish for a bit of fun now and again.'

'I know what you mean,' said Sukie. There was a pause, and then she added diplomatically that she supposed that the news shorts and all the rest were just designed to appeal to as many people as possible with the aim of keeping spirits up, and not to stop anyone having fun.

'I suppose,' said Pattie. 'But it's all so damn dull and it's all the same. What I wouldn't give for a bit of excitement.'

They looked around the cinema. With the lights turned up for the intermission, it looked shabby, and on the grubby side of sorry for itself.

'As I said,' Pattie muttered, 'what I wouldn't give for a bit of—'

'Excitement,' Sukie cut in, and Pattie laughed as Sukie knew she would.

A few minutes later Sukie was on her way back from the conveniences and was just picking her way down the row of seats towards Pattie, trying very hard not to step on anybody's toes, when she heard a child's voice say excitedly from somewhere nearby, 'This seat, Daddy. *This* seat. This one!'

She looked up to see a middle-aged man and a small child sorting themselves out as they made to sit down directly in front of Sukie and Pattie. As she sank into her seat Sukie had to apologise hastily to the man beside her whose foot she had just managed to stand on.

'If you are a very good girl, I shall be very proud of you,' said the man in the seat in front as he removed his Homburg hat. He had a kind voice, Sukie thought, as he added gently, 'You know you've got to be very grown-up for the next hour or two, and you mustn't talk and ask questions when the lights go down and it gets dark, don't you?'

'I *am* a good girl,' his daughter replied, very firmly, 'and I didn't want to see boring *Fantasia* again. I wanted to see *this* film.' Then she added, loudly, 'I am going to be QUIET AS A MOUSE, just you see, Daddy!'

'That's the ticket,' he told her. 'But can you be a little mouse with a pink nose and very long whiskers and a brown coat, and a mouse who also has a very bad cold and sore throat, and *who has completely lost her voice?*'

The little girl thought about this for a moment, then she looked up at her father and silently she mimed preening her whiskers.

Pattie nudged Sukie, and nodded towards the little girl, who was now arranging her coat and mittens just so on the seat beside her. She wrapped her scarf more tightly around her neck as she whispered, 'Mousie is wearing her scarf to help with the sore throat,' and the man smiled back at Mousie.

'How sweet,' Pattie whispered, and Sukie nodded in agreement.

All was well until towards the end of *Mrs Miniver*, and then out of the blue the little girl, who really had been very good up until then, began to sob uncontrollably and quite noisily just as on screen the congregation in the church began to sing 'Onward, Christian Soldiers'.

And then, to Sukie's astonishment, Pattie began to cry too.

Pattie didn't have a hanky with her – she hardly ever did as she wasn't the sort of person to think ahead, but luckily Sukie was able to find a neatly folded one in the pocket of her ancient but still serviceable coat, and she handed it to Pattie.

Sukie noticed that the man in front of her was searching in vain through his own pockets, and then his coat and the child's coat, presumably looking for a hanky for the girl who was hic-cupping between sobs.

Sukie had a rummage in her own handbag, and found a second handkerchief. She leaned forward and tapped the man on the shoulder, saying quietly, 'Excuse me, might this help you?' as she waved it at him.

'Thank you!' he whispered back, and a moment later the small girl was blowing her nose noisily into the scrap of cotton.

'Isn't he distinguished?' Pattie hissed into Sukie's ear when the lights went up, making it clear she was speaking about the man in front of them. 'Just look at that suit! I do like a man who is well turned out.'

'Shh,' Sukie replied, giving her friend a teasing nudge with her elbow. But Pattie was right – the man was striking. He appeared to be well into his forties, to judge from his dark hair with a steely glint of grey at his temples, but the skin around his eyes and mouth were pleasantly crinkled with laughter lines. The girl was clearly closely related to him if the aquiline outline of both of their noses and the cast of their hazel eyes were anything to go by.

'Thank you so much,' the man said, turning around. 'You got me out of a deep hole there. I've hankies galore in my other coat's pocket, although obviously not in this one, and we thought we'd see a musical but then when we got here Dot wanted to see *Mrs Miniver*...'

'It was the last film Mummy saw before she went away,' Dot interrupted, her small chin thrust out defiantly. 'She was very poorly, and then she went into hospital and then she never came out again.'

Dot looked at Pattie and Sukie as if expecting a reaction.

'Oh!' said Pattie, touching a knuckle to her mouth.

'Mummy told me this was her favourite film, and that one day I could see it with her. But then she died.' Dot's voice was sad.

Tenderly Dot's father put his hand on his daughter's shoulder. 'Yes, she did. Come on, poppet, let me help you with your coat and mittens, Dot.'

Sukie noticed Pattie nodding with approval at the way the man didn't try to divert Dot from talking about her mother.

The mittens ended up at Pattie's feet as the coat was wriggled into. Pattie bent down and picked them up, passing them across the back of Dot's seat. 'And how old are you, Dot? Or should I call you Mousie? You were an excellent mouse and for a very long time too.'

'I'm five, and my mummy would have been twenty-nine,' Dot replied proudly. Then she looked at her father to check she had her mother's age correct, at which her father dipped his head to let her know she was right. Then Dot said, 'And I have twin brothers who are four. I'll be six on my next birthday, and they will be five. And you can call me Dot.'

'Goodness, there are three of you. That's a handful for your daddy, I bet,' said Pattie, with a quick smile at him, before looking back at Dot again. 'But I expect that you are a wonderful big sister to your little brothers.'

'Dot most certainly is the very best big sister anyone could have,' said the man proudly as he tucked the velvet collar of his daughter's coat down at the back from where it had been standing up. 'The twins are with their aunt just now, so that Dot and I could have an outing, just the two of us, as that is what very good big sisters deserve. But if I'd remembered what the last song was, I'd have taken her somewhere else. We sang it at Miriam's funeral, you see, and that was only at Easter. Dot must have heard me talking about the film, which is why she wanted to come in when the lady in the ticket kiosk told us what was on, and I suppose she remembered the song from the funeral. It might not have been a very good idea for me to allow this, but I was rather caught on the hop.'

Sukie couldn't think of anything at all to say. This was very unlike her but the word 'funeral' unexpectedly looming into the conversation had instantly deluged her with overwhelming memories of Wesley's passing.

Luckily Pattie stepped into the breach. She leaned over and stroked Dot gently on the cheek, looking her directly in the eye as she said softly, 'Well, that funeral must have been a very difficult day for you and everyone else in your family, Dot. But just think that every time you hear that song as you grow up you'll be able to remember what a wonderful mummy you had, and what a good daddy you still have, and what lovely twin brothers you have too. I'm sure Mummy is very proud of you wherever she is now – I know that I would be if I had a little girl just like you. I've been feeling a bit blue lately, although about something much less important than losing a mummy, and I cried too exactly when you did, and so I think it must be a *very* sad moment in the film.'

The man cleared his throat in the way that men do when they are trying not to show too much emotion, and then he said briskly, 'Now, Dot, we mustn't keep these kind ladies from going about their business, and so let's get those mittens on, and then we'll see if we can find a cocoa somewhere.'

Pattie mentioned there was a small family-run cafe on Long Acre where she thought the Very Best Cocoa in London would still be being served as the cafe stayed open until quite late at night. 'We can show you where it is, as we have to go back that way,' she added helpfully.

And so the four of them found themselves walking through Leicester Square together and past the Underground station, with Sukie gradually feeling calmer after the surge of emotion to do with the thought of funerals and the consequent jolt of sorrow over the loss of Wesley.

The man introduced himself as Mr Jones, to which Pattie replied that she was Miss Yeo, and Sukie was Miss Scott, but that he and Dot could call them Pattie and Sukie, to which the man said that his Christian name was William.

'Are you sisters?' asked Dot.

'No, we're old friends, but you are very observant, Dot, as we are just as close as real sisters would be,' said Sukie.

'Sukie and I came to London together from the country, and now we share a bedroom and work together at a hotel not far away called the Edwardes. And we grew up together, and when I was your age, Dot, I couldn't wait to see Sukie. But she was a little older and best friends with my big sister, and so sometimes they were meanies and wouldn't let me play with them,' Pattie told Dot, with a glance at Sukie. 'But that's a long time ago, and now we are very good friends indeed, and' – Pattie nudged Sukie at this point, who was remembering with regret how she and Evie had indeed not always been very nice to Pattie when she was tiny – 'we hardly bicker at all.'

Sukie hoped this would continue to be the case.

By the time they had reached the cafe, Dot had told Pattie and Sukie all about her friends, and what their names were and what their favourite games were.

After thanking them very much for their kindness, William escorted his daughter inside the cafe. Pattie and Sukie waited for a moment and waved goodbye through the window as William and Dot took their seats, before lifting their own hands in farewell.

As they turned away Sukie slid her arm through Pattie's. 'Shall we go to the pub?' she asked.

'The Hercules?' Pattie suggested.

'The Hercules,' Sukie agreed, and they made their way to the Hercules Pillars in Great Queen Street. As usual the Hercules was bustling, fit to burst with its clientele of theatre- and cinema-goers, but the two friends were able to find a small table that was free, tucked away into a corner, on which they placed the two lemonades that Sukie had stood them.

'What a dear little girl, and such a nice man,' said Pattie. 'And before I forget, here's your hanky back.' Pattie reached into her pocket but when she looked at the crumpled mess of cotton she had pulled out, she added, 'On second thoughts I'll give it a launder first. I think I might not have been sleeping too well this last week or two, and it all felt a bit too much when they started singing.'

'I suppose that is the mark of a good drama – it's someone else's story you're watching but somehow it also feels as if it speaking about something to do with you.' Sukie smiled as she spoke to make sure that Pattie knew she wasn't criticising her in any way, and then she took the plunge. 'How are you finding it with you and John, now that the dust has had time to settle at least a little bit, and he's written you that letter?'

'Well, that letter was irritating to say the least. And I'll give him "alone time" and "big mistake". It won't be a surprise to you that every time I set eyes on him, I want to lamp him one, if you really want to know,' said Pattie. There was no smile on her face or in her eyes. Pattie sighed, and then added, 'And then a minute later I'm determined not to give him a moment where he can see that I'm not holding my head high and proud, as I want him to think that what he did wasn't of the slightest importance to me.'

'I think his black eye told everyone that that wasn't quite the case!'

Pattie sniffed agreement, and then admitted, 'I told everyone that a cork had come out of a bottle of fizz too quickly and caught him on the eye, and I know that nobody will have dared asked him about it to his face.'

Sukie thought that while it was true that probably not a single Eddy would have spoken directly to John about the fumbled goings-on on the Staff Room at the Christmas party – they were all far too polite for that, well, other than she and Mrs Bridge, of course, as they had dared to raise the knotty issue – it was probably wise not to remind Pattie that she had yelled very loudly exactly what she thought about John and his unnecessarily frisky behaviour right to his face. She had described too precisely what she had seen, in rather too much detail and right in front of several Eddies, and consequently the hotel rumour mill had been going great guns about this scandalous gossip ever since, although clearly not in ear-shot of Pattie.

'I think Evie, and Susan, are a bit worried about you, truth to tell,' Sukie said cautiously.

'They've no need to be, have they?' Pattie's voice sounded uncharacteristically spikey. 'I'm just as I ever have been, and the only thing that has changed is that John has turned out not to be the man I thought he was, and so it's lucky that *I* never took him too seriously. We had fun, but I always knew it wasn't going to last.'

Sukie thought Pattie's words sounded brave and devil-may-care, but the slight crack in her friend's voice towards the end of her statement belied the fact somewhat that Pattie hadn't been badly hurt by what he had done.

'I don't think anyone would blame you if you decided to forgive him this one transgression.' Sukie chose her words carefully. 'He seems very remorseful, despite the clumsiness of how he put things in the letter. And you two do get on well, you know.'

Pattie gave a scornful grunt.

Sukie took a slow breath and ploughed on. 'And we all know there'll be a shortage of men when this war ends, and I hate to think of you pushing him away purely because you're on your high horse right now, rightfully so or not, and then you find that you regret sending him away with a flea in his ear the moment you see him with somebody else. You know he's unlikely to be on his own for long, don't you?'

Pattie turned her eyes downwards to stare pointedly at her lemonade in silence, her lips pinched together. Her shoulders looked stiff and unyielding.

Sukie wondered if she was about to be told that she should be minding her own business, and so she added quickly, 'Of course, I completely understand if you don't want to talk with me about him today or to walk out with him anymore, and I'm sure he will too. It's more that I just don't want to see you cutting off your nose to spite your face if there is a chance that you two could still be happy together.' Sukie made sure her tone remained conciliatory. 'Or, to put it another way, you are in the position right now that if you did want to mend things, you can pretty much insist on having it all on your terms from now. And if you don't, well, there are plenty more fish in the sea for someone as lovely as you, and of course you never know where you're going to meet someone.'

Pattie's shoulders relaxed just a little at this, but she looked thoughtful, and indeed almost dreamy, and Sukie decided that as she couldn't quite read her friend's expression, perhaps it was wisest for her not to say anything further on the matter, and so instead she said, 'Fancy another,' as she held her glass aloft, 'as now you've reminded me how beastly Evie and I were to you when we were seven or eight, I guess I've a little making up to do?'

# Chapter Four

A couple of days later, at nine o'clock sharp, Sukie and Tracey Benn were shivering in the frosty shadows at an old bus depot in Peckham that had now been requisitioned as a place where volunteers could be assessed as ambulance drivers, or drivers of other useful vehicles.

Sukie's breath hovered in a little cloud as she blew on her fingers to warm them.

'Brass monkeys this morning,' said Tracey Benn, pulling her extravagantly collared, clearly pre-war fox fur coat a little more snugly to her towering but slim frame. A simple 'Tracey' never quite seemed enough for her extraordinary friend – who loved to dress either as a man or a woman, as the mood took her – Sukie had often thought, and so she was always Tracey Benn to her. Today Tracey Benn had a smart pinstripe suit on, a shirt and tie, well-polished brogues, a ladies fur coat, and a bright red felt fedora. It was a challenging look at the best of times, and most definitely so in the shabbiness of the Peckham vehicle depot. Sukie felt rather proud of her.

'Those monkeys are still tucked up in bed, nice and warm, don't you know?' said Sukie. She stamped her feet in turn, just in case Tracey Benn hadn't quite understood how nippy it was. 'It's too cold even for them.'

'Sukie, we drove here. And you have been out of the car for

less than five minutes,' Tracey Benn reminded her. 'You are not that cold.'

'Five minutes! Is that all?' Sukie laughed, and then to drive home her point about how chill the morning was, she thumped the top of her arms in unison. 'I do hope I'm going to be kept waiting around for a *really* long time as I am so enjoying this.'

It turned out that Sukie's wish was to be granted at it was at least half an hour before she was called forward.

She had urged Tracey Benn to go back and sit in her car as it was daft that they both got chilled to the bone.

Stoically, her friend had stuck it out alongside her, teasing, 'What? And miss the fun?! I couldn't bear not to see you being put through your paces in case you make a right hash of it.'

When Sukie had spoken to the required office to organise her driving assessment, she had requested very politely that if at all possible could she be assessed early in the morning as she was needed elsewhere as soon as possible, and she would be very grateful if they could take her other commitments into account. She hadn't elaborated but it was because Mr Bright had found that covering for her and Pattie's outing to the picture house had proved to be a bit too much for him just yet, and so Mrs Bridge had insisted he had a couple of days back in bed, saying that he must rest up and that she would fill in for Sukie while she was down in Peckham.

Just as Sukie was getting close to the point of having to have A Very Firm Talk with somebody about being kept hanging around – Sukie wasn't sure it really mattered who this gripe was with, as mostly she just wanted to get it off her chest that she felt she had been kept waiting long enough, and more or less anybody would be equal to this task – she was stopped in her tracks when an officious-looking man clutching a clipboard suddenly seemed to be coming her way.

He walked up to her and dramatically wobbled his salt and pepper moustache before giving Sukie a curt 'Ha!' in greeting, and then a toss of his head in the direction of a vehicle in a wordless pantomime of where Sukie should go. Although he was wearing a hat and a muffler, Sukie noticed that from the little bits she could see, unusually for these straitened times, his hair had been firmly pomaded into place. He clearly was someone who liked order and to be obeyed.

Sukie felt increasingly dubious about the assessment. It didn't help that she was alarmingly new to driving.

Between Christmas day and New Year's Eve, Tracey Benn had taken her out for a couple of lessons in her own shiny and pristine Austin Seven. Sukie had never driven before, but she had flippantly mentioned to her friend that she thought she'd be a good volunteer driver, and almost before she knew it, Sukie found Tracey Benn determined to teach her, and an appointment made at the Peckham depot for her to be tested.

In many ways, Sukie was pleased it was all happening so quickly. She was keen to get assessed before she forgot all that Tracey Benn had drummed into her, which seemed to Sukie to consist mainly of several almost identically worded instructions of 'look over your shoulder to check for traffic – your *right* shoulder, Sukie, not your left; if clear, it's clutch in and hand-brake off, let the clutch out slowly, ease your brake foot over to the accelerator; gently, steady, steady, straighten up; ease up on the accelerator, slow down, brake, brake, BRAKE, GODDAMN IT, SUKIE, BRAKE when I tell you to!'.

Sukie had had a princely three hours of tuition in total, but Tracey Benn assured her that would be two and three-quarter hours more driving experience than most of those who'd be at the assessment depot alongside her.

Sukie had thought her friend was joking, but when she'd seen the standard of vehicle know-how of the two women who were examined before her, as they crashed the gears and then ran right over the wooden crates they were supposed to reverse around, she understood that Tracey Benn hadn't been wholly wrong.

The vehicle Sukie had been nodded towards was a clapped-out truck with large crumbly patches of rust on its bumpers, rather than the smaller vehicle the previous two women had driven. The truck hardly looked roadworthy, and it had clearly seen a lot of use, and several bumps, since it had been converted to an ambulance, to judge by the scraps and deep dents in its metalwork that latticed the rusty bits.

As vehicles go, it was much larger than Tracey Benn's spanking Austin Seven, but before Sukie could get a worsening case of the collywobbles at the thought of driving something so big, Tracey Benn said a fortifying, 'Go, get 'em, girl' and gave Sukie a thumbs-up, and then a push in her back that was a little harder than was necessary to get her walking forward.

As she made her way across to the driver's door, Sukie took a deep breath to quell the butterflies in her tummy. While she had no qualms about fearlessly jumping a five-bar gate on horseback and was usually quite intrepid in the physical sense, she had never liked taking any sort of examination and tended to suffer with nerves beforehand. It had been a while since she had been tested for anything, and Sukie had forgotten quite how much the butterflies of apprehension skittered around.

But when she went to clamber up into the ambulance's cab, which was at a fair height above her head, Sukie realised she had a problem. Rather than having put on her tweed winter work skirt that morning, Sukie wished she'd instead worn her one pair of trousers as she battled to winch herself upwards, but the snugness of the skirt meant she couldn't lift her leg up to the first step of the cab. It was all very unladylike as Sukie hopped around on one foot while trying to push her skirt to the level that preserved her modesty at the same time as allowing freer movement of her legs. Almost immediately the butterflies were replaced by feeling foolish as Sukie could well imagine how ridiculous she looked as she hopped about.

A laughing Tracey Benn had to come and shove a shoulder under Sukie's buttocks to give her a final boost up. With a final push and a ringingly loud slap on her rump from her pal, at last Sukie was able to slither herself on to the worn leather seat behind the large steering wheel. She took a moment to pat her hair back into place, in a forlorn hope of looking as if she had *meant* to struggle to get into the cab in the way she had. Sukie knew she wasn't fooling anybody.

She turned the key in the ignition, rammed the gear stick forward and promptly stalled the engine. Rattled, she couldn't then remember how to start a vehicle.

Trying not to give in to a rising sense of panic, she wished she was a calmer person.

And then Sukie remembered how Wesley would always say 'easy' to himself in tricky situations of all types. It was worth a bash, and so, ignoring the man with the clipboard's fractious-sounding 'In your own time, Miss Scott, but remember we have a lot of people behind you to get through...' Sukie took a moment to gather herself. Then she forced herself to breathe out slowly before she said 'easy' out loud.

It worked. For now Sukie was able to turn the engine on, take her time putting the shift in gear, and then slowly let the clutch out as she gently accelerated. She almost looked like a dab hand as she drove across to the marked-out test area, even managing a neat double de-clutch as she moved up a gear.

Sukie had only been driving for five minutes, which was just time to rattle the cranky old vehicle twice around the yard, reverse around the tea chests, and do an emergency stop. She was getting into her stride and was, for the first time, about to clank the gear box up to third, the top gear, from its rumbling and painfully slow second gear, when a green flag was waved at her, which she knew meant that she should return to the others and park.

Sukie thought she must have driven very badly to have been halted after such a short time, although she wasn't sure that that the examiner had actually been paying much attention to how she had been getting on, as every time Sukie risked a peep his way he seemed to be busy peering at something in the street outside, and across at Tracey Benn, to take much notice of what she was up to.

Sukie slipped dejectedly down from the cab, finding it much easier to go downwards in the tweed skirt than she had gone upwards. She didn't like not being good at something but she supposed it was daft for her to have anticipated any sort of different outcome with only three hours' driving under her belt, Sukie reminded herself as her feet landed on firm ground and she looked for Tracey Benn.

Her thoughts were interrupted by an 'Ahem, Miss Scott?' from the moustachioed man with a clipboard.

'Your driving is acceptable, and so report back to the depot at this time next week to fill in some paperwork, by which time I should have sorted the rotas. I have allocated two four-hour stints weekly for you, either driving an ambulance or a mobile canteen. If I am not here, say you are one of Mr Watson's candidates, and can they find me please,' he told her.

Although Sukie had thought when they arrived that the examiner looked a bit of a jobsworth, with his trousers pressed to razor-sharp folds down the front of his legs and his overly polished brogues, Mr Watson turned out to actually be quite an obliging sort of chap, for he added in his nasal and sometimes squeaky voice that he would try to ensure that the pick-up of the vehicle she was to drive would be somewhere nearer to the Eddy.

'Ahem,' he concluded. 'I daresay this will be more convenient for you than coming down to Peckham each time. If there is a problem I will telephone the Edwardes Hotel.'

Sukie felt stumped momentarily and so she forgot to thank Mr Watson. In her opinion the driving examination had been far too perfunctory, and it certainly hadn't seemed like a test of anything much. In fact, she wasn't completely sure her ears weren't deceiving her and that perhaps Mr Watson and his clipboard were really telling her in a roundabout way that she had failed to come up to the necessary standard and that he had been telling her she would have to take the assessment test again.

Then a sneaky glimpse of Tracey Benn's smile and second thumbs-up confirmed to Sukie that somehow she had passed the standard of driving they required.

Sukie couldn't help grinning at the madness of such an unchallenging driving test. There was a war, of course, but they were really scraping the barrel, she felt.

Mr Watson held out his hand for her to shake and then he gave her an A-Z of London streets, and told her to mug up on the marked routes on the turned-down pages in the meantime.

'It shouldn't be too difficult,' Mr Watson finished with a final tremble of his magnificent moustache as he escorted Sukie and Tracey Benn to the gates of the yard.

Mr Watson looked as if he might be fibbing about this, to judge by the glint in his eye, Sukie decided. She told herself that if it turned out she'd been sold a pup, there were plenty of other jobs she could volunteer for.

Still, while the session had gone relatively smoothly for Sukie, the visit to the Peckham depot resulted in a less successful outcome as far as Tracey Benn was concerned.

She and Sukie had just got into the Austin Seven and were about to drive off, when Mr Watson rapped sharply on the driver's side window. Tracey Benn turned off the engine and wound the window down.

'I wonder if I might have a word...' he began.

And before Tracey Benn knew it, and much to Sukie's amusement when she saw the horror on her friend's face at the idea, Mr Watson had roped Tracey Benn and her car in for voluntary sessions where she would drive about visiting dignitaries or War Office workers with scrambled egg on their cap peaks.

This was in spite of Tracey Benn – a good few inches taller than Mr Watson – jumping out of the driving seat so that she could stand full-square before him as she rolled her eyes dramatically in horror at the thought. But although he wiltingly sought refuge for a moment behind his clipboard as she was dramatically drumming her metallic green fingernails in obvious pique on her folded arms, Mr Watson quickly rallied and stared Tracey Benn firmly in the eye, before retaliating by threatening to requisition the vehicle totally if she didn't seat herself in her car again and agree to what he wanted. Tracey Benn was so stunned by the firm timbre of his words that she obediently folded herself behind the steering wheel of her car.

Sukie had to bite back a smile when all Tracey Benn could say then in response was, 'I, er... I, er... , I er...' sounding to Sukie for all the world as if her words were on a record and the needle was stuck in a groove.

Then Mr Watson was apparently lost for words himself as he probably hadn't expected his opponent to acquiesce so quickly, and he and Tracey Benn were left staring at each other in stalemate.

Sukie knew he must have just noticed the tattoo of the coiled snake on her friend's middle finger between the first and second joints, with its tiny flickering tongue making it look quite sinister. This first glance of the small blue snake was always a showstopper in Sukie's experience.

Tracey Benn rallied with her arguments, but Mr Watson was made of sterner stuff than his dapper exterior hinted at, to judge by Tracey Benn's crestfallen expression when her excuses of why the car *shouldn't* be used were casually but firmly brushed aside.

To seal the agreement – on his side, at least – very quickly Mr Watson, with a last quiver of his moustache, scribbled something on his clipboard, and then thrust into Tracey Benn's hand through the wound-down window of the driver's door a billet-doux of when she and her car were going to be needed and where they should be.

'I bet those brass monkeys are chuckling away right now at the outcome of the Austin Seven debacle,' joked Sukie as they drove away from the depot.

'Are you saying you want to walk back to the Eddy?' retorted a glum Tracey Benn.

Back at the hotel, Pattie quickly regretted her innocent question, with which she greeted Sukie and Tracey Benn as they walked across the foyer, of how did it all go?

'You might well ask!' snapped Tracey Benn at Pattie, before Sukie could say anything. 'Me *and* my car have only been strong-armed into driving dignitaries about, that's how it went.

Or, more precisely, didn't. It's not that I don't want to help the war effort, you understand, but I prefer to keep my effort more behind the scenes, as it were, and most definitely not in public.' Sukie knew this was true as Tracey Benn was an extremely generous benefactor to many good causes, although she tried very hard to keep her philanthropic gestures quiet. Tracey Benn continued complaining to Pattie for quite some while, eventually grinding to a halt with, 'I suppose that I simply can't bear the thought of driving dull people about and having to make inane conversation with them.'

'Well, chauffeuring Sukie around should have trained you up nicely for that,' Pattie couldn't resist saying.

Even Sukie had to laugh. And Polly got in on the act with a couple of screeched 'You up nicelys'.

Tracey Benn groaned very pointedly and then turned to lope quickly up the stairs to her room.

Pattie laughed, and then asked Sukie how *she* had got on at the depot.

There had been a lull of hostilities over the previous four or five months as Jerry's attentions had seem to be turned elsewhere, and so neither of the friends had been volunteering for anything for quite a few months, other than the routine paper and metal collections that everybody did across the land. In fact, the bomb that killed Wesley had been one of the last times the streets around them had been worried, other than the freak incident of when the Capel had lost its roof.

But the rumours were growing that Jerry had a change of strategy in the pipe-line, and so Pattie was now keen to be involved in something too.

'Now that you've got your driving work, I think I need to do something too,' said Pattie. 'I'd feel embarrassed if you volunteer and I don't do likewise.'

Sukie thought this impulse to help the war effort was more her friend's way of distracting herself now that she wasn't spending time with John, but this didn't mean that it would be in any way less vital to keeping things ticking over on the home front.

'Well, if I were you, I wouldn't do the fire-watching from the roof of the Eddy, as I did last year,' Sukie advised when she and Pattie were getting ready for bed that night. 'We're on the cusp of the coldest months of the winter, remember, and when I did it, I can tell you that all the coats in the world, and then being topped off with Thing, are not enough to keep you warm. And I had chilblains for months afterwards, which Thing hadn't done a thing to prevent.'

'Thing' was the truly hideous knitted and crocheted double-thickness, voluminous 'blanket' that Mrs Bridge had concocted from scraps of wool to keep Sukie warm in the chill hours after midnight when she had been standing on the roof.

Indeed, so horrific a sight had she felt when she was wrapped tightly in Thing – the name Pattie had come up with for the woolly beast – that Sukie would quite literally shudder in embarrassment if any of the Eddies caught her enveloped in its many scraggy folds.

'Thing...' echoed Pattie, in the sort of voice that tells the listener something not very pleasant is being remembered.

'Thing,' uttered Polly, followed by a more questioning 'Thing?' Polly always came up to their room for the night.

There was a short silence before Polly added for all the world, as if he were pole-axed by distressing thoughts of Thing and consequently was in dire need of a pick-me-up, 'Rum?'

'Quite right, Polly,' said Sukie. 'Thing makes you feel like you need a tot of rum.'

The next morning Sukie had spent an hour or two in Mr Bright's office on the telephone dealing with various bit of administration when she became aware of an almost familiar voice talking to Pattie out on reception.

When at last Sukie could replace the telephone's receiver back in its place after helping an exceptionally talkative prospective guest, she realised that Pattie was still speaking to the same person, which was a bit strange as normally conversations at reception were kept quite brief.

Although Sukie couldn't make out the actual words, it sounded like a very engaged conversation between whoever it was and Pattie. It was definitely a 'he', Sukie could tell now that she was concentrating on what was going on on the other side of the door. In fact, although she couldn't place him, Sukie wondered if she did perhaps know the speaker as there was definitely a rumble of vague familiarity about the soft burr of his voice.

Sukie couldn't resist standing up and taking a peek at the reception desk through the small diamond-shaped window high in the varnished wooden door of her office, fully aware that she was at risk of turning herself into an over-inquisitive Mr Bright with this sort of behaviour. She hadn't liked the way he'd always been gawping through the window to see what was going on, and now she was acting in just the same way. Still, it was *very* tempting just to take a quick gander...

Sukie quickly stepped back out of sight when she glimpsed that William Jones, the widower from the cinema, was the person talking to Pattie, and they looked as if they were getting on like a house on fire.

Even though it had only been the briefest shufti, Sukie couldn't fail to notice that Pattie, side on to Sukie, had positioned herself on her high chair in a manner that her shapely legs were on clear display, and she was smiling very intently upwards at the older man.

William, on his part, was standing properly on the correct side of the reception desk, but he had an elbow propped quite casually on it and so he looked relaxed and as if he'd settled in for quite a chinwag. Afternoons were often quiet at the reception desk, and Sukie trusted that Pattie, if she were needed by a guest, would ensure that William stepped aside so that she could do her job.

Sukie went to sit back down at her desk. But before she did

so, curiosity got in the way, and she stepped forward once more to take a second look through the window.

This time she saw that even though they were virtual strangers, somehow they looked intimate and rather easy with one another, and that Pattie's laugh seemed the first natural one she had let out since the Christmas party. The sound of them talking went on for quite some time, certainly longer than Sukie would have expected.

When William finally said goodbye, Sukie made sure that she gave it ten minutes before she wandered perhaps a bit too casually out of Mr Bright's office.

Pattie was staring into space as she wound the clean and pressed hanky that Sukie had given Dot to use first around one finger and then another.

'Was that William I heard?' Sukie made sure her face looked as if she was asking an innocent question.

'Yes, he popped in to return your hanky,' said Pattie, not offering it to Sukie but continuing to run it through her open fingers. Sukie doubted she'd get the hanky back. 'The interesting thing is that he told me about a part-time volunteer position helping families who have become separated, or servicemen returning home to find their family homes bombed out, or organising things where family members have been badly hurt. It sounds very worthwhile, I thought, as it must be wonderful to reunite family members who thought they might never see each other again. And William runs the Covent Garden branch, as it turns out, and so he suggested I pop over there later on and then I could see if it were something I might like to be involved in.'

'That sounds very much as if it will play completely to your talents,' said Sukie.

It was obvious that William was interested in Pattie, and although Pattie was almost certainly young enough to be his daughter, and right now seemingly oblivious that he was father to three small kiddies, it appeared she might be just a little bit smitten with him too, to judge by the hanky-twisting.

What a turn-up for the books, Sukie thought. Pattie deserved a little harmless fun. William seemed nice enough, and Sukie hadn't detected anything in his personality to suggest that he wouldn't treat Pattie honourably.

But Pattie was only twenty-one after all, and if she did decide that she and John were definitively over, then pretty soon she was bound to meet someone her own age. William was destined only to be a distraction for a week or two, if that, Sukie was sure.

Still, Sukie doubted that Evie and Susan back in Lymbridge would feel as sanguine about the idea of Pattie appearing to be keen to volunteer under the aegis of an older man with whom Pattie was obviously smitten, if her gleaming eyes and flushed cheeks were anything to go by.

Sukie was sympathetic to why Evie and Susan might feel like that. On paper, William wasn't a good match for Pattie.

And as for what John would make of it all, well, Sukie decided not to ponder on that. Aside from the fact that it wasn't really any of her business – not that that usually stopped Sukie – whatever was going on between Pattie and William might burn brightly and then fizzle quickly, and then John would be none the wiser.

Or if this chance acquaintance between William and Pattie proved not to be a flash in the pan, Sukie had no doubt that there would be fireworks of one kind or another in the not too distant future, as it was a big age gap, and the fact William was a widower with three small children would mean a different life for Pattie than her loved ones might have chosen for her.

Either way, it was best that Sukie stood back a little and kept some distance, she told herself. It wasn't as if Pattie was going to pay heed to any advice that might be at variance with her own opinion, anyway. And there might come a time when Sukie would be needed to pick up the pieces, and this would be more easily done if she hadn't been too involved right from the off.

# Chapter Five

The next day was Twelfth Night, and for Sukie's celebration in the hotel bar to mark its passing, Tracey Benn had rustled up from somewhere a flattish and surprisingly large metal bowl, plus a trivet to hold the bowl up a little from the top of the bar so that the wood underneath wouldn't be scorched when the metal got hot. Tracey Benn really was extraordinarily good at knowing just where to go, or who to go to, in order to unearth exactly what they needed, and so Sukie thought that when she got a moment she ought to ask her friend for some tips so that she could learn some of these search-and-find skills.

Meanwhile Sukie rooted around in the depths of Mr Bright's office drawers until she came upon some coloured sheets of paper that hadn't seemed to have an obvious use. And so she'd cut the sheets into squares, which she'd placed in a basket on the bar, along with some pencil stubs; these were for guests to write down the nasty things from 1943 that they wanted to burn.

Although she had laughed it off at the time, subsequently Sukie had pondered Mrs Bridge's joke of the burning of the notes getting out of hand and causing an inferno if there was too much 'bad rubbish' that had happened to people and needed burning, and so she told John to make sure there were four of their red metal buckets of sand hidden beneath the bar on his side as one could never be too safety conscious.

'I'll make sure the soda siphons are full too, just in case,' John assured her.

Sukie smiled back, but it was only a little one. She didn't think Mr Bright would be too pleased with her if her idea for the burning ceremony meant it was the Eddy that ended up razed to the ground.

The night before the ceremony Sukie put notices around the hotel to let everyone know that the following evening there would be complimentary hot toddies in the bar at six o'clock, or warm milk and cocoa for children or those who didn't drink, followed by a ceremonial burning of the 'bad news' at six forty-five.

She'd asked that the pianist come in for five-thirty so that there would be a jolly atmosphere in the bar, despite the theme of 'good riddance to bad rubbish', and Sukie had suggested that John turn off most of the lamps as they could light candles to give the bar an ambiance. She assumed it would mostly be guests who attended, as although the Eddy was making a name for itself with the pre-theatre crowd, early January was traditionally a very quiet time in the theatres, and so several theatres were taking a well-earned break.

So the 'good riddance to bad rubbish' part of the evening seemed taken care of. Sukie was struggling, though, with how to mark the 'making a wish for nice things to happen' part of the evening.

Then, at lunchtime, Tracey Benn had bustled into the office with a surprise for Sukie. It was a large box.

Sukie opened it to find 150 crisp and freshly cooked sweet-wafer fortune cookies, nestled in crumpled tissue paper so fine she could see right through it. These fortune cookies came from a Chinese restaurant a little way away in Soho, complete with messages of good fortune handwritten on tiny scraps of rice paper that had been tucked inside the wafers.

'My goodness – what a treat!' cried Sukie. 'How on earth did you manage to swing this? I had no idea this sort of thing was available.'

'It isn't.' Tracey Benn smiled. 'Unless you are friendly with Raymond, our friend from the Pink Sink, that is, and you know that he and I go way back. And he has fingers in pies all over the city, of course, and he had such a good time at our party that he told me to tell you that this is his thank you present to us. He says Chinese restaurants and fortune cookies will be the bomb after the war.'

Sukie gave her friend a brief but heartfelt hug of gratitude. It meant that people could be urged to make their wish for the coming year as they broke open a fortune cookie; the messages inside were merely icing on the cake to what Sukie hoped would be enjoyable for all. She must remember to break open her own fortune cookie, Sukie told herself.

Meeting Tracey Benn had been a life-changing experience for Sukie. Without Tracey Benn, who exuded glamour and confidence, Sukie thought she would have found it much harder to shrug off her feelings the previous year of being a country mouse in a big city than she had.

From the off Tracey Benn had seemed to find something in her that was worth cultivating, and because of this Sukie had started to believe in herself too in a different way to how she previously had. While Sukie had always been reasonably confident, understandably she had felt very low in the immediate wake of Wesley's death. But as luck would have it, not long afterwards Tracey Benn had checked in to the Eddy as a guest, and then somehow she had never left.

And without Tracey Benn, Sukie knew she would never have had her eyes opened to a place like the Pink Sink, which was an outrageous club where homosexual men could spend time with each other, without fear of prosecution.

Sukie fondly remembered Raymond, the Pink Sink maître d' and the provider of the fortune cookies, happily chatting to Mr Bright in the Eddy's bar as the Christmas party caroused merrily along in the basement below, Mr Bright seemingly oblivious to Raymond's glamorous but low-cut ball gown from which the pelt of his manly chest curled provocatively around the delicate décolletage of the gown as the two men shared substantial slugs from a bottle of whisky.

If somebody had told Sukie when she first arrived in London that she wouldn't turn a hair at such a sight, she wouldn't have believed it possible; but it was, and she hadn't.

At five o'clock Mr Bright toddled weakly from his bedroom to sit in his office for an hour, although Sukie made sure he didn't really have anything to do, other than signing a few cheques, which she had already written out for him, cheques she had already logged in the cashbook and the accounts ledger.

Mr Bright looked to have perked up a little after he'd dealt with the cheques, and so Sukie quickly ran through some of the changes to the running of the Eddy she had implemented in his absence, which were mainly to do with a new way of organising the staff rotas and an idea of training everyone up so that they could do two jobs in case of illness or staff shortages (the memory of John's face, when she'd made him spend an afternoon on reception, was still amusing to think of), and a simplified way of showing the balances in the cash-in and cash-out ledgers, so that it was clear whether the Eddy was in the red or the black on a daily, weekly, monthly or annual basis.

'Capital, capital, Miss Scott,' said Mr Bright, when he'd finished running his finger slowly down the pink and blue lined column in the ledger, in which Sukie had written the running totals. 'I think you will have to go through it again once I am back in the office to bring me fully up to speed, but on a brief precursor those suggestions look to me as if they will all add immensely to the smooth-running of the Edwardes.'

Sukie looked at him with gratitude, as she knew her changes had been quite bold and had the potential for Mr Bright to think she was getting above her station. While she couldn't pretend that she hadn't enjoyed having the free rein to implement her ideas that Mr Bright's illness had afforded, Sukie absolutely didn't want him to think that she felt he wasn't up to the job of being the manager of the Eddy (even if it was clear at this moment that he wasn't), or that she was trying to step on his toes in any way and come over as too domineering, as nothing was further from her mind.

'I've just had an idea, Mr Bright,' she said. 'Why don't you say a few words to welcome everyone to the Twelfth Night ceremony? I'm sure all the Eddies would love to see you there. The guests too, of course, as they are always asking after you. And I'd really love to watch you stand tall at the helm of the Eddy as you guide us into this New Year.'

'Miss Scott, I, er...' he began, and then to Sukie's surprise he made as if he wanted to review Sukie's arithmetic in the ledger again. He fumbled for his hanky, and after a quick check on his pocket watch on its chain across his waistcoat, he blew his nose and at last, somewhat recovered, he looked up at her.

Mr Bright's eyes were glistening and this made Sukie wonder if he were blinking away a tear. Her heart went out to him as he really had been through the wars over the last couple of months, and it had taken only the smallest of comments on her part to cheer him up.

'*Nothing* would give me more pleasure,' he said, patting down the pockets on his waistcoat. 'Now remind me what is going to happen, and when.'

'I look around me on this dark January night and see friends old and new,' said Mr Bright, getting on for an hour later, once everyone was assembled. He looked pale and more than a little shaky as he stood before a packed bar, his weight leaning heavily on his stick, and Sukie wondered whether her idea that he give a speech had been a good one.

He'd put his weight on her as they'd slowly made their way to the bar. Realising how wobbly he was, she had tried to get him to sit down on a high bar stool to open the evening but he had refused, and Sukie hadn't found it in herself to press him too much that he should take a seat as she felt he might be embarrassed if she did; it might seem she was questioning his authority.

She caught Mrs Bridge's eye, though, and so the housekeeper moved closer to him, just in case he did totter.

'And certainly I think we probably all have words we want to write down and then burn as a way of clearing the decks of the hurts of the past in order that we can start anew.' Mr Bright looked down at his trembling hands clutching his stick, and then he said, 'I know that I have quite a lot I want to write down that I wish to burn. But before we get on to the business in hand, please allow me the indulgence of saying a big thank you to all of the staff at the Edwardes Hotel for running such a tight ship in my unavoidable absence. Everything seems to have gone like clockwork...'

As Mr Bright continued speaking, Sukie allowed her thoughts to drift away, thinking of all the things that *hadn't* gone to plan while he had been laid up. There'd been the great turkey black-market fiasco that she really hadn't approved of once she had discovered it and which she then had had to stamp on in the run-up to Christmas (or, more accurately, stamp on for *next* Christmas, as by then all the contraband birds were in the Eddy ready to sell on illicitly), and of course there'd been John's fumble with the young woman on the Staff Room that had caused Pattie to swing her mean right hook.

Sukie hoped Mr Bright would never find out about either of those incidents, as he would be very disappointed in them all if he did, she was sure.

Mr Bright showed no signs of ending his welcome, and Sukie crossed her arms and nonchalantly rested her behind on the back of a chair no one was sitting in.

Through a daydream she heard Polly scream a faint but clearly furious 'Where's the rum, Mr Bright?' He was obviously most peeved at being exiled to the manager's office, with the door firmly closed on him as Sukie was always worried about him and too much cigarette smoke if there were a large number of people in the bar.

There had been some funny shenanigans when John and

Pattie had brought the parrot into the hotel too, that was for sure, she remembered.

People began clapping suddenly, and with a start Sukie realised everyone was looking at her, and that it must be very obvious that she had no idea as to what had just been said.

Pattie was now standing before her, her arm linked with a suave-looking William, and their coats still on and noses pink from the cold. Pattie grinned at Sukie and explained, as people smiled at Sukie for being caught so obviously on the hop, 'Miss Scott, Mr Bright thanked you for your contribution to the running of the hotel, and then he said why don't you burn your own "good riddance note" to kick us off?'

'Oh my giddy aunt, I'd better write it first,' said Sukie, and deliberately she made a silly face that provoked more laughter.

Then she stood up straight and announced in a much more business-like way, 'But before I do that, let's raise our glasses to our wonderful Mr Bright, and wish him health and happiness in 1944, with the sincere hope that he's back in the office every day before too long – we've missed him, Eddies and guests alike. For anyone that hasn't done so – and that means me too, you won't be surprised to hear! – please now take a piece of paper and write down something you want to say goodbye to. It can be anything, anything at all; nobody will know what you have written. Then each piece of paper will be added to our small pyre on the bar. And after your note is burned, please choose a fortune cookie, and as you break it open, then do make a wish. And inside each fortune cookie you will find a goodwill message for the New Year. But, as I say, all best wishes to you, Mr Bright.' And with that Sukie raised her glass in the hotel manager's direction.

There was a round of applause, and at long last Mr Bright was persuaded to sit down, much to Sukie's relief. At last the business of the night could get going.

With a stony face and eyes that kept flicking to Pattie and William, John grumpily officiated over the burning of the notes, although fortunately he took good care to ensure the inferno stage was never reached.

Mrs Bridge, wearing the smart russet-coloured cardigan Sukie had got her for Christmas using Sukie's own precious clothing coupons (Mrs Bridge had been very kind to her ever since she had arrived at the Eddy, and Sukie wanted her to know that she appreciated how caring of her the older woman had been), made sure everyone got a fortune cookie. With a reminder of 'remember not to tell anyone what you wish for', Mrs Bridge helped several small children who were guests stand in turn on a chair so that they could place a piece of paper with a scribble on it into the bowl.

To her surprise, Sukie couldn't quite decide what she should put down on her own note, and she found herself dithering, which was unlike her, and so she told herself she had to be selective because if she wrote down everything that had been horrible about 1943 then she might have a note of *War and Peace* proportions, and she must remember her piece of paper was only a couple of inches square.

Eventually she wrote simply 'the war' on her piece of good riddance paper, which she then carefully folded in two, and then folded again. It quickly shrivelled to ash in a swirl of blue and orange flame.

And then she reached for a fortune cookie, and as the wafer snapped as she broke it apart, Sukie made a wish, which was: 'Wesley, I wish you peace at rest'.

Instinctively she reached for his engagement ring at its place on the gold chain around her neck, and then remembered with a pang that the ring and the chain were now cushioned safe in her embroidered hanky case upstairs. And she remembered too her promise to herself she was going to move forward, and not hanker dangerously after a past that had hurt and almost destroyed her.

She sighed, a trifle sadly, and then caught John's eye as he put his own note into the metal bowl. He looked from her and balefully over to where Pattie was standing with William at the other side of the room, and then he turned back to Sukie with a hurt expression.

Sukie tried to give a sympathetic shrug, but she was still slightly too much in thrall to the moment of thinking about Wesley and his loss, and so she felt her face more wonky than anything approximating something that could comfort somebody else.

To distract herself, Sukie looked again towards Pattie, this time studying her friend carefully.

Pattie and William appeared to be very wrapped up in each other as they chatted, and to judge by Tracey Benn's raised eyebrow, and then Mrs Bridge's, Sukie and John weren't the only people to have noticed Pattie's obvious attraction to the distinguished older man. Or the awkwardness of Pattie's deliberate and very public slight to John.

There wasn't anything Sukie could do to affect the scene playing out before her, and so she reached for another fortune cookie and passed it to Mr Bright. Behind him she saw Pattie and William break open their cookies, and laugh merrily at the messages inside. Chef tried to pass a cookie to John, but he was too busy glowering at Pattie and William to notice Chef's gesture.

Sukie turned her gaze away as she didn't want either Pattie or John to think that she was scrutinising them any longer, and she couldn't help but notice Mr Bright's wish as he was laboriously jotting it down in a very weak hand as he sat beside her. 'I wish to recover all my strength and faculties. And that Miss Scott has a better 1944 than she did 1943' were his shakily written wishes.

A lump came into Sukie's throat. Mr Bright was really a much more caring person than he liked others to think. She touched his arm and smiled down at him, and he grinned back and said that it was almost time he went up to bed, and he rather fancied taking a tot of rum with him.

Polly would be proud, Sukie thought.

She decided that she should make a new wish as somehow

her first wish wasn't sitting quite right, although she worried she was overcome with what felt like selfish thoughts.

She'd always tried very hard to be a good person, the type of girl who always had the backs of her colleagues and loved ones. But she felt in this communal moment of renewal and putting to bed of old cares that perhaps sometimes this had slightly been at her own expense. Sukie had an intoxicating thought then – perhaps her previous way of going about things wasn't going to be quite enough for her over the months, and years, stretching ahead. She felt for the first time that she might be able to find a way to make time and space for 'Sukie' alongside trying to look after everyone else, and to make sure she had Sukie's back too, even if only in small ways.

The sounds around her shrank down to a murmur as Sukie was enveloped by her thoughts. She looked at the fortune cookie as she pondered quite how to word what she was feeling, and then once she had done so, she closed her eyes and solemnly said to herself, 'I make a wish for imagination, so that I can work out what it is that I actually do want, the fortitude to try and achieve this with kindness and generosity, and the strength to think calmly about what I cannot change. In short, I wish to be a stronger Sukie, a full-blooded woman, but still one who knows also how to be caring and thoughtful.'

She opened her eyes and saw Mr Bright break open his fortune cookie. 'You will run far tonight,' it said.

'Hmmm,' Sukie told him with an ironic raise of her brow, as they both stared at his walking stick. 'Maybe I got your fortune cookie instead.'

But when Sukie cracked her wafer cookie open, she did wonder if the perfect fortune cookie had found its way to her after all.

For as she read the slip of paper she felt as if the presence of Wesley and his zest for life was near. And it seemed as if his spirit was taking hers by the hand, and feeding into her new-found feelings of resolution – or was it even optimism? – at the thought of her own life lying waiting before her and how she must be brave and grasp her opportunities.

'There is in the worst of fortunes the best chance of a happy ending', the saying on the ribbon of paper gifted to her by the cookie insisted, and as Mr Bright shuffled his way to the bar to ask John for his glass of rum, Sukie hoped with all her heart that these words were going to prove to be true for both herself and Mr Bright.

# Chapter Six

Over the next few weeks the days remained short and the nights long and increasingly bitterly cold, and it felt as if they almost merged with one another, with the dim daylight and dank weather not so very different from the hours of darkness each night.

In what felt like an inappropriately short time to Sukie, Pattie seemed obsessed with William and how wonderful he was and what fantastic work he and his team of workers were doing matching up long-lost relatives, and so on.

'He knows so much, on just about everything,' Pattie repeated for the umpteenth time. 'I just can't fault him. And his staff at the voluntary depot all look up to him. He's *so* funny too, and very clever. Everyone thinks so. And of course he is devilishly handsome.'

Sukie tried not to look bored as she put a rubber hot water bottle into her bed and slipped into her nightie. Most of Pattie's conversation these days was about William, and frankly a little of this was proving to go quite a long way, Sukie had discovered. She'd written as much to Evie, who had replied in an equally dispirited fashion only that morning, wondering if Sukie might have a go at tempering Pattie's high spirits as far as William was concerned.

'Those kiddies are simply adorable, and really well-behaved. Have I mentioned that? He is an outstanding father. And have

I told you that he makes a wonderful cup of tea too?' Pattie ploughed on regardless.

'Tea-making is a good skill to find in a man,' said Sukie, wondering how to interrupt the flow of adoration to broach the subject of whether Pattie had jumped into this relationship too fast.

'Isn't it?' said a beaming Pattie, missing the note of withering irony in Sukie's voice.

'Pattie, I don't want to be irritating, but do you think that possibly you are rushing things a little?' Sukie said gently after Pattie had stood in silence for a while, her arms wrapped around her slippers, deep in thoughts that were presumably of William if the big smile on her face was anything to go by.

'Whatever do you mean? It feels as if we've known each other, well, um, for ever!' Pattie said back very quickly.

'Not wanting to split hairs, Pattie, but really it's only a month or two since you both met, you do know?' Sukie pointed out. 'You're taking things frightfully fast and spending an awful lot of time with William, aren't you? And it's not that long after John and the Staff Room incident, mind, and you were terribly cut up about that, if you remember. And now you've thrown the baby out with the bathwater, and simply flung yourself into being with William and his family with what looks a bit like complete abandon. There's a lot to take on with William, you know, as those children won't always be well-behaved. And some people might think also that he's quite mature, while you are yet to bloom properly—'

'Rubbish!' interrupted Pattie. 'In fact, I don't feel like I'm spending *nearly* enough time with him. Or with the children. And as for the age thing, I never had you down as small-minded, Sukie, but now you're making me think otherwise! I'm perfectly fully-bloomed, thank you, although I detect Evie's voice coming out of your mouth... And you seem to be forgetting that your own experience with men is actually less than mine, partly as you keep deliberately avoiding them in case what happened with Wesley were to happen again.'

With that Pattie flounced dramatically from their bedroom, her wash bag in hand as she thumped noisily down the corridor on her way to the bathroom, leaving Sukie in no doubt that she was immensely vexed.

Sukie sighed gloomily. She thought a large part of William's attraction had happened precisely because Pattie *was* on the rebound from John. Still, she'd done her best to urge caution, but Pattie seemed determined that she was going to leap in, hook, line and sinker. And the jibe about Sukie not risking another broken heart had certainly found its mark, giving Sukie a real pang with its dagger-prick finding its home with unerring accuracy, forcing her to acknowledge there was more than a ring of truth to Pattie's words.

There were a tense few minutes when Pattie returned. Although they didn't say anything out loud to each other, if the looks they darted towards the other's bed were anything to go by, it was the closest that Sukie and Pattie had ever come to having a proper squabble.

Meanwhile, John, in retaliation, started to flirt outrageously with Mavis. She was Mrs Bridge's daughter (not that they advertised this fact particularly) and sometimes Mavis would stand in on the bar if John was on as maître d' in the dining room, even though she had an office job during the day.

Pattie didn't appear to notice, or care what John was up to, or if Mavis was returning his obvious advances, and so Sukie thought that as a strategy of getting somebody's attention, it wasn't working out as John had intended.

This peculiar stand-off went on for several weeks, during which time Sukie wasn't sure whether to offer a word of caution to Mavis (in case she didn't know that John was hurt over how Pattie was behaving, and that him fawning over her was very probably only his way of dealing with his loss of Pattie), or of admonishment to John (to say it wasn't very fair of him if he was going to mess about hurtfully with somebody else's feelings as a way of trying to get Pattie's attention).

Eventually Sukie decided to say nothing to either of them, at least for now. Mavis had always struck Sukie as being reason-ably worldly-wise and, Sukie thought, Mrs Bridge would step in with the words of wisdom if things looked to be getting out of hand concerning John's treatment of her daughter. And he wasn't a callous person by nature, Sukie believed, even allowing that he was a man who was a bit too single-minded and – as the Staff Room incident showed – self-centred at times. Sukie suspected, all the same, that if she did say anything to either of them then the only result would be that she would be sent away with a flea in *her* ear, which would be irritating in the extreme when she only had their best interests at heart.

'Steer well clear,' reiterated Tracey Benn as she watched Sukie give an unimpressed Polly a sponge bath in the scullery one day. 'They're all grown-ups, and they'll have to get themselves out of their own pickles if it all goes a bit wrong. Nobody – and I mean nobody – is going to listen to you anyway.'

'Thank you for that!' said Sukie, not meaning it at all as she was momentarily quite put out at her friend's bluntness about nobody caring what she thought, even though her friend's statement accorded with her own feelings.

Tracey Benn stared back with a gimlet eye. 'Well, they're not going to listen to you, and you know that, and so you might as well get over it. And Pattie is right about you deliberately avoiding men, you do know that, don't you?'

'I'm *not* avoiding men,' insisted Sukie. 'Well, not often.'

'*Are!*' said Tracey Benn firmly.

'Avoiding men,' echoed Polly.

'Shut up, the both of you,' said Sukie in pique. 'I just want to avoid potential quarrels among the Eddies.'

'Shut up,' Polly replied, and pushed over the small bowl of warm water with which Sukie had been dousing her cotton rag to clean his feathers.

Soon Sukie had other things to think about besides Pattie and William and John and Mavis, as Mr Bright's health dipped, and so he had to endure a series of hospital visits as they experimented with different medical regimes and medication. Sukie had to increase her own hours each day, and she told herself she should dig in as a temporary manager for a while longer, and so she began to wonder if she should try to employ another receptionist as she found she was often having to do a couple of hours a day there as well, on the days she wasn't doing her voluntary work.

And, as Sukie and John expected after the rumours they'd heard, Jerry began to bomb Britain again, and so once more there was the sound at night of defensive ack-acks and muffled explosions, and if one looked upwards through the blackout there would be strong anti-aircraft shafts of beaming into the night skies trying to highlight Luftwaffe planes. Fortunately, this latest German offensive wasn't as harsh or concentrated an onslaught as the Blitz of 1940, and soon the press had dubbed it the Baby Blitz.

But that wasn't to say that these weeks of night-time turmoil didn't have any teeth, no matter how tame people deemed it to be in comparison with those dark days of the Blitz proper that broke the Phoney War, when on many nights literally thousands of people had died as the bombs had rained down. Sukie found it hard to get enough sleep, and the dark circles under the eyes of many of the Eddies suggested she wasn't alone in this.

Sukie was now driving a mobile canteen two afternoons a week, which was quickly upped to three. Her driving improved from session to session, and as she got more experienced, her confidence behind the wheel grew, just as Tracey Benn had promised would happen.

She found that she very much enjoyed dispensing hot drinks and food to those clearing up after a strike. Certainly those she was feeding were always delighted to see her, and Sukie found this hugely rewarding.

She loved dropping down the side to the canteen and lining up the cups, which she would then fill with a huge teapot. Often the men and women clearing the roads, or checking over bombed-out buildings would look exhausted, and be covered in brick dust, the skin around their eyes showing pale where they had had to close their peepers as they shovelled the rubble.

Quite often she noticed a particular man who seemed to be directing operations, and he always had a cheery smile for her, and so Sukie took to keeping back a large enamel mug just in case she saw him as she thought he deserved a little extra tea. She liked to see the way he'd wrap his strong hands around the mug with a 'Right you are!' and then a 'Thanking you' a minute later when he handed back the empty mug. He never wasted a moment, and Sukie always watched the way he led by example, his quick return to work hurrying up even the most lazy of the rubble-clearers. If he were the last to arrive for his tea, and the last to go, he'd always help close the hatch door, and then slap twice on the wood so that Sukie would know she could drive on to the next place on her route.

It was impossible to predict how her driving stint would go each time she settled herself behind the steering wheel. Sometimes Sukie found the London streets she wanted to make her way down were blocked by huge potholes if they had taken a hit from a bomb, or there could shards of glass everywhere (Sukie had been told not to drive over glass if she could help it as there was a rubber shortage now that the ports were blockaded, and so tyres must be eked out for as long as possible), or sometimes she had to navigate around huge mountains of rubble (the A-Z of London streets would be well-thumbed on those days, as she would detour through grimy back streets).

At other times she didn't have much to do if her volunteer session followed a quiet night at the hands of Jerry. Twice chemists' shops on her routes were hit, and each time Sukie heard rumours of a ferocious black market quickly developing in stockpiled face powder being sold on to local women by the spivs who had managed to purloin the precious booty. However, Sukie never saw any of the rumoured cosmetics, and soon she believed these stories to be apocryphal.

Once she was told to drive an ambulance rather than the

mobile canteen, but that was mainly ferrying people with flesh wounds to a field hospital to be stitched up. Sukie didn't care for the sight of blood much, or the groans that people would make when hurt, and so she breathed a sigh of relief when the next time she turned up for driving duty it was back to the old and dented mobile canteen for her.

All of this Sukie pretty much took in her stride. The country was still at war, and occasionally she was aggravated by her long hours at the Eddy and there not being quite enough staff to do everything that needed to be done comfortably, but she refused to let herself be bowed down. Sometimes she felt she couldn't face yet another tinned sardine on toast for her supper, and she suspected that many people felt as she did: a little worn down by the length of time the war had gone on, but determined to do their bit for as long as they had to.

What was more discombobulating though was that somehow Sukie found that she wasn't seeing as much of Tracey Benn these days, in part as the Austin Seven was in great demand and its owner didn't trust anybody else to drive it, and in part as Tracey had become quite adept as slipping unobserved out of the Eddy.

In fact, Tracey Benn was behaving quite strangely, almost as if she had a secret, and although Sukie gave her every opportunity to explain herself, Tracey Benn refused to be drawn out.

And Sukie wasn't seeing much of Pattie either, other than when they settled down in the bedroom they shared at night. Pattie's volunteer work at William's organisation very quickly took up every spare moment she had, although Sukie couldn't tell how much of this was work, and how much was pleasure.

Sukie didn't feel jealous that her friends were giving her less attention, although she did feel a little at sea at not having her normal buddies around to spend time with.

She missed their company, and felt a little lonely occasionally, which was odd considering that she was surrounded by people all day long, but it was true nevertheless.

It took her a while to admit this even to herself, and she most definitely felt too shy about this to let either Tracey Benn or

Pattie know that she felt a trifle down in the mouth about them having more interesting things to do than spend time with her.

This feeling of melancholy bothered Sukie in the evenings especially.

She took to playing bridge for an hour with Mr Bright in the hotel bar, telling herself she was trying to keep his mind active, even though deep down she knew that every evening when she asked him if he fancied a hand of cards, it was more to keep herself occupied than it was to make sure he was entertained. It didn't help much that Mr Bright tired quickly and would soon retreat to bed.

Then Sukie would have a cup of tea with Mrs Bridge, but as the housekeeper got up each day at six o'clock at the absolute latest in order to oversee the chambermaids preparing their cleaning trolleys, it wouldn't be long before Mrs Bridge would be yawning conspicuously too.

# Chapter Seven

It was still early evening, and at the far side of the bar, a distinctly jaded Sukie was giving Polly some attention, which he was lapping up greedily. Lavishing affection on Polly was Sukie's way of feeling a bit less at a loose end. But it wasn't working terribly well as a strategy, not that it was the parrot's fault. She definitely felt bored, but not the sort of bored that reading a good book or listening to the wireless would salve.

'Miss Scott, if I may,' murmured a low male voice near Sukie's ear.

Sukie jumped at the sound of the man's voice, as her thoughts had been miles away, and then she felt a little foolish at being caught out so.

It was Simon, the rather dashing young man that Tracey Benn had picked to dance with Sukie at the Pink Sink, and who then had escorted her around the dance floor at the Eddy's Christmas party.

He was smiling at her, and he looked very dapper in a dark suit, his hair combed and shining under the dim wall lights of the bar.

Simon had worn army uniform the two times they had met previously. Sukie had understood, through the red-lined crown uniform sign on his neatly buttoned jacket, two things: he was a major, and that at that time he must be active on duty in the

UK as no uniform signs like this were allowed in active service abroad.

It was still not the done thing to ask a man in uniform what they did, or where they were stationed, and so Sukie realised she didn't actually know very much about Simon. And as they had danced together in such a casual manner, and it had felt to Sukie to be still too soon after Wesley's passing to be thinking of this sort of thing, she realised now that hadn't asked Tracey Benn about him afterwards either. She assumed that his working role had changed now that he was in mufti, but again she knew better than to bring this up.

Behind Simon, Sukie could see John's head craning forward in her direction in order that he could get a better gawp at Sukie and her acquaintance.

'Simon! What a nice surprise,' said Sukie warmly, ignoring John. 'And you do know that it's Sukie and not Miss Scott, don't you?'

He grinned. 'May I stand you a drink, Sukie?'

'How lovely,' she said, and then she lowered her voice to a whisper. 'It's been *very* dull in here tonight, and so you are a sight for sore eyes.'

'Nowhere could be dull with you in it,' Simon replied. He managed to say this in such a way that it didn't sound as corny as it might have coming from someone else, and so Sukie decided this was a point in his favour.

Simon turned and appraised the busyness of the bar, which had a mighty eight patrons in it. John had had to pick up a glass and a cloth very adroitly, so that Simon didn't notice him staring.

Simon leaned forward, and whispered back to Sukie, 'But I see what you mean as to the lack of excitement, and so what about if we pop over the Strand to the Savoy? You look present-able – indeed, *most* presentable – and so you could come just as you are.'

He was so close as he spoke that Sukie could feel his breath in her ear, and instantly she felt a corresponding tightness in her chest.

It had been such a long time since she had experienced a sensation in any way similar to this that, in part as it was all happening so unexpectedly and so quickly, she couldn't quite make up her mind as to whether she liked it or not.

'I... I, er...' Sukie floundered to a halt, feeling put on the spot.

But she couldn't think of a good reason not to go with Simon to the Savoy, which was only several minutes' walk away, other than that she was still in her work clothes (and, aside from the fact that Simon had already neatly circumvented that particular argument, in any case she didn't have anything smarter to wear hanging in her bedroom closet upstairs, aside from the silk evening dress that Tracey Benn had given her that Simon had seen at both the Pink Sink and the Christmas party), and she felt a bit miffed that she didn't have a lipstick to hand (but then nobody had lipstick these days, the pre-war lipsticks having been used up long ago).

Fortune favours the brave, Sukie told herself, and she remembered her promise to herself in the New Year that she must always be at pains to live in the moment as much as she could.

'How delightful,' she said at last.

They walked through to the foyer of the Eddy, Sukie making sure she ignored John as they passed.

She pressed her lips together and then bit them hard to get a bit of colour going. After pinching her cheeks and running her hands quickly through her hair, Sukie looked at Simon again, and said, 'Will I pass muster, do you think?'

'Absolutely.' His smile was dazzling.

She opened the hidden cupboard in the hotel foyer and took out her coat.

Suddenly the evening was looking up, Sukie decided.

Despite all the wartime scrimping and saving, the Savoy had managed to retain the unique but unavoidable whiff of money about it. There was a sense of hushed opulence about it that only top-class hotels could achieve, even in such straitened circumstances.

This was something that the slightly lower tier of hotels, such as the dear old Eddy, strived very hard to replicate, although without any real hope of ever quite being able to match up.

A smartly dressed doorman with almost blindingly white gloves held open the doors to the foyer for Simon and her, and they stepped inside and then paused to take in the view before them before they crossed the polished marble floor.

Sukie came from a modest family background, and what she saw around her now almost felt overly sumptuous for her to be fully comfortable with, as she couldn't quite forget the large number of people in London who'd been left with next to nothing over the past four years, and to whom such a sight as this before them would, quite literally, seem like a foreign land.

Here, there was gilt in abundance, large and ornate mirrors, and thick portions of carpet under their feet that had been laid to break up the large expanse of flooring. Of course, the Eddy had gilt and mirrors and springy carpet too, certainly in excess to what most ordinary people had in their homes, while the sense of place that greeted a new guest at the Eddy could be described, at best, as a most comfortable pleasure craft of a hotel, as a boating analogy, while what Sukie now spied stretching away into the distance at the Savoy was more top-end transatlantic ship of the line.

She breathed in deeply to savour the moment, catching a trace of luxurious pot-pourri as she did so, and then she and Simon were escorted to two comfy chairs in a snug of a bar. Before they sat down properly, their coats had been discreetly whisked away in a manner that screamed top-class staff training to Sukie's now-practised professional eye.

'Whatever my guest would like, and a large Talisker for me, if you still have any. Thank you.'

Sukie liked the confident way Simon spoke to the waiter. She knew from John that someone being concise and clear was a good thing.

Then she let the side down rather as she just couldn't decide whether she fancied more a small sweet sherry or a port and lemon, asking for first one and then the other, at which Simon indicated to the waiter with a raised brow that he should serve her with both.

Sukie opened her mouth to say no, it was far too extravagant. But Simon didn't seem at all fazed and was looking at her with encouragement, and then she thought, what the heck, how often am I at the Savoy? And as part of her began to plot out already how she would describe all of this in a funny way by letter to Evie the next morning, the rest of her grinned up at the waiter, as she said, 'I do apologise. I've not had a night out in nearly a year, other than once being taken to the Pink Sink, and so I can't make up my mind.'

'In that case, shall I make it a *large* port and lemon for madam, *and* perhaps a *large* sherry too?' asked the waiter with almost (but not quite) a coquettish rise in his tone, causing Sukie to suspect that he may well know all about the Pink Sink and quite what went on there.

She laughed out loud. 'Goodness me, no, thank you, as that would make me squiffy and I have to be up early. Single measures, please.'

The waiter nodded and moved soundlessly away.

Simon had the sort of expression on his face that suggested a squiffy Sukie might not be the worst outcome he could imagine.

Then, once he had her to himself again, he seemed slightly at a loss for words, and so there was a moment or two when neither of them said anything and Simon concentrated on hoicking down on each of the cuffs on his shirt so that the shirt's arms weren't ridden up in any way, before he asked her, 'Was that true about you only having been away from the Edwardes that one evening?'

'At night-time, yes, quite true, I'm afraid, as I'm rather a dull person these days and have decided that I am perfectly happy being a home-body. Tonight is a very rare experience for me, although I confess to very occasionally kicking over the traces by going to the pictures of an afternoon.' Sukie deliberately kept her voice light and as if perhaps she was making a joke, although actually she realised that she was feeling increasingly sombre as the unacknowledged weight of losing Wesley was nudging at her all of a sudden.

This was best dealt with head-on.

And so, before Simon could steer the conversation on to other topics, and although she couldn't quite look Simon in the eye as she began, Sukie said more seriously, but in as matter-of-fact a way as she could manage, 'Actually, I lost my fiancé very suddenly quite early last year. And of course sometimes I have to work evenings at the Eddy, and so somehow the weeks have slipped by without me doing anything much that led to me being away from the Eddy often, and especially if you don't count my volunteer stints as a driver of a mobile canteen. If I'm honest, I spent a long time after Wesley died feeling like I didn't want to go out at all.' Now Sukie found she could look up. 'The reason I was at the Pink Sink that evening you and I met was because Tracey Benn took me there as I'd told everyone I planned to organise a Christmas party at the Eddy and then I was panicked at the thought of putting on an event that was, in my opinion, destined to be very forgettable. And so Tracey Benn thought therefore that the Pink Sink might give me ideas, and be something of an eye-opener. I'd come from a very small village on Dartmoor, you see, and had led a very sheltered life with hardly any party-giving experience. Or experience in attending them either, for that matter.'

It was the first time Sukie had broached the loss of Wesley to a man who conceivably might be interested in her, and now that she had brought it out into the open it felt as if a weight she hadn't known she was carrying had been lifted from her. And, sneakily, she was just a little proud too of the way with which she had dealt with such a potentially emotional moment.

She was pleased too that Simon didn't look at all put out or shocked, for what she had said wasn't the light and airy conver-sation that young ladies were advised to speak to young men on early association, Sukie knew, and it was gratifying that Simon hadn't tried to interrupt her in order to move the conversation to less contentious grounds.

He looked sympathetic and quickly said in a low voice, 'I'm sorry to hear that, Sukie.'

She gave a tentative smile back.

'And was your sojourn to the Pink Sink an eye-opener?' he asked her then, a distinct twinkle in his eye as he spoke in a more upbeat manner.

'Oh yes! It think it's safe to say that it was.'

Sukie's reply was quite lively, but then they fell silent for a little while as the pair of them watched the waiter place their drinks down on the low table, and a small bowl of something salted, although she couldn't immediately identify what it was that the bowl contained.

'I think you'll find it's thin slices of fried beetroot and parsnip with a little salt,' Simon told her, correctly guessing what she was thinking.

She dipped in cautiously, expecting the worse, but found the salty snack delicious.

Sukie angled her face towards Simon, conspiratorially. 'Actually, a lot of what I saw at the Pink Sink was a bit too much for what I could imagine carrying over to the Christmas party at the very dear to me but resolutely staid old Eddy. However, experiencing an evening of jazz music at the Pink Sink was an unforgettable education nonetheless and one that I very much enjoyed, and so I doubt I will ever forget it.'

Simon gave her an affable smile. 'I know what you mean. I too thought it a very, er, lively place when I first went.'

Sukie thought it was time to get off her chest another thought that she had just had, now that they had started to talk about the Pink Sink.

She said cautiously, 'If I'm honest, I was struck by how *comfortable* the male patrons were with one another, if you take my meaning? I'm sure many of them were and indeed still are married, but they seemed very *happy* to be able to dance cheek to cheek with another man if they so wanted.'

This was about as far as Sukie dared to speak on the subject, and she hoped that Simon would twig what she was driving at.

His dark eyes regarded her thoughtfully. 'I know what you are really asking,' he said in a more forthright way than she had expected, even though he took care to keep his voice light, 'and so let me assure you that I am not of *that* persuasion. I like to spend time at the Pink Sink as I find it relaxed and more fun than most other places in town, with the best music London has to offer; and of course there's the irreplaceable Raymond, and I appreciate the wit and humour of the people who go there. But I never spend time alone with anyone I bump into there, as I am not there for *those* reasons, if – to quote you – *you* know what I mean? And I assure you too that one day I hope to find a wife and then be very faithful to her in all ways, and hopefully this will happen sooner rather than later.'

Sukie knew that this sort of thing between men was quite common. Evie had almost got engaged to a lovely architect, whose family were pushing for him to make a decent marriage before the rumours of his homosexual proclivities became a scandal. Sukie didn't disapprove of such behaviour, but as something that could wreck a marriage and was, of course, illegal, it was a hurdle best avoided, she felt.

Anyway, if Simon claimed such behaviour wasn't his bag, of course she should believe him, Sukie felt.

'Well,' she said, deciding to lighten the moment, 'haven't we started off in a bold manner, what with me saying I spent a lot of time recently grieving the death of my fiancé, while you have had to tell that you like women and not men? Whatever shall we talk about if we ever decide to have a serious conversation?'

Simon laughed, and then Sukie pointed playfully from one of her glasses to the other, and back again, with a 'eeny meeny miny mo', choosing the port and lemon.

'Let's toast "saying what we mean",' said Simon.

'Saying what we mean,' Sukie echoed, and their glasses softly touched.

As they sipped, they looked into each other's eyes.

It was an oddly frank moment, and Sukie experienced something akin to a shiver. It made her feel very alive and quite tingly.

What a peculiar, unexpected evening, she thought, and it's come from nowhere. How strange and exciting life can be, and just when it seems at its most dull.

They broke eye contact, and then naturally slipped into an easy-feeling conversation. As they chatted, Sukie began to look at Simon with greater attention.

He was tall, which she liked, and fair, which she was less certain about, even though his colouring was actually quite similar to hers. Previously, she had only liked dark-haired Lymbridge boys and then men when she was older, and of course Wesley had been black; in comparison to all of her beaux, Simon looked very different.

He certainly was a suave man, to judge by the expensive jib of his suit, and she guessed that he was probably in his late twenties, and so would be four or five years older than her. She admired the precise folds in the Windsor knot of his tie, and the crisp whiteness of his freshly ironed shirt; it was the end of the day and yet on him both looked box-fresh and professionally pressed.

'Simon, if you want a wife who is going to be everything to you, may I ask why you aren't married already as you're very much the age to be bringing up a young family? Have you just not found the right girl?'

Here they were, laying out all their cards on the table. Even though they hardly knew each other, her interest was piqued, she realised. In fact, Sukie felt as if she was going for broke and needed to know Simon's precise romantic situation, and for once she knew why she was feeling this way.

She'd seen couples with their arms wrapped around each other check in at the Eddy, the men with that indentation on their finger where a wedding ring had been slipped off, and this had always struck her as a tawdry way of going about things.

Simon didn't wear a wedding ring, and there was no indentation on his finger, but she knew that some married men chose not to wear one, and so she wanted to be clear about how available he was.

'I thought I was to be married, once,' Simon confided, 'and then she realised she loved my best friend.'

'That sounds awkward.'

'Not so much, really, at least not as much as one might expect. It turned out that I wasn't too bothered, and so I don't think I ever cared for her in quite the way I should have. I doubt that we'd have been happy together if we had gone ahead and she hadn't been brave enough to tell me her true feelings before it got to that point, which I know she found very hard to do at the time,' said Simon. 'And she and my friend are made for each other, anyone can see that. They have four children now, and run a huge farm. I'm godfather to their eldest, a son.'

Sukie raised her glass to clink against Simon's again. 'It sounds as if honesty is the best policy.'

Simon volunteered that he worked in Whitehall, at which Sukie nodded but didn't probe further. If he wanted to say more on this he would, although she assumed that he wouldn't, as most people still stuck to the guns of the government's mottoes: 'careless talk costs lives' and 'loose lips sink ships'.

They began to chat then about more trivial matters, such as their favourite food and the wireless programmes they liked to listen to, and what books they had read.

And by the time they had moved on to funny things that had happened to them and various horse-riding anecdotes, they had completely failed to notice that they were the only people left in the snug, or that their waiter, positioned by the door, risked a look at his watch every now and again as he wondered what time they would decide to call it a night.

The next morning Sukie awoke with a pounding headache just as Pattie closed the bedroom door on her way down to breakfast.

By the time Simon walked her back to the Eddy at around two in the morning, she was a little tipsy, having proved persuadable to several extra drinks despite her earlier protestation, conveniently having forgotten her early start the next morning. As she tried to gauge the extent of her headache, Sukie was relieved that after the first drink she had had the presence of mind to stick to port and lemon, and not mix it with more sherry, as that would have led to something even worse than she was feeling now.

After nipping down the chilly corridor to the bathroom, she trotted back to the bedroom, blew her nose and then she took two aspirin, drank the glass of water on her bedside table, and then Pattie's too. Her alarm clock told her she had twenty minutes until she had to get up.

As she slipped back into bed and allowed herself to revel in the memory of how, on their way back to the Eddy, Simon had guided her into a darkened doorway and then slid his hands gently around her waist to pull her close, and as he bent his head down towards her, his lips had softly pressed down on hers.

Sukie glanced over at her hanky case that was lying on her bedside table, which had Wesley's ring and the gold chain wrapped safely inside.

She realised that she didn't feel guilty about kissing Simon.

She ran a finger across her lips as if to bring back the sensation of Simon kissing her; it was a tingly sensation of the sort she wanted more of.

And then Sukie snuggled down the bed for a precious fifteen minutes of snoozing, a smile on her face at what a lovely evening it had been.

# Chapter Eight

Almost without realising it Sukie and Simon drifted into spend-ing their spare time together, and one day Sukie looked up and out of her office window as she was getting ready to finish work for the day to notice that the days were lengthening and there was the scent of spring in the air.

Mr Bright was much stronger, although he was engaged a lot of the time away from the Eddy on mysterious 'appointments'. But he wasn't so busy that he didn't notice that Sukie and Simon were spending a lot of time together, and so he took to calling Simon 'your young man, Miss Scott'.

Mrs Bridge described Simon as 'a nice boy', which, as gener-ally she took rather a dim view of men, Sukie decided was a firm stamp of acceptance by the housekeeper of Simon as an appropriate partner for her.

'I completely approve,' said a more enthusiastic Tracey Benn to their faces, when Simon came to pick up Sukie one evening. 'Two of my favourite people together – what could be nicer?' she added.

Simon and Sukie grinned at her, and Tracey Benn smiled back, and then, juggling the keys to the Austin Seven, she said there was somewhere she needed to be but she hoped they were going to have a topping evening.

Pattie was a bit more basic as regards to the arrival of Simon in Sukie's life. 'About time too, Sukie. What does Evie think?'

'Evie says if I'm happy, then she is too,' replied Sukie.

'And are you? Happy, that is.'

'Yes.' Sukie paused. Pattie had asked a serious question, and Sukie thought it deserved an answer where she did more than pay scant lip service to it, and so she added, 'Well, I think so. Simon and I get on like a house on fire as we always seem to have something to say to each other, and I like it that we make each other laugh.'

'Hmmm,' said Pattie, clearly not wholly convinced. 'But does he electrify you in the way that Wesley did? I mean, William only has to look at me, and I want to tear his clothes off, and so I suppose that I want you to feel like that about your Simon.'

'*Pattie!*' Even though they were alone in their bedroom when they were talking, with the door shut, Sukie couldn't help but look behind her to check there was nobody else in earshot who could hear Pattie being so brazen. 'I'm not sure that he is "my Simon", or that I want him to be. More importantly, from what you say, does this mean that you and William have now progressed to having, um, er, relations?'

'We have and we are!' yelped Pattie, and then went on to describe in perhaps a little too much detail exactly what she and William got up to once his children were in bed and asleep, and how very much Pattie enjoyed it. 'Well, you must know what it's like, as you and Wesley were engaged, and you had all those lads in Lymbridge mooning after you too,' Pattie finished. 'I'm not particularly religious but I think to experience the full love of a man truly is a gift from God.'

Sukie swallowed, and then admitted quietly, 'Actually, those Lymbridge lads were always kept very much at arm's length, and Wesley and I never went that far. We wanted to, very much, in fact, but we felt that until we were married people would judge us too harshly if anybody ever found us spending a night together. I wish now that we had done, and that we had thought: damn anyone who notices the difference in the colour of our skin. But at the time it seemed important that we wait until we were married. And then it was too late.' And then Sukie said in an even quieter voice, 'In fact, I've never been with a man, or even really done more than kiss.'

Pattie moved to sit beside Sukie on the bed, putting an arm over her shoulder. 'I think you are right that if you and Wesley had slept together, and you had become pregnant with his child, and you were not yet married, then you and he would have had a very sorry time of it at the hands of other people. It's a shame some horrid people think like that when all a woman has done wrong is to show some love. And for many, the fact of no wedding ring will always be a huge problem no matter what race the lovers are, as would a baby born to a couple of different nationalities, even if that couple *were* married. I know you knew all of this when you took on dear Wesley, and so it must have been very difficult for you both.'

Sukie's eyes were threatening to fill with tears. She hadn't expected Pattie to be so thoughtful about how it had been for her and Wesley.

Then Pattie looked at Sukie with a naughty expression on her face, before she said, 'And when you do go all the way, Sukie, whether it's with Simon or with some other lucky man, you are going to love it. There's no feeling on earth like it, I promise!'

There must have been something in the air that day as that very evening Simon announced that a friend of his had said they could borrow his flat, if Sukie felt they were now at the stage where they should spend a night together.

While she had a flutter of excitement at the mere thought of them lying in a bed together, Sukie wasn't utterly convinced otherwise that she did feel like that, not really.

While she was very fond of Simon and she enjoyed their embraces, her skin didn't ripple with pleasure when he touched her, and certainly not in the way an accidental nudge from Wesley could make her feel. And while she always liked to re-member Simon's kisses the following day, she didn't think that she felt desperate for them, not in the passionate and heated way that Pattie had described, and that Evie had told her about too.

Every moment in Wesley's arms had felt incredibly intoxicating, but always tempered, Sukie saw now, by her determination that they didn't go 'too far', which had been ultimately a passion-killer for both of them, to the point that now Sukie wondered about the intensity of what she and Wesley had shared.

In addition, Sukie also felt a little peculiar that Simon had been talking about her in these terms to his chum; for why would anybody want to stay in a flat with their friend, unless it was for them to sleep together? It felt base, somehow, and Sukie rather wished Simon hadn't told her so bluntly about the flat and its owner.

But then, hadn't she and Pattie talked about having relations with Simon? And she had tolerated too some knowing nods from Tracey Benn, which had managed to comment very effect-ively on what might or might not be going on between them under the sheets.

So Sukie had to admonish herself immediately for having been both a prude and a hypocrite for criticising Simon for doing what she had also been happy to do.

Interestingly, Sukie found then that now Simon had brought the idea of them having sexual intercourse out into the open so blatantly, there was an answering tickle of something insistent from Sukie's own body, and she felt her neck flushing.

And this made her think about her virginity, and she saw that in many ways it had come increasingly to feel more of a burden rather than something precious to bestow on a 'special someone' (as Sukie had heard two of the chambermaids describe it rather mawkishly only the day before).

So, while she had reservations, she worried that if she and Simon didn't go to the flat, she was going to get herself into a proper stew, and would regret not going there before too long.

'Let me think on what you've just told me,' Sukie said to Simon, as this was all too complicated to try to explain to him, and she wanted to consider a bit more what it was that she actually felt. 'I wasn't expecting you to come out with that right then, but it's an interesting and possibly provocatively attractive proposition that I need to mull over.'

He nodded relatively cheerfully, and she liked that he didn't try to force her.

The next morning her mind was made up.

There were many much less personable first lovers around than Simon, she had decided, and in fact most women would love to be in Sukie's position. Simon was handsome and appeared to like her, and she was fond of him, and she was sure that he would take good care of her.

She *would* do this.

It was time that Sukie Scott became a proper woman, Sukie told herself. And before the morning was out she had informed Simon of her decision.

# Chapter Nine

Now that they had made their minds to move to the next level, they had to wait for a few weeks until Sukie could get a night away from the Eddy without it being the centre of gossip.

Simon had suggested that perhaps they should aim for an afternoon liaison instead, but Sukie said she had romantic notions of their first time, and as she was sure it was going to be lovely, she wanted them to be able to wake up together.

Actually, she hadn't quite been able to tamp down her caution, but she wanted Simon to think she was enthusiastic at the idea of what they were planning to do and indeed was very much looking forward to it. And the more she and he talked about how and when they should meet, the more she felt an answering worm of pleasure wriggle below her waist at the very idea. It was only when she tried to imagine the actual act itself with Simon that she felt decidedly wriggle-free.

As luck would have it, Pattie had headed back to Dartmoor for a weekend, and she had taken William and his children with her to meet Evie and the rest of Pattie's family.

While it was still frowned upon to travel about on frivolous journeys as petrol was rationed and the trains were often stuffed to the gills with evacuees being moved around, or troops in uniform on manoeuvres, William had to visit departments like his that were operating down in Bristol and then Plymouth on a fact-finding visit so that he could use any of their ideas that would then help him better organise finding lost relatives back in London.

The tors of Dartmoor, and Lymbridge, were quite close to Plymouth and so Pattie had leaped at the chance of combining his work commitments with giving the children a few days in the countryside to let off steam, as well as showing him, and the kiddies, where she had grown up. She was keen to introduce them all to her family, although Sukie wondered privately how the Yeos would take Pattie's pash on such an obviously older man, and moreover, one with a very young ready-made family much in evidence.

Still, the West Country visit of Pattie and William and co. meant Sukie could have a night away from the Eddy with nobody (almost definitely) being any the wiser, unless she chose to tell them what she was up to. And she certainly wasn't about to do that.

With an appropriately innocent look on her face, Sukie waved William and Pattie off on their way early on The Day, after having given Dot, with strict instructions to share with the twins, a small box of barley-twist boiled sweets that by chance just the day before a guest had pressed into Sukie's hands as a thank you gift for making his stay so pleasant.

Pattie said to the children that they could each have one sweet now and then she'd look after the box for them to prevent any bickering, and then as William put the car into gear Pattie mouthed with a knowing nod, 'I'll save the rest in case we have travel sickness to deal with,' and Sukie gave her a playful grimace back at the hideous image that immediately sprang to mind, causing Pattie to give a cheery hoot of laughter.

In mid-afternoon, when she and Simon had arranged to meet, Sukie was left hanging about for what felt an exceptionally long time as she stood patiently beside one of the huge black lions in Trafalgar Square that supported Nelson's Column as she waited for him to arrive.

She had just got thoroughly chilled when he finally ran up to her from Whitehall, apologising profusely and saying that something had come up at work that meant he had had to stay longer than he had intended, and he hadn't been able to let her know he was going to be late. He kissed her on the cheek while giving her a quick hug, while Sukie tried not to look too shivery.

Then, on the way to the flat where the deed was to be done, they had to stop off in order to collect bread and a tin of baked beans from Simon's digs in Warren Street, which fortunately was roughly on the way, so that they would have something to eat for their supper.

Sukie normally thought of herself as a right old greedy guts, but she had completely forgotten to think about anything as mundane as food, which Simon didn't look too impressed by, and so Sukie guessed that he felt she should have planned ahead for their victuals.

Sukie wanted to say that this sort of rendezvous was so new to her that she didn't know what he expected of her, and that she had been imagining much more interesting things . . .

But then she took a look at his face, which was staring off into the distance slightly as if he was contemplating a very oner-ous task he had to do, and so she decided to keep mum as she didn't want Simon to feel that she might be making fun of him or what he expected of her or, indeed for that matter, of himself.

The flat for their clandestine engagement turned out to be in the basement of a dark and foreboding-looking five-storey terraced house on a dingy Camden street. It belonged to somebody – Simon didn't tell Sukie his name – whom he played cricket with in the summer months.

As they cautiously made their way down the crumbling steps to the flat's front door, Sukie asked Simon what was in the bag that he was carrying, and then she grimaced, although not at all in the playful manner that she had earlier when with Pattie, as he replied it was towels and bed linen.

It all seemed so seedy somehow (and potentially messy, if the towels were anything to go by), Sukie couldn't help but feel.

However, when she saw how squalid the flat was inside, she

was glad that Simon had had the foresight to think ahead as he had, as she wouldn't have wanted to lie in the crumpled and grimy bed linen she could see on the bed.

Simon's friend clearly didn't have a woman-who-did, and nor did he spend much time on housework or on putting things away once he had used them, if the clutter everywhere was anything to go by. Although she tried not to be judgemental, Sukie suspected that she wouldn't be terribly impressed by Simon's friend if she ever met him.

She made up the bed with the clean linen, leaving the used sheets and pillow cases in a pile in the far corner of the room, pulling a chair in front of them so that she wouldn't see what lay now in the corner of the room unless she really looked.

It felt too early to be thinking of making use of the bed, and so feeling peculiarly at a loose end, and as evening opening hours had just begun, they decided to go to the public house at the end of the road for a drink.

It wasn't a particularly hospitable pub and Sukie noted how sticky the tables felt and the large number of cigarette burns pitting the surface. She thought there must have been a time in her life when she hadn't noticed this sort of thing, which had made the rough edges of the world look a bit less disappointing, but after more than a year at the Eddy, Sukie knew those days were past for her, and probably for ever.

They hadn't been in the ladies' bar for more than half an hour when a fight broke out over in the main bar.

'I don't think it's a serious set-to,' said Simon. He tried to smile at Sukie as if to reassure her, but Sukie thought that he looked subdued and anxious, although almost definitely more concerned with what was to come than anything to do with the noisy scuffle and the scrap of chairs being pushed back on the tacky linoleum floor across the room. It was as if he was the one who needed the reassurance more than she did.

'Neither do I,' Sukie replied. 'I think they are letting off steam as much as anything, but perhaps it's a sign that it's time for us to go to the, er, um, flat.'

'Yes, let's go, we probably should do that,' Simon said and he stood up abruptly, a little, Sukie thought, as if he just wanted to get it over and done with.

For a moment she lost confidence, and wondered if she did actually want to go to bed with Simon. But then she told herself that if she didn't, immediately she would feel the weight of her virginity more heavily than at present, which she really didn't want to happen, and that she might as well grit her teeth and bear it.

Simon's expression suggested he had seen her brief hesitation.

But then Sukie reached for his arm, saying firmly and with as much enthusiasm as she could muster, 'Lead on, Macduff', and suddenly the awkwardness between them lessened and they looked at each other almost as if they were about to set out on a great adventure.

When they got to the flat, although Sukie tried her level best to be positive about it, she now thought it looked even more filthy in the fading light of day. She had expected a friend of Simon's to have had a home that was more comfortable, and certainly more clean. But Simon guessed what she was thinking when he saw her looking around again, and so he told her how much each week his chum had to pay for the flat, a sum that totally horrified Sukie, it was so large.

She realised that she was lucky to be able to live at the Eddy, right in the centre of town and in very warm and comfortable surroundings by comparison to this.

Nothing was going as Sukie had imagined, and she felt a wave of despondency threatening to engulf her. Her tummy had a unpleasantly sinking feeling inside and not the happy tremor of pleasantly fluttering butterflies she had been expecting.

She tried to buck up her mood, but the temperature in the flat was quite nippy and the fire Simon was trying to light wouldn't take, and their beans (heated on a tiny gas stove in the corner of the room) on bread (as without the fire, they couldn't turn the bread into toast) were only decidedly so-so.

However, what Sukie felt worst of all was that conversation between herself and Simon, normally easily flowing between them, had dwindled since they had entered the flat for a second time to something awkward and uncomfortable that was punctuated by nervy periods of quiet, the loud ticking of a 1920s clock on the mantelpiece testament to these aching silences.

It was time to call a halt. And so before they became too dispirited by the whole affair, as Simon stood up and made as if to clear their supper things away, Sukie said, 'Come on, Simon, why don't you leave that for now? Shall we do what we're here for? It's got to be more fun than this.'

They undressed with their backs to each other, and then slipped under the covers, neither daring to look at the other, although Sukie caught a glimpse of some soft downy hair low down on his belly.

She thought about this as at first they lay on their backs and stared at the ceiling, and then Sukie reached out a hand across one of Simon's heavily starched sheets that now, in the chill of the flat, felt almost icily damp.

Agonisingly slowly she edged her hand over towards Simon. Gently her fingertips found his, and slowly Sukie entwined her hand with Simon's.

It was a while later before they found the courage to reach properly for each other, and then it happened suddenly and with more than a hint of clumsiness.

Sukie wasn't sure about Simon's expression as he had moved above her in the dim light from a candle in a saucer on the chest of drawers. She thought that it had looked very much like he was in pain and doing something he didn't want to do, particularly when it ended in something like a howl. Then he'd rolled away and promptly fell asleep, which she hadn't expected either.

She couldn't imagine Wesley and her having such a cold-feeling experience, and she felt mournful and sad, until Simon woke up after ten minutes and put his arm around her and pulled her close.

She and Simon did it again an hour later, in part as Sukie thought she might have missed something important the first time through her naivety and so she wanted to analyse the act a bit more, now that she had a rough idea of what it might be. But although it was a bit less underwhelming for Sukie than it had been earlier, again she found the essence of herself curiously removed from what she was actually doing or, more exactly, what Simon was doing to her body.

It was as if she was a bit player in somebody else's drama and she didn't know what she should do or, importantly, what she wanted to do.

A church clock struck nine.

'Goodness, it's got chilly in here,' said Sukie.

'It has,' said Simon.

'I think I've been spoiled at the Eddy. We don't have heating in the staff bedrooms but I think warmth rises from the lower floors and so it's never really cold like this.' Sukie wished she could stop babbling and saying the first thing she could think of to fill the silence, but conversation felt awkward between them once again now that they had done what they had come to do. She couldn't imagine them discussing the sex they had just had.

'Simon, I hope you don't think I'm terribly rude, but I wonder if we could call it a night and go home. I know we'd planned on staying...' Sukie said tentatively.

'Yes, I think we can go,' Simon chipped in quickly, and Sukie tried not to dwell on how relieved he sounded.

On the way back to the Eddy, Sukie told herself once again that she wouldn't let anybody know what she and Simon had just been up to, and that included Evie and Pattie and Tracey Benn.

She certainly didn't feel like bragging about the sojourn in the flat. It all seemed so insignificant and disappointing, and not at all the life-changing and climactic event that Sukie had hoped that it was going to be.

As they walked towards Covent Garden, Sukie looked at Simon, and again tried to find in him the handsome and debonair man she had so enjoyed drinking with at the Savoy.

But what she saw instead was a pleasant man, but one who she couldn't quite fathom and whom she mightn't be terribly attracted to.

In that moment Sukie was struck by the thought that perhaps Simon was exactly as he always had been, and that instead it was she who had changed now that she had been deflowered. And it had been the act of *deflowering* that for her had been much more about why she had wanted this sojourn to the flat to happen, than it had been about having sexual intercourse with *Simon*, or in making either of them euphorically happy.

Maybe therefore it wasn't Simon's fault at all that she hadn't enjoyed the experience much.

After all, if she couldn't fathom if she properly desired Simon, let alone why the act itself had all felt such a damp squib to her, then it was impossible to have expected Simon to do so either, Sukie realised gloomily.

# Chapter Ten

Sukie stared at herself long and hard in the mirror that hung in her and Pattie's bedroom. She was tired and a little grumpy, as she hadn't slept very well, although that might partly be down to Polly perching on her pillow and staring intently at her face from three inches away at one point.

She looked exactly the same now that she was no longer a virgin as she had done when she was.

She shouldn't be surprised by this, she knew, but it felt odd all the same.

Sukie laughed wryly. Of course that was a good thing, as none of the Eddies would guess.

But she felt very different somehow – about herself, about Simon, and actually about her place in the world in the general sense – than she had this time just a day previously, and it seemed strange that that sense of difference wasn't obvious to anyone who cared to look for it in her face or in the shadows under her eyes.

Now, everything around her seemed to Sukie as if shaded with levels of complexity she'd not noticed before. And she knew that only time would tell whether that was a good thing or not.

She told herself not to worry about it any further as she couldn't do anything about it, and went to brush her teeth.

But a knock on Sukie's bedroom door a minute later, with

the request that she come down to the kitchen as quickly as possible, abruptly pushed aside these philosophical thoughts.

Downstairs, there was some shocking news – news that told Sukie that certainly nobody was going to be giving her a second look that day.

For, the moment she saw Mrs Bridge, Sukie realised something unpleasant had happened; it was the squint buttoning of Mrs Bridge's knit, with the buttons out of alignment that gave it away.

And the moment Mrs Bridge spied Sukie, she told her in a breathy and emotional way that the Eddy had been broken into overnight.

'Lawks-a-mussy, what a horror, although nothing much seems to have been taken, and the safe is secure, an' so is the upstairs petty cash box,' Mrs Bridge garbled, the housekeeper's white-knuckled fist clutching her old grey cardie close to her heart, belying the assertion that 'nothing much' had been taken.

Sukie thought that at the very least Mrs Bridge's ease had been stolen, and she felt very badly about this.

The housekeeper looked anxious and very pale as she stood by the kitchen table, and so Sukie asked her to sit down, and then Chef, who was tut-tutting over the theft, pushed a cup of sweet tea towards Mrs Bridge, reminding her this was good for shock, and Sukie suggested that he make some toast for Mrs Bridge too, which he scurried off to do.

'I didn't know anything about it until this morning,' said Mrs Bridge. 'But when I looked around after, I realised what had happened – I woke up and the alley door was swinging open, an' I think the sound of this were what stirred me, an' the old bolt was lying plain to see on the floor, and an old jemmy, so that all and sundry could have wandered in and murdered us in our beds stone-dead. And then I found that my downstairs petty cash box for housekeeping is gone, and so are the tins of salmon I'd been saving for Good Friday that were at the back of the pantry, and a pair of my good drawers were missing too.'

At this revelation of her underwear having been taken, Mrs Bridge fanned herself furiously with her hand.

Chef and Alan, the maître d' who'd suffered a stroke in the autumn and who was now easing himself back into work with breakfast duties only, had both been listening to Mrs Bridge's description and quickly made themselves scarce by heading to the cooking grills immediately after the housekeeper brought her own underclothing into the conversation.

'Your *drawers?*' said Sukie incredulously, thinking she must have misheard as this seemed so absurd.

Mrs Bridge nodded. 'Yes, I'd rinsed out my drawers and they were drying on the back of a chair in my sitting room. As you know, my sitting room door is right next to the door into the pantry, and so I expect the robber, God rest his heinous soul – but wouldn't I love to get my hands on him for five minutes! – must have opened my door and saw there wasn't much of value there, other than my drawers, of course, which he probably thought were a pillowcase, seeing as the waistband was towards the door, an' then he went into the pantry instead. Chef said he wouldn't have wanted to risk going too far into the hotel, not once he'd found all that salmon, as it's a good haul he'll be able to sell on, and like a fool I'd left my housekeeping petty cash box on the shelf beside all the salmon – there was a whole seven and six of coins in it, which would have pleased the dratted charlatan no end, I don't doubt – and so I think the robber went back to my sitting room at that point and took my drawers in which to carry the booty away with him. Before he made off quick down the back alley.' Mrs Bridge had been talking so fast that her words were almost running one into another, and occasionally she had lost her diction, so rapidly was she speaking, but eventually even she had to stop to take a gaspy breath.

'Oh dear,' said Sukie, and she stroked the housekeeper's arm in comfort.

Mrs Bridge's tiny bedroom was just behind her little private sitting room, and so it was a wonder she hadn't been woken by the break-in as it happened. It was a good thing she hadn't, though, Sukie was convinced – one well-aimed blow from a jemmy, and it could all have been much, much more serious.

Sukie felt, though, that she didn't need to say that Mrs Bridge had been very lucky that the perpetrator hadn't wanted to harm her in any way. That bedroom was incredibly vulnerable at night, Sukie could now see, because during late service and first thing, the kitchen and scullery areas tended to be quiet, and so very often Mrs Bridge would be the only person on that floor during the depths of darkness, and any cries for help she might have made – if the burglar had proved to be of a violent disposition – would not necessarily be heard by the night cover of doorman/receptionist upstairs.

While Sukie thought about how to beef up the downstairs security, she couldn't help but hear the Eddies' chatter about what had happened.

'We could all have been murdered in our beds,' said a new chambermaid.

Sukie sighed. She thought the girl should have known better than to say something so dramatic and unlikely.

'Murdered!' screeched Polly, and Sukie looked at the chambermaid with an exasperated expression.

'The Min. of War talks all about the Dunkirk spirit on the home front,' said Alan, who'd sidled up to them again, 'but a whole lot less about the robbers taking advantage of us all in the blackout.'

'Well, if he'd come face to face with Mrs Bridge, they'd have heard her yell down in Whitehall, of that I'm sure,' said John.

And so on as the Eddies egged each other on, until Sukie said very firmly, 'Right, that's enough! Of course what has happened is unpleasant and unsettling, and especially so for Mrs Bridge. But if you all go on like this it will spread all through the Eddy, and then somebody will panic, and then where will we be? Hear me well – I don't want a single guest to be worried, and so all this chat stops NOW. Understand?'

Everyone nodded.

'Murd—'

'Polly!' admonished Sukie with a cross look at the bird. He raised a claw at her as if in supplication.

A baby-faced bobby turned up an hour after Sukie had telephoned Holborn police station, and after he'd begun with the music hall saying of 'Hello, hello, hello', which Sukie couldn't tell was a joke or not (she thought he probably wasn't intentionally trying to be funny as he looked a serious young man), he depressed her by talking about the shortages of bobbies on the beat.

'Petty crime is becoming a right problem round here, with robbings and hoistings every day,' he added, unhelpfully, 'and we don't have enough peelers to stop it.'

Mrs Bridge got the wrong end of the stick, thinking his use of the word 'petty' meant he thought her petticoat had been taken too. 'No, no, he took my best drawers an' not my petty,' she said to put him right as she lifted her blouse away from her décolletage and wafted it quickly, as if the mere thought of a stranger grabbing her underthings was making her hot.

The bobby looked confused, and so Sukie told Mrs Bridge to describe exactly what had happened.

He and Sukie caught each other's eye when Mrs Bridge got to the part about her drawers playing a crucial role in the theft. Manfully, he managed not to snigger, but when he then asked to see the door into the alley where presumably the burglar had made his entrance, Sukie noticed his voice was pitched at a higher register than it had been a minute beforehand when he had been asking his more routine questions, which Sukie put down to the effort of him not laughing in front of the clearly still very upset housekeeper.

Sukie indicated to Chef that the bobby be offered a cup of tea and a biscuit. The fact that he had taken care not to hurt Mrs Bridge's feelings had rather endeared the policeman to Sukie, and she felt he deserved a little treat, even though he was still on duty and this was against the rules.

John usually took care of a lot of the Eddy's handyman duties, but his shoulder was playing up and meant he couldn't step in, which was a little tiresome as Sukie wanted Mrs Bridge to see that the back door was urgently being repaired. She thought that might restore a little of the sense of security the housekeeper deserved.

But when Sukie mentioned to Tracey Benn what had happened – Tracey Benn being the one guest that Sukie didn't mind knowing about the break-in – and added that she was just about to telephone around to get a repair man in, Tracey Benn said 'Rubbish!' in a very authoritative way to Sukie.

She disappeared for ten minutes before returning, having whisked herself into a heavy-duty Rosie the Riveter blue boiler suit in the meantime, clomping down the stairs to the basement level at the front of the hotel with a wooden box of tools, her sturdy brogues making an almost musical clanging sound on the metal stairs.

'How on earth do you *always* have the right outfit?' said Sukie incredulously.

'First thing I learned as a Brownie.'

'You! A Brownie? I do *not* believe it.'

Tracey Benn tapped the side of her nose and then held up the crossed first and second finger of left hand. 'Me and Olave Baden-Powell are like this!'

'Oh, look at that!' said Sukie suddenly, pointing out of the barred window of the kitchen. 'There's a pig flying by.'

Tracey Benn saluted the imaginary pig and then, with impressive efficiency and with a minimum of fuss, she fitted a second bolt to the door to the alley, and a new mortice lock, explaining to Sukie the way to do it, making it all look very easy.

Sukie looked on in awe as she wouldn't have had the first idea as to how to go about this.

As Tracey Benn deftly twisted the final screw into place, she said to Mrs Bridge, 'It's always handy to know how to keep the rowdies away from one's smalls,' with a comically raised eyebrow at the mere thought of the purloined drawers.

Mrs Bridge was by now recovered enough from her ordeal to reply instantly, 'I think we'd better say mediums, if not larges'.

And she and Tracey Benn and Sukie enjoyed quite a chuckle about that, which they then agreed was a good moment and that it really was true that every cloud did contain a silver lining if only one looked hard enough to find it. Although Sukie thought it was a pity that Tracey Benn's final, 'and of course a silver lining in a cloud stops anyone getting their knickers in a twist,' was a little wasted on the housekeeper, who didn't appear to find the inference amusing, or maybe by this time she had just had enough of them laughing at what could be taken as being at her expense.

Fortunately Tracey Benn was diverted then as, with a briefcase in hand and a bowler hat on his head as he was clearly on his way to an appointment off the premises, Mr Bright bustled down to inspect the new lock and its fitting, and he stood looking on as Tracey Benn gathered together the tools she had used and returned them to the toolbox, repeating appreciatively, 'Capital, capital,' until Sukie coughed to break Mr Bright's train of thought.

He and Tracey Benn left to go upstairs to the dining room together, with Mr Bright saying, 'Thank you so much, Miss Benn – now have whatever you fancy,' and Tracey Benn cooing seductively back at him, 'Now *there's* an offer, Mr Bright,' in a deliberately provocative manner that Sukie knew was designed to make Mr Bright harrumph in embarrassment, which he duly did.

Mrs Bridge and Sukie smiled at each other; they were in agreement that Mr Bright was the sort of chap who was always going to be wrong-footed by somebody as bold and quick-witted as Tracey Benn. But it was amusing to witness the myriad ways that Tracey Benn naughtily couldn't resist achieving the hotel manager's 'harrumph' time after time, much to the gentle discomfort of Mr Bright.

Sukie had once called her out on her rather flippant treatment of Mr Bright, but Tracey Benn had assured Sukie that the hotel manager enjoyed her quips and that she would stop speaking to him in that way the absolute moment she felt he didn't.

And when Sukie had watched Mr Bright with Tracey Benn, and saw how pink he got and his little smiles as he shifted his weight from foot to foot as he tried and failed to think of a clever reply to whatever Tracey Benn had just said to him, she was inclined to agree.

'Are you feeling a little more yourself now, Mrs Bridge?' said Sukie as the sound of Mr Bright and Tracey Benn going upstairs faded. 'Please let me make you another cuppa as you are still looking a bit shaken. Your bedroom is right behind your sitting room, I know, and so that nasty thief would have been very near to you, and I do appreciate that's not a very pleasant thought.'

Still, while she wanted to show solidarity with the housekeeper, there was quite a large part of Sukie that was terribly tempted to joke further about Mrs Bridge's knickers being in a twist.

But a look at the housekeeper's still-worried face told Sukie it was too soon to be inserting this sort of humour quite yet into the situation, although she thought that at some point she might be able to.

'It gave me a right turn when I saw my drawers had gone, I can tell you,' said Mrs Bridge, who was as yet still oblivious as to the absurdity of a thief stealing her underwear.

Sukie replied that she was sure she would have felt similarly, and then she stressed that before the day was over she would make sure that Mrs Bridge's bedroom window was further secured against entry from the alley, and a bolt had been fitted to the door of the sitting room too, so that the housekeeper could feel more secure once she had gone to bed at night by making sure her sitting room was barred to intruders. And that Sukie would make it a top priority to replace Mrs Bridge's missing drawers with the very best she could find.

They chatted for a while, and then had another cup of tea as a pick-me-up, after which Sukie a little reluctantly stood up and said she really must get to work.

Before she left the kitchen, Sukie leaned down and gave Mrs Bridge a comforting hug, and told her to take an hour or two to gather her thoughts, at which Mrs Bridge assured her, 'I feel fine now, pet, thank you. Don't you worry about me.'

The older woman looked much calmer now, and so Sukie couldn't resist adding just before she went out of the kitchen door, 'I know you had a funny turn, Mrs Bridge, when you realised what had happened during the night, but I bet it was nothing to the turn the burglar will have had when he realised what he had grabbed to put the tins of salmon and the cash box in!'

# Chapter Eleven

Sukie telephoned a couple of locksmiths to ask advice, and arranged for one to visit the next day when Mr Bright would be there to give an audit of the weak points of entry to the Eddy. Then she began sorting the morning's post when the phone rang.

It was Evie!

She had never telephoned Sukie at the Eddy before, and so Sukie knew instantly that something serious had happened.

'Thank goodness, Sukie – I am *so* glad that it was you who answered the telephone,' said Evie in a very fretful manner.

Evie didn't sound at all like herself and Sukie felt a corresponding twist of apprehension that wasn't too far off a panicky twinge. For all the world it sounded like incredibly bad news was about to be broken.

'Evie, is everything all right?' Sukie cut in, hearing the tremble of worry in her own voice. 'You and Peter are okay, and Nellie?'

'We're fine...'

Oh heck, it had to be Pattie then.

There hadn't been a car accident, had there?

'Pattie?' Sukie asked.

'Oh, she's here, and very full of beans,' said Evie, 'and she has been showing off William and the kiddies left, right and centre. And everyone else is well too, so don't you worry about any of that.'

Sukie felt a wave of relief.

Still, despite these assurances, Evie definitely sounded very concerned, and Sukie wanted to know what had happened.

'But Pattie is why I'm telephoning,' said Evie, a morose tone peppering her words now.

Sukie heard behind her friend's voice the chinking sound of glasses touching each other as they were picked up, and she realised that Evie was telephoning from the bar of the Haywain, a fact confirmed by Evie then dropping her voice to a whisper so that nobody nearby could hear, even though Sukie knew the public house only opened in the evenings and this meant it would only be the landlord, who everyone called Barkeep Joss, who was sorting out the glasses.

Evie went on, 'All hell has been let loose as Father discovered that William is *five years older* than he is, and so there's been a terrible ding-dong, and William has driven off with the children in what I suppose is a huff, and Pattie has been left screaming blue murder at everyone. Or at least she was last night when Pa told her she was throwing her life away and making a big mistake. And first thing this morning before breakfast, Ma tells me that Pattie stomped off for a walk with Shady, and nobody has seen her since. Mother hates an argument, as you know, and apparently Shady wouldn't stop barking after they were shouting at each other, and so nobody at Bluebells could get much sleep. And James threatened to punch William's lights out. Julia said that she thought Pattie was being very brave following her heart, and then Mother had a say about her for sticking her oar in, with Ma shouting at Julia that the family had already suffered enough shame through her behaviour and, well, you can imagine how that went down.'

'Like a lead balloon,' Sukie agreed gloomily.

Shady was the family dog, an ugly but lovable mutt, and James was Pattie's younger brother. The irony was that his own lady friend Jane Cornish was a whole twelve years older than he; he'd not quite been sixteen when they had met, and they were still going strong over two years later. And Julia was the sister between Evie and Pattie, and she had, scandalously, lived proudly for several years now in a gloriously unmarried state with the almost terminally dull Leonard Bassett.

Evie ended with, 'And last night Ma told Pa off, after which he shouted at her, and she shouted back, and then he went to the Haywain and, Mother says, didn't return until closing time, by which time he was well in his cups. They're not talking, and Mother is weeding the same bit of vegetable patch again and again, and Peter took Nellie over just now and says Ma is pulling out the half-grown vegetables and not just weeds, she's so angry. It's such a bind, and we just weren't expecting it.'

As Evie spoke to Sukie of all these familiar and very dear to her Yeo family members, Sukie felt an almost overwhelming rush of homesickness, and a longing for a walk down the mossy lane that ran through Lymbridge. She'd been an only child, her parents dying in a car crash when she was small, and although Sukie had technically been brought up by an aunt who was now in Canada, really she regarded Susan and Robert Yeo as her parents. They had treated her always pretty much as one of their own brood, and Sukie had loved spending time at Bluebells.

Evie, normally a very calm person, sounded extremely rattled, Sukie thought, and so the family argument must have been a right humdinger.

The Yeo family weren't the type of people to quarrel much. There was plenty of friendly bickering between them, of course, but in all the many hours Sukie had spent at the family house, she never remembered hearing raised voices, in part as Robert and Susan were very skilled at pouring oil on troubled waters. And they would always encourage everyone to remember that the best thing to do would be to follow the Yeo mottoes of 'live and let live' and 'least said, soonest mended'.

Sukie had adopted these mottoes as a mantra for her own life, and she thought they were good, sound sense.

With a quick calculation, Sukie realised that if he were five years older than Robert, therefore William must be fifty if he was a day, and although personally she'd always thought William rather a nice man (and he certainly didn't look his age), she could see why Robert had taken umbrage at his youngest daughter 'throwing her life away' on a man close on thirty years older than she was.

Sukie doubted that Robert, normally such a kindly and mild-mannered man, had intended his words to upset Pattie and William quite so much, or that he for a moment thought that his comments would end up pulling the whole family into the argument. But that was what happened with things that were said in the heat of the moment, Sukie knew. Like Pandora and the box, once unleashed, who knew where an argument might lead?

'Sukie, I know it's terribly difficult for you as you are always so busy, but I wondered if you might come to see us, as I think you will have thoughts on this that might calm everybody down?' said Evie, her voice pleading. 'I spoke to Mr Smith just now, and he is in London at the moment, driving back down to Lymbridge later today, leaving at lunchtime, and so if there's any way you could come with him ...? And in any case, I really want to see you. Please, please come, my dearest Sukie.'

While she was homesick for Dartmoor, this wasn't good timing, Sukie thought, as there was always so much more to do at the Eddy than she had time for, and she wanted to keep an eye on poor Mrs Bridge in the wake of the burglary, and to deal with the locksmith booked for the next day. In addition, she'd been preparing the accounts for the accountant to show to the tax man and had hoped to get those off this week, plus she wanted to design a newspaper advertisement to promote an upcoming series of cookery demonstrations on cooking on a ration that Sukie had organised for the Eddy after Easter.

But immediately thoughts flooded Sukie of how staunchly supportive of herself a heavily pregnant Evie had been when she had come all the way to London to be at her side after Wesley had died and she was feeling very low.

And then Sukie reminded herself that there never would be a good time to take a break from the Eddy. If she promised Evie she would come in several days rather than today, there was bound to be a new drama at that time that would make it easier not to go.

She doubted that either Mr Bright or Mrs Bridge would quiz her as to why she wanted a leave of absence so abruptly – they were the sort of people who if she said that Pattie and her sister Evie needed her with them for a few days, they would think that of course she had to go. Certainly in over a year of working at the Eddy, she hadn't had a single day completely to herself as holiday, and both of them had said at various times that she really should make sure she got a little time to herself now and then.

And so, provided Mr Bright and Mrs Bridge were agreeable, and Mr Bright thought he could handle the locksmith, she thought a break would pep herself up.

A couple of days down in the West Country, wouldn't that be the very ticket?

Mr Bright was so much better now than he had been, that Sukie was pretty sure that he and Mrs Bridge could muddle along without her for a couple of days, even in spite of the break-in. And although Pattie wasn't on reception, they had the former receptionist from the Capel standing in at the moment, and she certainly knew what she was doing.

Then Sukie realised that there was an ulterior and unacknow-ledged motive lurking beneath all this that was adding gasoline to her favourable thoughts about going to see Evie.

For if she were in Lymbridge, it would mean that she had a bona fide reason for not seeing Simon for a few days, and in turn this would mean they could both regroup their thoughts and feelings after the previous evening's goings-on in the squalid Camden flat belonging to his friend.

'Sukie, you've gone very quiet,' prompted Evie.

'No promises, but let me have a word with Mrs Bridge and Mr Bright, Evie, and I will ring you once I've spoken with them,' said Sukie. 'And I need to make sure there is cover for my shifts driving the mobile canteen. But if there's any way I can swing it, and I can cadge a ride with Mr Smith today so that I can come and see you all, then I certainly will.'

Evie's answering gulp of relief made Sukie absolutely determined that she would go.

It had been far too long since she had breathed in the heather-laden air of Lymbridge, and with that dart of homesickness from earlier still puncturing her heart so determinedly at the sound of her best friend's voice, Sukie felt that there was no place she would rather be at that moment than sitting right beside her very best friend.

Mr Bright, Mrs Bridge and Tracey Benn all thought it was an excellent idea that Sukie went back to Dartmoor.

Mr Bright and Mrs Bridge could man the fort at the Eddy, they assured her, Mr Bright promising Sukie that he would take extra good care of Mrs Bridge in her absence, and that he would deal personally with the locksmith's visit tomorrow. And Tracey Benn assured Sukie that she would make sure she was also there for when the locksmith came. In addition, she'd be happy to drive the mobile canteen in her place, and she'd better go and telephone Mr Watson from the Peckham depot immediately so that he could rejig the rota for the Austin Seven pick-ups.

Sukie was just about to lift the telephone receiver to get in touch with Mr Smith, who was a lovely man now married to Sukie and Evie's former headmistress, and who had to divide his time between London and Lymbridge, when the telephone rang, and Mr Smith turned out to be on the other end of the line, and quickly they agreed that he'd come to collect Sukie at one o'clock.

It was well past noon already and so Sukie ran upstairs and threw a few things harum-scarum into her cardboard suitcase, including her handkerchief case. She didn't like to think of Wesley's ring being left behind. She knew her clothes would be crumpled but she didn't really have time to fold them properly as the morning had almost gone. Sukie sighed and told herself that before she wore them, she could press the clothes that she was now heaving into the suitcase any old how, and she closed the lid and pressed its two case-toggles closed.

Sukie ran out of the bedroom and was halfway down the stairs when she remembered that wrapped in tissue paper in her underwear drawer was a very tiny teddy bear that she had seen in a toy shop not long after Christmas and had bought for Nellie. She thumped back up the stairs and added that to the suitcase. Then she thought of a new pair of nylons she had just got on the ration, still in their cellophane wrapping, and she popped those inside too as a small gift for Evie.

Sukie was just about to go down the stairs again when she realised that she didn't have her toothbrush with her, nor her comb, and so she had to dart to get those, saying out loud to herself, 'Sukie Scott, you'd forget your own head if it wasn't screwed on'.

Not too long afterwards Sukie was ready in reception, having said her goodbyes to Mr Bright and Mrs Bridge, and Tracey Benn, and was waiting in the warm for Mr Smith's black car to pull up outside.

She was idly scratching Polly's chin as he sat on the small perch at the side of reception he was allowed to use if he'd been very good, when Sukie was trying to go through a mental tick-list of everything that she had done, and that she should have done.

Although everything seemed to be in hand, Sukie had a nagging feeling that there was still something she had forgotten to do.

With a jolt, she remembered.

Of course.

Simon!

She had completely neglected to inform him that she was going away. In fact, she rather felt that she hadn't thought of him once that morning following Mrs Bridge's revelation of the burglary.

But before she could do anything to rectify the matter, Mr Smith honked his car's horn from outside, and Sukie ran out and placed her suitcase on the back seat.

'I'll just be five minutes, if that isn't too much of a problem, Mr Smith – I've just this second remembered something important that I very much need to do. Many apols,' she said, and Mr Smith smiled and calmly reached for a newspaper as he told her not to hurry on his account.

Sukie hurried back inside the Eddy and scribbled a telegram: SIMON STOP BEEN CALLED AWAY URGENTLY STOP I WILL LET YOU KNOW WHEN I AM BACK STOP SUKIE STOP

She gave it to Mrs Bridge to send to Simon's flat, and she promised to pay the housekeeper for the cost of sending the telegram when she had visited Dartmoor and was ensconced once more back at the Eddy.

Sukie felt a bit bad on Simon's behalf that her words might read abruptly, but she hadn't had time to think of a better way of putting things. It was too late now, anyway, as she and Mr Smith really needed to be making tracks if they were to get there before midnight.

She was just coming out of the office after a final check that everything was as ship-shape and Bristol fashion as she could leave it, when Polly called a perky 'Rum' in her direction, and then Sukie and the parrot's attention was caught by an insistent noise coming from the stairs up from the lower level.

It was Mrs Bridge, who fairly galloped into the foyer to press into Sukie's hands a basket containing two Thermoses full of hot tea, some sandwiches wrapped in waxed paper, a couple of hard-boiled eggs with a little twist of salt, and a brown paper bag with four still-warm biscuits she'd baked, saying it was just a 'little nothing' and 'only some tiffin for the journey' for Sukie and Mr Smith to share.

Sukie kissed the housekeeper on the cheek warmly to say thank you, and then with a final wave at anybody who was in the foyer, she raced outside to take her place in the passenger seat beside Mr Smith.

How exciting. She was well and truly ready for a few days out of London.

Best of all, she was on her way to Dartmoor, and Evie!

# Chapter Twelve

Mr Smith was a safe but cautious driver, and it took them a long time to drive down to Lymbridge, but it would have done so anyway as it was a long way to go.

There wasn't too much traffic, once they had left London, although Sukie and Mr Smith commented on the large number of police vans for transporting crooks they saw, which Sukie called Black Mariahs (a phrase she had picked up from Tracey Benn), and Mr Smith paddy wagons, as they made their way out to the suburbs of the city.

Around Salisbury they came across a lot of army lorries, with men in the back, that were crawling along in a manner that seemed sluggishly dawdling to an impatient Sukie. They had no choice but to slow down to the speed the lorries were moving at, and as she wound the window down for a while now that her hair wasn't at risk of getting windblown, Sukie noticed how fresh the air was compared with London, even though she was getting the occasional whiff of the lorries' exhaust fumes too. Mr Smith and Sukie supposed the army lorries were taking new recruits on training exercises.

As they drove, Sukie found it disorientating that all place names and signposts had been removed, which had happened almost immediately after war had been declared. She knew that this had been done in order to confuse Jerry should there be an invasion, but she wondered how ordinary people found their way around. She and Pattie had gone to London by train and so she'd not noticed the lack of signage as much then, as it seemed easier to know where you were somehow. And of course she was by now used to seeing the London night-time buses driving along with headlights dimmed, curtains at the windows and only the softest of blue lights inside, and with conductors who didn't shout out the bus stops any longer. But for those who needed to travel any distance by car, it didn't look easy, especially as one had to apply for a licence if a map needed to be brought, as did the newsagent who was selling it.

'How do people manage to not get lost?' Sukie wondered out loud. 'I suppose the fact they often don't is more a sign that people are not moving around as much as they might ordinarily. And for servicemen being relocated, I would think the services can use maps.'

'I think that's so,' agreed Mr Smith. 'It took a bit of getting used to when I first had to drive around. But now I know the route between London and Lymbridge so well, that I feel I could do it blindfolded.'

As they drove Sukie thought at first that any workers they saw in the fields were all women, as she knew the Land Girls were still very active in farming the land, but the closer she looked, the more Sukie could see occasional men, usually with a black piece of cloth sewn on to their garments.

'Those are prisoners of war,' explained Mr Smith. 'Do you know that apparently there are thousands of them now living and working all over the land. They get the same rations as our troops, and the trusted ones can work outside the POW camps for a decent wage. I hear we treat them very well, and that includes the Germans – it's to encourage those holding any of our men overseas to treat them properly too. There's even a football team of Italian POWs down near Plymouth, which plays our lads when they are home.'

Sukie twisted in her seat to get a better look at the POWs. They appeared to be very much like British men, and somehow the sight of how ordinary they looked made the war, already nonsensical as far as Sukie was concerned, feel even more so.

'I wonder if there is somebody just like me, somewhere abroad, catching her own first sight of POWs, only of course it would be our boys who are the POWs?' Sukie mused. She hoped that all the POWs, wherever they were and on whatever side, were in good shape and were being well cared for, although she knew that it wouldn't be until the war had ended that whether this in fact was the case would become clear.

It was a sobering thought and Sukie fell very serious for a while. But the day was lovely and it was exciting to be heading home to Lymbridge, and soon Sukie felt her spirits lifting once more.

The longer they were in the car, the more Sukie noticed how pretty the English countryside was and how it looked, the lack of signposts aside, very much as it always had – other than there occasionally being an airstrip in what once would have presumably been a field.

Sometimes she could see that people had given over their gardens to vegetable patches, and many had their own pigs, chickens and rabbits for food, but Sukie noticed too that people were taking pride in the villages and towns they drove through, with some flowers and brightly-coloured hanging baskets.

She supposed it was another way of keeping morale up and showing Jerry a touch of defiance, in that life was continuing very much as normal no matter what Jerry's best efforts to the contrary had been. Sukie thought this was a bit like the government encouraging women on the home front to do their hair nicely and to make an effort with the way they dressed.

Mr Smith and Sukie stopped several times to stretch their legs and spend a penny. Mrs Bridge's picnic was very welcome, and they watched the dipping sun in front of them as they ate their boiled eggs. And so the long drive passed pleasantly enough.

'Sukie!' cried Evie as she ran down the front garden path to greet her friend, not bothering to close the front door even though it was dark and they needed to be mindful of the blackout.

Sukie thanked Mr Smith profusely for bringing her down to Dartmoor with him, and said please would he let her contribute a little something to the petrol, but he waved her away with a smile and slipped the car into gear to drive to the other side of the village where he lived.

Sukie and Evie held each other tight.

It was a moonless night and quite cloudy, and as they hugged Sukie saw the huge expanse of velvety blackness of the sky arching over them far above, very occasionally interrupted by a small shine of starlight. It seemed a much bigger sky than in London, but Sukie knew that was because they were high on the moors, while in London there were many buildings that vied to interrupt one's eyeline.

There was a lovely soft silence all around too that gently enveloped them, and Sukie realised that she had forgotten this quality of quiet about Lymbridge. She must have got very used to the constant background hum of Covent Garden, where it was rare that everything was totally silent.

Sukie breathed in deeply. At last! Here was the peaty, heathery scent of the moorlands she had been longing for.

It was the smell of childhood, of good times with Evie, and the first heady months of falling in love with Wesley. There was nothing in the world to match this wonderful aroma, Sukie thought.

She realised she was crying, and she looked at Evie's face, softly lit by the open front door, to see that Evie had tears in her eyes too.

'Come on, Sukes, let's go inside before somebody shouts at us for breaking the blackout,' said Evie, and they walked arm in arm up the garden path, with Sukie carrying her suitcase and Evie Mrs Bridge's basket.

The minute they got over the threshold Sukie saw Peter sitting on one of the bottom treads of the stairs, with Nellie standing upright with her back to him as she looked towards the door down the passageway, one foot waving in the air and with her tiny hands out beside her as she clutched her father's fingers for support.

'Come to Mummy, Nellie,' said Evie, placing the basket beside her as she crouched down with her arms outstretched towards her daughter, 'and show Sukie what a big girl you are now, and how clever.'

And with a smile that showed two small baby teeth beneath her upper lip, Nellie chuckled and then waddled three or four steps into Evie's arms.

Sukie applauded, and Nellie's smile widened into a laugh.

And, just as suddenly, the little girl was overtaken by shyness and she hid her face in Evie's chest.

Peter stepped over, and after kissing a hello on Sukie's cheek, he lifted Nellie away, and picked up Sukie's case to take upstairs too. 'You'll see Sukie tomorrow, Nellie, but right now it's time for Flopsy bunnies and the lettuces. Or is it the cabbage patch? Let's go and find out.'

'Night night, Nellie,' said Sukie in a singsong voice, and as she smiled and waved at the toddler, the last thing she saw that evening of Evie's daughter was a shy grin back at her from over Peter's shoulder as he carried her up to bed.

'She's adorable, and she looks just like you,' Sukie told Evie as she followed her friend through into the kitchen.

Evie and Peter's house was a small cottage, and Sukie could remember it from her childhood when for a while the village school's ancient caretaker Mr Cawes had lived there before he moved in with his daughter and her family a couple of years before. Sukie recalled how it had always had a spectacular display of riotously coloured hollyhocks in the front garden every summer, and a host of bright pink lupins.

'Sometimes she's adorable!' agreed Evie. 'But this motherhood malarkey isn't all beer and skittles, I can tell you. I don't think I'm a natural, and as to how Ma and Pa went on to have four of us, it doesn't bear thinking about.' She filled the kettle up and placed it on the stove, adeptly lighting the gas as she did so.

'I don't believe you for a moment – you and Peter are clearly parents who've taken to it like, well, like ducks to water,' Sukie told her. 'But how are you, Evie? And how are all the others? You worried me when we spoke earlier.'

'Well, it's all pretty much as I told you this morning, although Pattie turned up to see me at tea-time very tight-lipped, and so goodness knows where she'd been all day,' Evie said. 'Everyone is furious with everyone else still, as far as I can tell. I'm trying *very* hard not to take sides, and so I said to Father when I went over for lunch that if he goes on like this he's just going to push Pattie and William together. And I told Pattie that Pa is being like this because he cares about her and he's only being extra protective as she is the baby girl of his children. But you know Pattie – she wasn't having any of it.'

'Where are William and the children staying?'

'We had them here the first night, which was a bit of a squeeze. And luckily they are down in Plymouth for tonight and tomorrow night, and then they'll all be at the Griffin in Oldwell Abbott. And Pattie is sleeping at Bluebells, even though Julia and Leonard offered to have her; she said although she'd prefer not to be at Bluebells, the thought of being with the dreary Leonard overnight would definitely drive her to murder.'

Sukie and Evie both thought about the Griffin, and they shared a look that was halfway between a frown and a hoot of gaiety. For the Griffin was where Julia and Leonard Bassett had gone to consummate their relationship, not caring who knew about what they were getting up to, and the fallout was still gossiped about in Lymbridge.

This was because the abrupt revelation of this blatant un-married canoodling had caused Evie and Julia to argue fiercely, and then end up rolling in an enraged tussle on a table-top in the ladies' bar of the Haywain for all to see, as their heated debate about what Evie had felt at the time to be scurrilous behaviour on Julia's part, and for her to carry on so openly and shamelessly, had degenerated into fisticuffs, shouting and hair-pulling.

Sukie began to chuckle at the memory. It was a while before Evie joined in, but eventually she was laughing as hard as Sukie.

Evie admitted it hadn't been her finest hour. 'Barkeep Joss still reminds me of it very regularly. And goodness knows what Nellie will make of that when she's old enough to understand, as I know someone or other won't be able to resist telling her about Mummy and her bar-room brawl.'

'It's only funny because you are the least likely person in the world to do something like that,' Sukie consoled Evie. 'And Nellie will be proud she has such a lively mother prepared to kick up such a fuss about what she believes in.'

Evie's 'Hmmm' was dubious.

The whistle of the boiling kettle brought Peter back downstairs after tucking Nellie in, and within five minutes the three of them were sitting down to rabbit stew and mashed potatoes, and the obligatory cups of tea.

Although Mrs Bridge had packed a lot of food into the basket and she had felt stuffed when she and Mr Smith had finished the picnic, Sukie was now ravenous, and so she had seconds and then thirds, saying she was lucky they were all such good pals as this meant that she didn't have to act like a lady and pretend she didn't have a man-sized appetite. It was a treat for her to enjoy a meal that didn't have to be rationed, as the veg was home-grown and the rabbit had been shot that morning on a patch of grass on the moor.

Once she had given her plate a final wipe clean with a last piece of bread. Sukie looked towards Peter. 'What do you make of William?' she asked.

Peter glanced at Evie, and then he said, 'I rather liked him, actually. He seems intelligent and quite wise and a sober sort of chap – I'm thinking in temperament more than if he likes a tipple – and he's clearly besotted with Pattie. I am sure he is very aware that Pattie is a lot younger than him. And I'm only saying this because we are here and not at Bluebells, as this wouldn't be what Robert and Susan want to hear, but I suspect he might be quite a good influence on Pattie, as she seemed more grown-up and confident than I remember. I think it is serious on his part.'

Evie was nodding as Peter spoke, and so Sukie gleaned Evie agreed with her husband's assessment of the situation.

Sukie thought about what Peter had said, as Evie added, 'And Pattie claims it's most serious as far as she is concerned too. What do you think about all of this, Sukes? You'll have seen more of it than we have.'

Sukie debated whether Evie's assertion was in fact the case.

Pattie and Sukie had never really spoken about exactly what Pattie felt for William, Sukie realised, in part as Pattie spent every moment she could with him. Well, Pattie had had an awful lot to say about William's good qualities, whether Sukie had been in the mood to hear them or not, but the more Sukie thought about it, the more she saw that actually Pattie hadn't been too forthcoming as to whether she loved William or not, although she had made it very clear that she was in awe of him. Up until meeting William, Pattie had been one of those lively people who didn't seem to take life too seriously, and she had appeared to be content with her and John's not particularly demonstrative relationship, and so Sukie had assumed a similar attitude on Pattie's part and not probed too deeply.

Once upon a time, Pattie had liked to go out dancing and to public houses much more than Sukie had done, even when Wesley was alive, and she'd got to know the nightlife of London better than Sukie. But when whatever it had been between Pattie and John had ended so suddenly after the Staff Room incident, Sukie saw now that subsequently she had found Pattie more distant to talk with about matters of the heart than previously, and so she hadn't really pressed her. Pattie had been brittle and a trifle touchy in the days immediately after the severing of the relationship, although she had put up a good front of showing John that she wasn't interested in him any longer.

Sukie had to admit to herself that she might not have tried hard enough with Pattie back then, or more recently, and that actually she hadn't been paying her much attention at all.

Sukie felt that while she had been wrapped up in herself, and busy at the Eddy, this wasn't really much of an excuse for neglecting her friend.

Still, it wasn't long after Christmas and the New Year when Pattie had been at her touchiest, and this had been precisely when Sukie herself was a bit frazzled in the gloomy come-down after all the festive excitement, and immediately following the Twelfth Night ceremony when she had been preoccupied with not letting herself think about Wesley as much as she had.

Sukie thought back to her Twelfth Night wish, which now she thought boiled down to her becoming a woman in her own right, happy to enjoy her successes and able to live with her failures without too much rancour. She thought she had made some steps to achieve an equilibrium that might be described so. But it was the other part of the wish – the care and considera-tion bit – where Sukie felt she had been found wanting.

To her shame, Sukie realised now that she had never spent time with William and the children when they were with Pattie, and so she didn't really know how they all got along, or what William was like as a person.

She wasn't sure why she hadn't made steps to do so, especially considering how important William and the kiddies were to Pattie, and how important Pattie was to her. But what this meant was that while she felt as if she knew *of* William, it was more because Pattie had mentioned him in passing quite often than anything else. This felt a failure of, well, *something* on Sukie's part, although she wasn't quite sure what. Maybe being more sympathetic, she wondered.

Her Twelfth Night wish seemed simple on the surface but was fraught with myriad opportunities to slip up, or where lip service seemed initially a better option but was really ultimately only an expression of laziness or a lack of sympathy.

She had a way to go before achieving the full expression of her wish, Sukie decided.

'I don't think I've been a very good friend to Pattie. I'm embarrassed to say that I know very little of William, really, and I do feel that for Pattie's sake I should have made more effort with him. He seems nice enough, I suppose,' said Sukie seriously, 'and Dot is a lovely little girl, obviously well brought up and extremely polite. We all met by chance at a cinema one afternoon, and I do remember that I very much liked the way William allowed Dot to talk to me and Pattie about her dead mother without him trying to change the subject or tell her everything would be all right when quite obviously it wouldn't, even though people say this sort of thing to small children all the time.

'I would have to admit that Pattie seems calmer now that she has met William, although if pressed, until now I would have said that was more because she wasn't with John any longer. I have thought in the past that when she was with John, she was a little jumpy through always having a niggle of doubt about him and his intentions, thinking that potentially he was a bit of a ladies' man. On the other hand, that could well be more my opinion of John, because I can't quite get over seeing him jump up so hurriedly when Pattie and I caught him with that other woman at the Christmas party. Goodness, I don't know, Evie. From what I can make out, William is reliable and pretty solid, and Pattie says he owns his own house just across the river near London Bridge, and so he has a certain substance to him. I'm sorry – I don't know that I am going to be much use to you, Evie.'

'Just having you here is tonic enough,' said Evie. 'But I think the fact that you haven't seen anything particularly worrying about William will be at least of some comfort over at Bluebells. All the same, William is hugely older than Pattie, isn't he? Imagine that if they do marry, when she is fifty she'll be lying in bed with somebody at her side who is in their eighties. And if they were to have their own children, he's going to look like a granddaddy at any school meeting.'

Sukie hadn't thought about it quite in those terms before, and it certainly was a picture that seemed at odds with Pattie's youth and liveliness. She wondered whether Pattie had ever thought along these lines too.

It was hard to think that she hadn't, especially as she now knew that William was substantially older than Robert.

What a change to Pattie's life there had been since the start of 1944.

# Chapter Thirteen

The next morning was Saturday, and Evie had arranged a surprise for Sukie.

Just as Sukie finished the last mouthful of boiled egg for her breakfast there was the sound of horses' hooves outside.

Evie smiled at Sukie, who ran to the front door.

Outside the garden gate was their friend Linda, which was really exciting.

Linda was mounted on a small but sturdy pony distinguished by a mane and tail of busby bushiness, and she was holding the reins of an equally small and very rotund pony on one side of her, and a rather nice-looking but quite big hunter on the other.

'Surprise! Jodhpurs time!' yelled Evie right beside Sukie, and Sukie bellowed back at her just as loudly a really thrilled, 'Yippee!'

They ran upstairs to get ready to the sound of Peter telling a now squalling Nellie, startled from a nap by their shouts, that Mummy was a big silly to make such a loud noise and wake her up so rudely.

Sukie had to borrow a pair of Peter's trousers, and wear six pairs of socks to make his hiking boots fit, and Evie had to struggle into her jodhpurs rather, and tussle quite hard with the waistband button to do it up.

'Clearly not got my figure back after Nellie, then, as I've not had these on for months,' she laughed, and then undid the button and reached instead for one of Peter's belts to make sure her breeches stayed where they should be.

Sukie was thrilled to have such a treat. She loved horse-riding, and was an excellent equestrian, but she hadn't had the chance for such a long time.

'It was Peter's idea,' said Evie, and Sukie turned to wave at him and Nellie, who were in the garden seeing them off, Nellie's tears having given way to chuckles. Sukie stretched up to give Linda a hello hug.

It was such a lovely morning, sunny and crisp, with little curls of steam rising from the ground as the spring sun burned the droplets of dew off the sod.

The horses were a motley selection, but Linda said they were the best she could rustle up at short notice, and Sukie should have the hunter as he was the friskiest and Sukie the most experienced rider.

Sukie swung herself up easily, and then she and Linda had a laugh at Evie's expense, as Evie's mount was so plump that the saddle kept slipping around every time Evie put her weight in the stirrup. Sukie dismounted and pulled his girth up a couple of holes. As the pony was virtually spherical around his middle and therefore his withers wouldn't hold the saddle in place, she held the opposite stirrup so that Evie could get on after quite a bit of hopping and then a grunt as she hauled herself upwards, with a 'Well, that was elegant' once she was finally on-board.

It was glorious out on the moor. The granite tors rose up imposingly nearby and those in the distance looked hazy in the sunlight. The ground felt springy and well-drained, with lots of give in it, and all the horses were raring to go, although Sukie made sure that as leader she kept the canters sedate as she knew that Evie and Linda were more nervous and didn't enjoy galloping nearly as much as she did.

Linda had been the first of their trio to get married, and she now had two children and juggled bringing them up and working as a farrier, shoeing horses and making simple iron gate accoutrements in her forge.

'Look at the size of my arms,' said Linda, flexing her biceps to show Sukie an impressively muscled forearm and upper arm. 'That's what shoeing carthorses, and having two little ones, will do for you. And helping Sam lug around the forage on the farm and sheering the sheep.' Sam was Linda's husband, and he hadn't been called up because of running the farm and the need for food production.

Sukie laughed and showed Linda her own slim arms. 'That's what pushing a pen in a London hotel will do for you! I don't know how you do it all, Linda. It's hugely impressive.'

'It's easier now Sam has built me a forge at home as quite a lot of people can come to me,' Linda explained. 'I have the mobile forge for those a long way away, but I try not to do that too much. And Sam goes and looks after a lot of the sheep and cattle hooves I used to trim, as I showed him how to do that. We have very interesting chats in the evening about foot rot and laminitis, and field rotation – you're missing out on all this country fun up in London!'

'Do you come across much of a meat black market?' Sukie asked.

'It's hard to say as the Min. of Ag. is eagle-eyed these days and knows most of the scams, so I doubt there's much going on around here to do with large animals. But maybe if a cow calves twins, that might go down as one, and so on,' said Linda. 'And it's probably a battle of wits concerning poultry and egg production.'

'Well, even at the Eddy last Christmas there was a huge turkey black market to do with a Norfolk farm sending illegal turkeys that were sold under the table. Those involved made a tidy sum, and didn't seem to feel bad, although I did as I kept imagining that this was taking the meat away from some on the ration. Anyway, I've said they can't do this turkey wheeze again, which went down like a lead balloon,' said Sukie.

'Wise you stamped on it,' Evie said, and added after a pause, 'You'd all be up before the beak otherwise.'

Sukie and Linda groaned in unison.

They ended up near the Grange, the recuperation hospital in quite a grand house where Peter ran a top-secret government research facility in the building's basement. There was a point-to-point course in the grounds – Sukie having previously won a hotly fought race there against all comers earlier in the war when Evie and Peter were only at the stage of flirting with each other – and so Sukie couldn't resist giving the hunter a pop over one or two of the point-to-point fences.

He was very obliging and Sukie liked him, and so she took him to a level piece of ground to open his pipes with a short, flat-out gallop, returning to the others laughing and with the hunter foaming, with sweat on his neck, and with her eyes bright with the joy of the moment and her curls all over the place.

As they turned for home Sukie thought briefly of Simon, as he'd told her he liked to ride to hounds, and she felt that there was a million years between her at that moment, with the Devon sun on her back and the now tiring hunter walking out calmly on a long rein, and the Sukie who had been lying on those cold sheets with Simon in the horrid flat, even though there was only thirty-six short hours separating the two events.

The hack was over far too soon for Sukie, but Linda had horses to shoe that afternoon, and Evie said that Susan was expecting them at Bluebells for lunch, and so they were dropped off at the gate to Bluebells, and the last thing Sukie saw that visit of Linda was the comical sight of her making her way along the single road through Lymbridge, leading a rangy giant of a horse on one side of her own diminutive steed that had the wiry waterfall of mane and tail, and a squat roly-poly pony with an apple-shaped rump on her other side.

Sukie pulled Evie to her and said a heartfelt thank you, that was wonderful, and Evie embraced her back, agreeing it had been a perfect ride as they walked inside Bluebells to wash their hands and change.

Downstairs, there was no sign of Pattie, and Susan shook her head to indicate to Evie and Sukie that it was best if they didn't ask.

Susan enveloped Sukie in a bear hug, and then told her in the way that only people who are very fond of one can, that Sukie looked exhausted, much too pale and nothing more than skin and bones, and Sukie replied with a smile that it was lovely to see Susan too.

Robert came in and shook Sukie's hand warmly, telling her, as he always had, 'You're a sight for sore eyes, and still a handsome maid,' as he sat down to take his gardening boots off. Sukie grinned back; she adored Robert.

Evie and Susan were pantomiming, meanwhile, where Pattie might be, and quickly Sukie understood that Pattie was in her bedroom upstairs but she wasn't coming down any time soon.

Robert shook his head and sighed in annoyance, and then made to stand up as if to go and get her. Susan raised her brows at him and breathed in audibly through her nose, and so he sat down with a put-upon look on his face.

Susan ignored this as she ladled potato soup into bowls.

Halfway through the meal they heard the resolute sound of someone barrelling down the stairs, quickly followed by the slam of the front door and the speedy clomp of Pattie's disgruntled footsteps as she marched out of the garden.

'Thank goodness for that,' said Susan. 'We've been walking on eggshells all morning and hardly dared say anything.'

They then all began to talk about Pattie and William, with Sukie assuring Susan and Robert that as far as she could tell William was an upstanding man, and that although obviously he was older than Pattie, he did seem to be very fond of her.

Robert muttered, 'Those two will be getting hitched over my dead body, mark my words,' and Susan snapped at him, 'You're jumping the gun as it's not got to that stage yet. And anyway, that's just the way to get them together and lead to the hitching.' Then she and Robert stared crossly at each other over the kitchen table.

Although it's never nice to see a couple argue, Sukie felt a tremor of pleasure at what was unfurling before her. To Sukie, this showed that she was regarded as 'family' by Susan and

Robert Yeo, as indicated by the way that they felt they could act exactly as they wanted before her, without trying to be polite or show their best side.

It felt a privilege, even if a bit of a peculiar one. Sukie smiled a little bashfully at Evie, and Evie nodded back at her in a way that told Sukie that Evie understood.

That was an even better feeling, and for a moment Sukie felt the prickling sensation of tears that might fall, as she felt loved and very lucky. Although she was extremely fond of her new family of Eddies, Sukie felt in the moment that this was where she belonged.

In spite of the threatened tears, it was a wonderful sensation of warmness.

Sukie looked again at Robert and Susan. Although they were cross with each other at that moment, she could see that they were still very much a husband and wife team, and were clearly a couple who adored each other.

Sukie's mood deepened without her wanting it to, and she found that she lost the drift of what the others were saying.

She was thinking that while she had lost Wesley, she had likewise never felt for a moment when she was with him that they weren't on the same squad, ready to face the best and the worst that life had to throw at them, as they stood united and side by side.

She knew what that feeling was, and she prized it.

In comparison, she saw now that she had never come close to that feeling of closeness and oneness when she had spent time with Simon, and certainly not that one time they had cavorted naked in the flat.

But was that such a bad thing? she wondered. She had been so devastated when Wesley had died, that perhaps it was more sensible to have a cooler sort of relationship as there might be less chance of getting hurt that way.

This meant she didn't want to write Simon off just yet, Sukie discovered, perhaps a little to her surprise.

The marriage of Susan and Robert Yeo was an inspiration,

and yet Susan had once told Sukie and Evie that it had taken a long while for her to fall in love with Robert, but that she had never worried about it, believing strongly even back then that some things were too precious to rush.

Sukie considered if she and Simon had pushed things on too fast. There had never been the instant physical sensations that she had found with Wesley, even though she had never given in to them, but that didn't necessarily devalue what she and Simon could have in the years stretching ahead, Sukie understood. There was every sign that Simon was a thoroughly decent chap and it was very possible that they just needed more time to get used to one another. She'd met Simon exactly when the loss of Wesley still felt acute, and she hadn't been at her most robust, and nor was she used to spending time with people who were above her in the social scale, as it was impossible to ignore the fact that, similarly to Tracey Benn, Simon was very well-bred and, of course, far too well-mannered ever to mention her more lowly social status.

Had she been too swayed, expecting the fireworks Pattie had promised?

In order to be fair, therefore, to them both and not risk throwing something out that could be good, Sukie decided that almost definitely she should try harder to think of herself and Simon as a unit or, more precisely, a unit in the making. As for them having a relationship, that wasn't 'there' yet, but some might think there were promising beginnings nonetheless.

The second time she had had intercourse she had liked it more than the first, Sukie reminded herself. Who was to say what she would feel on their tenth time, or their hundredth?

Sukie thought of how every time she saw Simon's handsome face and well-proportioned body walk over to her, she was struck that he really was incredibly presentable, and that most women would give their eye-teeth to be with him.

She wasn't foolish enough to doubt that there was a tremendous currency in that, or that happy and fulfilling long-term relationships hadn't sprung the world over from much less promising beginnings. And of course, as she had said to Pattie earlier in the year, there was going to be a terrible shortage of eligible men available once the dratted war was over, and so this was another point in Simon's favour, as if Sukie rejected him there was no guarantee that she wouldn't end up a lonely and scratchy old maid.

Of course, after the business in the flat, an experience on which he probably held downbeat reservations just as much as Sukie did (and she felt awkward now that she had been so at sea during the whole evening, to the extent that she had pretty much laid there and left all the hard work to him), and so it was very possible he might be thinking anyway that it was time their relationship was over.

Sukie told herself she would only have herself to blame if that were true.

But maybe that was life: a series of lovers, none of whom could quite stay the distance for a whole variety of reasons. Either way, if that was true or if it wasn't, perhaps now was the time that Sukie needed to find out what would happen next.

With an effort she tuned back into what Robert and Susan and Evie were talking about, and tried not to think about herself anymore. She didn't want to be that person, the friend who was always only thinking about her own life.

But as she and Evie walked back to Evie's house after lunch, Sukie asked that Evie excuse her while she nipped into the Haywain to telephone London.

Barkeep Joss was delighted to see her, and slipped a small glass of sherry on the house in her direction as Sukie first called the Eddy to check all was well there, which it was, the locksmith apparently having made some very good suggestions, once he'd stopped being frightened by Tracey Benn.

Then she telephoned Simon's office, which she had never done before, although Simon had assured her that it was perfectly acceptable if she ever needed to ring him at work, as he had a direct line to his desk and so only he would answer if she were to ring.

'Whitehall 3121,' said his voice.

'It's Sukie,' she said quietly, privately questioning what his response would be.

'How good you sound,' he replied warmly. 'How very good indeed. Tell me what you have been up to, and when we can see each other again.'

'Well,' she began, 'I'm down in Devon. But before I tell you about that, let me describe what happened to Mrs Bridge's drawers...'

And with that they fell to chatting with all the ease that they had in the Savoy that first night. In fact, Simon seemed so delighted that she had called that nearly all the doubts she had about him and about their time at the flat melted away.

Sukie walked back to Evie and Peter's house feeling happier about the prospect of her and Simon than she had for a while.

# Chapter Fourteen

Sukie and Evie took Nellie for a walk later that day, in large part so that Peter could have a little peace and quiet, and possibly even a doze by the kitchen fire in his slippers and with the newspaper on his lap.

As they went along, Nellie sat up proudly in her perambulator, for all the world looking like a miniature queen surveying her grateful minions as Sukie pushed her through the village.

They got to the primary school and turned inside the school yard, shutting the gate behind them that enclosed the tarmacked playground. Evie had been a teacher at the school before her pregnancy and the headmistress, Mrs Smith, had said to her that she was very welcome to let Nellie have a run-around there whenever she wanted as it was such a safe enclosed space for Nellie to play, especially as there wasn't a communal children's play area in Lymbridge and Evie and Peter only had a small garden that was, these days, pretty much devoted to growing vegetables.

Nellie was lifted down and allowed to explore at will, which she did mainly by shuffling along on her behind with her two legs stuck out in front of her.

'Fingers crossed this will wear her out a bit, and hopefully she won't find any mud to roll in,' said Evie, as she and Sukie sat on the miniature kiddie's bench in the playground, the sun warm on their backs.

'Tell me about Simon,' Evie added, once she had retrieved a small pebble that Nellie had found and was now about to put in her mouth. 'Pattie says he's very handsome.'

'He *is* good-looking, that's true,' said Sukie, but although she smiled, somehow it didn't quite ignite her eyes, Evie noticed.

Sukie ground to a halt as she didn't really know what to say to Evie about him.

'Are you keen?' Evie asked.

'To a degree, I suppose.'

There was another short silence.

Evie looked at her intently. 'That's not terribly enthusiastic, Sukes.'

'Well, I do like him,' Sukie told her. 'Any fool would, and I'm no different. He's decent and kind and thoughtful, and a good dancer too, and – usually – we have lots to say to each other, and I enjoy spending time with him.'

'He sounds perfect. I sense, though, that there may be a "but" coming.'

'There is. I was so bowled over when I met Wesley, and then Pattie is simply thrilled to spend time with William, and although I've always felt quite cool about Simon, I listened too much to Pattie, and convinced myself that I was over-romanticising how I'd felt about Wesley. And then Pattie promised me that when Simon and I did decide to move to the next level too, I would feel as she does, which is pretty amazing by all accounts—'

'Whoa!' interrupted Evie. 'So they have definitely gone all the way then?'

Sukie nodded, adding miserably, 'I'm surprised you didn't see the fireworks right down here in Lymbridge, if Pattie is to be believed, and I guess she is, as what would be the point of her making that up?'

Evie lifted Nellie on to her knee, and then as she jiggled her leg to make Nellie laugh, Evie leaned over to take Sukie's hand. 'And you and Simon? That sounds like a big development.'

'Oh Evie, it wasn't at all as I imagined.'

'Wesley and—?'

'Wesley and I never took the risk, and so it was my first time.' She took her hand from Evie's so that Nellie could hold her forefinger. Sukie's voice softened as lifted her hand up and down as Nellie hung on, and she added, 'I'll always be sorry that I never showed Wesley how much I felt.'

Evie nodded to let Sukie know she understood, and she shifted Nellie to her other leg, which was closer to her friend.

Now that she had begun to speak, there was no stopping Sukie. 'When I heard Pattie being so excited about the bedroom shenanigans between her and William, I asked myself what on earth I was waiting for. Simon is very presentable and I *am* fond of him, and I was curious about what it would be like with him, and it's true too that I didn't want to be the lonely party of one among my friends who had never gone all the way any longer.

'The first time of me and Simon being together was the night Pattie and William caused such a stink at Bluebells – we chose that night as Pattie was away and I didn't want her asking for a blow-by-blow account – and so it was only a couple of nights ago.

'William borrowed a flat, which was a horrible place, and in fact the whole process of "the arrangements" I found distasteful. And we both went all strange and quiet beforehand, and it was much too planned, and pretty hideous all around.

'We did it twice but I really don't know why people make such a fuss – it wasn't unpleasant as such, but just not particularly pleasant. And now I think I was expecting too much, and then when I didn't like it, my lack of enthusiasm meant that Simon didn't enjoy it much either, although I'm not too sure that he really knew what he was doing either.

'In fact, we'd been going to stay in the flat all night, but I suggested we went to our homes, which we did. And I've not seen him since, and I don't know what he thought about it.'

'Oh dear, Sukes,' said Evie. 'That does sound a bit grim. Don't write it off totally, though. It doesn't sound disastrous. And I think it can take a bit of time to find your feet...'

'Did *you* love it from the first time?' Sukie thought her voice had something of an unappealing whine to it.

'Well, yes, I did,' Evie admitted. 'But don't forget that Peter and I had a very long build-up to the main event, and so I practically felt as if I was going to burst with longing for him. You and Simon haven't known each other for a huge amount of time, remember, and of course poor Wesley's loss won't have helped, as I am sure that got in the way a bit. I think it sounds as if you are being very hard on yourself. And on Simon too.'

'Maybe.' Sukie's voice was doubtful. 'I had wondered that, so I telephoned him from the Haywain.'

'And was he pleased you had?'

'He seemed to be.'

'What about you?'

'I was glad I'd rung him,' Sukie said. 'But I suppose the real question is whether we do *it* again, and if we do, whether he and I enjoy it more. I can't guess the answer to that as I really don't know that I want a repeat performance.'

'Maybe you should both talk about all of this before you do it again. Perhaps you could tell Simon what you'd like him to do to you next time to make it better?'

'*Evie!*'

Sukie's exclamation of horror at the thought of Evie's suggestion was so loud that old Mr Cawes, who was walking past, stopped to stare at them.

Then Nellie uttered a distinct 'Evie' in echo of Sukie's, although in a much less agitated way.

Evie kissed her daughter on the top of her head, and she beamed across at Sukie. 'Nellie has just said her very first word, and how wonderful you were here to hear it! You've performed a small miracle here as she hasn't done any of the mum-ma's or dad-da's we've been prompting her with. And if you can do this, surely having an honest conversation with a very nice man that you feel you could maybe come to care about deeply shouldn't be utterly impossible for you?'

Sukie smiled, but deep down inside she was wishing she felt as confident about the whole matter as Evie obviously did.

# Chapter Fifteen

That evening Pattie came over to eat with Evie, Peter and Sukie, but she slightly mis-timed her arrival, as Nellie had been on the point of dropping off – the playtime in the playground having worn her out just as Evie hoped it would – but immediately as she heard the door Nellie began to wriggle and try to sit up in bed, and it took Evie a while to settle her.

Pattie was pleased to see Sukie, joking with a nod towards her fellow Eddy, 'I see they decided the Yeos had to draft in the heavy artillery.'

'All present and correct. But less of the heavy, if you don't mind,' said Sukie.

It didn't take long for Sukie to see that Pattie remained unrepentant over the brouhaha her and William's arrival had caused.

'Honestly, I wouldn't have inflicted such a nightmare on poor William if I'd have known how feeble they were all going to be. One minute there was me assuring William how open-minded every single one of the Yeo family is, and that nobody is even the slightest iota one bit fuddy-duddy. And then my promises of a warm welcome and wall-to-wall bonhomie were all shot to pieces in no uncertain terms, as it seemed only a moment later Father had come over all Victorian, and was acting as if William was the devil incarnate, and Ma was nearly as bad, and James and Julia too. I felt most embarrassed by them, and for them,' said Pattie, and then in case anyone had been left in doubt how she had felt, she gave a dramatic shudder.

Evie came into the kitchen and went to wash her hands, while Peter set the kitchen table. 'I think it was a bit of a shock,' Evie then told her sister in a very calm manner, so much so that Sukie knew Evie was trying to diffuse Pattie's emotions, 'as although before you all arrived you'd let Ma and Pa know that William was a father already and was a widower, the fact of them having been given those facts, and then the both of them actually seeing it all in practice are two very different things. I'm sure with a bit of time they'll get more used to the idea.'

'That's all very well for you to say ...' said Pattie in a petulant way, which Peter neatly sidestepped as Pattie drew breath to say something else by sliding a large slice of Woolton pie on to her plate, and urging Pattie to have a huge helping of greens.

Sukie exchanged looks with Evie to say she'd noticed that Evie hadn't mentioned the biggest hurdle as far as Robert and Susan were concerned, which was William's age.

Sukie gave the tiniest of shakes of her head back to her friend, and so Sukie understood that Evie felt this was too touchy a subject to risk raising at the moment.

'How is William now? Have you spoken to him?' said Peter, and Sukie noticed that Evie stretched her leg out to touch her husband's in a silent nudge of thanks for helping out with the tricky conversation.

'I have indeed telephoned him, and for a long time. He's very calm, the dear of him, but then he always is. Calm *and* a dear. And he refuses to condemn either Mother or Father for not giving us their blessing, even though I tell him I am utterly appalled at their brazen attitude. He says it went pretty much as he thought it might do, and that we'll have many such bridges to cross,' said Pattie. 'But I'm so cross and furious on William's behalf that I can't forgive Ma and Pa, as they were simply vile, and they never got to see the many wonderful things about William. And if that wasn't bad enough, James got uppity too, and so he's also in my bad books – not that he's a leg to stand on as Jane is almost old enough to be *his* mother – and then Julia didn't help even though she weighed in on my side, but she managed to do that in such a way that all the issues that Ma and Pa have swept under the carpet about Julia and the odious Leonard Bassett living together unwed were dragged out into the open once more. Honestly, in my worst nightmares, I never thought it would go to hell in a handcart quite as it has done. William is so wonderful that stupidly I thought the moment they met him, they would see what a remarkable man he is.'

'Well, if you look at it from Robert and Susan's point of view,' Sukie began cautiously, 'I suppose to them you and William are in quite a fresh relationship still, and...'

Pattie's eyes looked furious and as if she was ready to be hurt all over again, but this potentially dangerous moment was averted by a masterful stroke of good timing before Sukie could well and truly put her foot in it – and she was very aware that she and Pattie had to go on sharing their bedroom back at the Eddy, and so Sukie really didn't want them to come to blows – by a loud and cheerful 'Cooee!' heralding them from out in the hall, followed by, 'Surprise!'

Nellie gave a wail from upstairs at being unceremoniously woken up, and Peter sprang up to hold the kitchen door open, and with that Tricia wheeled Timmy and his wheelchair into the kitchen with a practised and easy-looking manoeuvre.

Tricia flung her arms effusively around Evie and then Sukie, and lastly Pattie, and Sukie noticed how readily Evie smiled at Tricia as she stood up to go and see to Nellie.

Timmy waved at everyone with an extravagant and affable 'holloawa' and then he took a bottle of port from his lap and with a flourish slapped it on the table, saying, 'Let's get some glasses charged.'

Aside from Pattie having thus neatly been diverted from talking about William, Sukie was heartened at this sight of Tricia and Timmy, even though once she would never have believed that possible.

Sukie smiled hello at Timmy and looked around at her friends.

Everyone around the table looked full of beans and as if they were enjoying being the age they were, war or no war. They had come a long way during the course of the war, and Sukie was comforted by how they had all changed for the better in her opinion.

It could very easily have turned out differently. Several years ago Evie had been engaged to Timmy, but he was a jack-the-lad and he had managed to impregnate Tricia during a drunken fumble outside the village hall when Evie was officiating at a Make Do and Mend evening. Before anyone knew of Tricia's pregnancy, Timmy had gone overseas to fight, and then his service ended abruptly when his spine had been shattered and he had almost lost his life. Although they struggled on for a bit despite Tricia's obvious pregnancy, inevitably his and Evie's engagement had ended, and later Tricia and Timmy had gone on to marry, with Tricia not caring a jot that Timmy was now confined to a wheelchair for the rest of his life. And now they had three children despite Timmy's paralysis, a second pregnancy after the arrival of baby Hettie having given them twins.

At first Evie had thoroughly disliked Tricia, and so had Sukie, although more in support of her best friend than because she found Tricia dislikeable. They hadn't known Tricia before she became pregnant, and they were horrified at the obvious result of Timmy's peccadillo. Aside from allowing Timmy to do what he had with what they supposed had been very little prompting, at the time Tricia had only been a lowly dairy parlour maid and this meant – Sukie and Evie gossiped meanly to each other – she was nothing in comparison to Evie, a schoolteacher with a good education and a promising career. Tricia had, Sukie and Evie agreed, a blowsy, upfront way of speaking that they assured each other was 'common', and this, along with the illegitimate pregnancy, indicated that Tricia was 'no better than she should be'.

But these quickly turned out to be harsh and unfair judgements, and now both Evie and Sukie felt immensely guilty about the unkind way they had judged Tricia before they had taken the trouble to get to know her.

Tricia had the last laugh, of course. While she didn't sound particularly intelligent on first acquaintance, she soon proved herself to be whip-smart, quick-witted and easily able to hold her own.

It wasn't long before Sukie had to admit shamefacedly that Tricia was very bright but without the advantage of a comfortable upbringing. And this meant she'd left school at fourteen so she could contribute to the family coffers with a decent wage, and the extra years of study that Sukie and Evie had enjoyed had never been an option.

Tricia was kind and resolutely energetic and cheerful, and she had never held Evie and Sukie's snooty opinion of her – which they had made sure she knew about – against them.

And Tricia was brilliant at handling Timmy, who understandably got frustrated sometimes at being stuck in his wheelchair. She didn't let him get away with anything on account of his limited movement, and she refused to accept that what had happened to him was a disability and so she made sure he was out and about in Lymbridge as much as she was, and that all of his old friends treated him exactly as they always had.

Evie had said, as Sukie pushed Nellie in the pram back from the primary school, that she and Tricia spent a lot of time together as they were the only two young mothers in the village, as Linda lived several miles away. Tricia had given Evie lots of practical advice with Nellie, Evie said, and the fond way she spoke of Tricia told Sukie the old hurts of how Tricia and Timmy had got together had been long forgotten by Evie.

'Will you let Nellie stay with our three, and she can sleep over?' said Timmy. 'Mother's there in charge, and then we can all go to the Haywain. I know Nellie is in bed, but she's not asleep.'

'Obviously so!' said Sukie, and they all laughed as they listened to Nellie bawl in a way that told everybody that she wasn't very happy about not being included in whatever was going on downstairs.

'I'll nip up an' give Evie a 'and wi' 'er,' said Tricia.

Ten minutes later there was blissful silence as Tricia and Evie took a now only hiccupping and slightly grizzly Nellie over to the new house a couple of hundred yards away that had been built for Tricia and Timmy.

It was a dwelling that had been brilliantly designed especially for a disabled man in a wheelchair – by ironically enough – the young architect Evie had nearly got engaged to after her and Timmy's engagement had been broken, and Peter had looked to be promised to somebody else.

By the time Tricia and Evie returned from leaving Mrs Smith, who was Timmy's mother, in charge of all the children, great inroads had been made into the bottle of port by all of those in Evie and Peter's house waiting for them to come back.

Once the bottle was finished, they all trooped over to the Haywain, where quite a night was made of it, in part as Barkeep Joss used the local bush telegraph to let all the regulars know that Pattie Yeo and Sukie Scott were in town, and were ready for a good old knees-up, and this meant that within an hour people had come from far and wide in order to join in with the fun.

Even Julia and Leonard Bassett turned up, as did James with Jane Cornish, and then at ten o'clock Robert and Susan made an appearance as a way of burying the hatchet with their youngest daughter, and Sukie noticed that they and Pattie spent some time speaking in a way that suggested they weren't arguing, although they weren't necessarily agreeing with each other either to judge by Pattie's arms staying resolutely firmly folded across her chest.

The whole night ended in the wee small hours of the following morning with a huge sing-along, with Peter bashing out the tunes on the Haywain's slightly out of tune Joanna as the public house's clientele roared out the words to a host of popular songs, ending with a rousing but very drunken rendition of 'We'll Meet Again'.

The last thing Sukie remembered before she slumped on her

bed in all her clothes was drunkenly hugging Peter to say she loved him for making Evie so happy, and him smiling back at her, looking dishevelled and young enough to be a schoolboy.

There were sore heads all around the next morning, and some very late rising, with Evie and Peter admitting they were very glad they didn't have to sort Nellie out, and Sukie promising to herself that she was never going to touch a drop of alcohol again.

When William had finished whatever it was that he had needed to do in Plymouth, he returned to Lymbridge, and Evie headed rather reluctantly over to Bluebells for a very strained tea there that Robert didn't attend (crying off that he 'had to do something very important with the Home Guard', not that anyone believed him as he'd always been very able to give the Home Guard a miss before, if he fancied).

Sukie had been invited, but she didn't go, as she didn't want either William or Pattie to feel they were in more of a goldfish bowl than they already were.

'Wonderful,' said Evie, 'you can babysit Nellie for me instead.'

Evie later told Sukie that it had been a polite affair, although she felt rather as if she had been through the wringer after it as everybody had been trying so hard to keep the conversation on safe topics. All in all, it was quite a tortuous hour, said Evie, and one that was only saved by Dot and her little brothers being so sweet that Susan had to soften a fraction.

While Evie was over at Bluebells for the dreaded tea party, Sukie found Nellie quite wore her out, as no sooner had Sukie started to read to her then she wanted to do something else, and immediately her lower lip would tremble with impending tears if she wasn't allowed to do what she wanted. This happened a lot of times, causing Sukie to wonder if Pattie had any idea really what she would be letting herself in for if it did remain serious between her and William. His children were older, granted, but if Nellie was anything to go by, they would all be very well versed in getting their own ways.

Sukie spent some time showing Nellie what was in the pantry (which wasn't much, and Sukie realised she had got very used to seeing the Eddy's much better stocked kitchen shelves, aside from the gaping hole where the tinned salmon would have been, naturally). Sukie then had to explore the scullery with Nellie, but it was all to no avail, and in the end Sukie had to take her out to the vegetable patch, where – ignoring that Evie was likely to be peeved that Sukie had allowed her daughter to get dirty – Nellie proved happy to sit in the mud and slap the ground beside her.

Sukie found this babysitting to be simultaneously exhausting and boring.

At one point she looked at Nellie and tried to imagine whether if she had a baby daughter, would it be easier looking after her than she was finding it with Nellie? It was hard to imagine having a child, though, or Simon being a father, Sukie discovered.

Nellie gave a wail, and Sukie wondered if it was of the 'I need a clean nappy' variety that Evie had mentioned in her letter of a while back. She hoped not.

When Evie returned, and Sukie said she'd found keeping a small child entertained was more exhausting than running a whole hotel, Evie looked back at her sternly and quipped, 'Your point?'

Sukie told herself that she must remember that she hadn't much enjoyed looking after Nellie, lovable as she was when seen sitting on Evie's lap.

If given a choice right now between spending a morning dealing with irritable guests at the Eddy and fractious Eddies themselves, or in trying to amuse one small toddler, Sukie knew what she would choose. And it wasn't entertaining a young child.

Pattie must need her head examining, Sukie thought.

# Chapter Sixteen

The next morning, just as Sukie was playing with Nellie as Evie washed up the breakfast things, there was the staccato beep of a car's horn from the road outside. Sukie ran down to the front door to check who was there.

As she'd expected, it was William, with his car already loaded up with Pattie (who looked to be about to dole out the barley twists), and Dot and the twins.

Sukie felt a pang of homesickness for Lymbridge, although she hadn't yet left. She'd enjoyed being there very much, and spending time with Evie and everyone else. It was all such a picture, the pretty village nestled as it was high on the heathery hills of Dartmoor, every bit as lovely as Sukie remembered. And she felt rejuvenated after several days with no work and being thoroughly spoiled by Evie.

But as Sukie went to put on her coat and hat, and rushed to spend a final penny before the long journey back to London, she realised she was also rather looking forward to arriving back in the hustle and bustle of London again, and seeing her fellow Eddies.

She wondered what everyone had been up to, and what Polly had said, and whether there had been any dramas in her and Pattie's absence.

While Lymbridge had a special place in Sukie's heart, she

knew now that so did the Edwardes Hotel and everyone who was in it.

Immediately before she made her way down the garden path to the car, Sukie gave Nellie her teddy bear, and Evie her stockings.

Evie made sure that Sukie had the wicker picnic basket that Mrs Bridge had put the picnic in for the way down. It was groaning afresh with food for all six who'd be in the car, and Sukie felt a prickle behind her eyes at her friend's thoughtfulness.

'I really am missing you already,' Sukie told Evie, as the trusty old cardboard suitcase was squashed into the boot of the car alongside what looked like a lot of luggage. William's children were only small but obviously they didn't travel lightly. 'It's been lovely to see you all, Evie, and very heartening to watch what a great advertisement you and Peter are for married life. And Nellie is the dearest sweetie ever to have drawn breath. Although possibly one of the hardest to entertain.'

Evie and Nellie stood in the garden, with Evie lifting Nellie's hand so that the little girl could wave goodbye.

As Sukie settled herself on the back seat, Evie started to sing 'We'll Meet Again'.

It was a nice idea, but singing wasn't (and never had been) one of Evie's fortes.

Sukie and Pattie roared with laughter at the horrified look on Nellie's face as she turned to stare at her mother with a furrowed brow, and then her face started to crumple. Howls were not far away.

William put the car into gear and they drove slowly down the lane, and both Sukie and Pattie furiously waved goodbye to Evie and Nellie.

Everyone other than William stared over their shoulders until they had got well past the very last glimpse of Lymbridge, and then they were all quiet for a little while as they turned to face forward again and took a moment to compose themselves.

They were still navigating the twisty single-track country lanes of Dartmoor, when Pattie said, 'I'm taking it as a good sign, Sukie, that Father and William stood smoking outside together as I was inside saying goodbye to Mother. I know it was all eleventh hour on Father's part, but I suppose we must be grateful for small mercies.'

'I didn't know you smoked, William,' Sukie said.

'I don't,' he replied as he changed up into third.

Sukie was still smiling about this when she fell soundly asleep a mile later, despite Dot chattering away nineteen to the dozen right beside her right ear in the very insistent voice of a small child.

There was a surprise for Sukie on the way home.

She was gently shaken from a deep sleep by Pattie, who was saying in her ear very quietly so as not to wake up the twins, who were both flat out and dead to the world beside her, 'Sukie! Sukie, wake up, we have something to show you.'

Groggily Sukie stumbled from the stationary car, rubbing her eyes as she did so, and she followed Pattie to where William and Dot were standing to the side of a little coppice.

She was disorientated and out of sorts, and she felt as if she staggered slightly rather than walked as normal.

But once she reached William's side and looked to where he was pointing, Sukie had the most wonderful vision before her.

For there, looking resplendent in a patch of sunlight, was Wesley's bench, complete with its shiny brass plaque in memory of him in the centre of the uppermost rail at the back.

Sukie went across and ran her fingers over the bench, enjoying the sensation of the carefully turned wood in her hands. Gently she traced Wesley's name on the plaque.

She had a lump in her throat and didn't trust herself to speak as she felt so overwhelmed with emotion, in part as it was all so unexpected.

She sat down on the bench then, and for a moment she had the curious sensation that it was almost as if Wesley were reaching out to caress and then softly envelop her. She leaned back and closed her eyes, and took a deep breath. It was wonderful.

Pattie and William had the good sense not to say anything, but just to let Sukie revel in the moment in whatever way she wanted.

Sukie smiled at them in gratitude, although she didn't yet dare to say anything.

Then she looked at the view in front of her from where she was sitting, and her breath felt taken away, before a sense of peace and well-being calmed her.

The sight before her was unbelievably stunning, stretching far into the distance from the high viewpoint on which the bench had been positioned.

The spot has been chosen carefully by his mother – it was where Wesley had spent happy hours with his brother playing when they were little.

Sukie had asked that Wesley's mother think of somewhere beautiful for the bench to go, a place where people would want to sit and think of their own lost loved ones.

Sukie thought that even if she had known Bristol like the back of her hand (which she didn't, as she had never been to the city), she could never have chosen a better place. This was glorious, and she thought she must write to his mother to tell her so.

William fetched his camera, and he took a picture of Sukie sitting there and looking thoughtfully at the vista stretching away below, and then one of Sukie with Pattie beside her.

Sukie jumped up to insist that she take a picture of William and Pattie, and then William, Pattie and Dot all sitting in a row on the bench (the twins were still both sound asleep and so everyone decided that it was best that they weren't disturbed).

The roll of film in William's camera was now all used up and so they all went back to the car, and Sukie found her voice vibrating with emotion as she sincerely thanked William and Pattie for being so thoughtful as to bring her there.

She went to get in the back of the car beside Dot, but Sukie realised she needed just a couple of minutes more on the bench, this time quite alone, and so she begged that they indulge her for just a little while longer.

Pattie told Sukie to take all the time she needed.

Sukie went to the back of the car and opened the boot. She found her suitcase and removed her embroidered handkerchief case.

She carried it back to the bench and sat down again, taking out the engagement ring and kissing it, as she thought of Wesley.

Then she slipped the engagement ring on to the third finger of the left hand and reached inside the hanky case for the delicate gold chain on which the ring has been suspended for so long, dangling its small but beautifully cut diamond close to Sukie's heart.

She held the chain up to the light, and saw the sunlight pick out the finely wrought details of the chain's craftsmanship, back-dropped by the superb views in front of her.

As she said, 'I'll never forget what you and I had, Wesley', Sukie had an idea.

She crouched down.

And then she lay herself prone on the bare earth beside the bench, right where the feet of people who had sat on the bench had already worn a slight furrow on the ground.

Sukie looked up at bench the from underneath. As she spied the end of a bolt sticking out from the corner joint of the bench, with quick fingers she wrapped the chain around the bolt end in silent and private tribute to her lost love. It was a secret marking of the spot that she hoped nobody but she would ever know about.

She kneeled in a silent prayer for a moment, and then she laid her forehead slowly to the bench, her hands on the brass plaque where Wesley's full name was etched.

Sukie was calm and peaceful as she re-joined Pattie and William in the car several minutes later, and silently placed the hanky case (now with the ring back in its place within the folds of Wesley's handkerchief) back in her case.

Although they raised a questioning eyebrow at each other,

there was something calm and satisfied about Sukie's demeanour that made Pattie and William think it best that they didn't mention the blades of grass that they could see on Sukie's back, or a grubby mark on her leg where it looked as if she might have kneeled on the earth in supplication.

# Chapter Seventeen

Tracey Benn happened to be standing outside the Eddy when William turned into the street to drop off Pattie and Sukie. She was leaning over to speak to somebody through the wound-down window of a car, her elbows resting on the car door and her hands in the car, and laughing quite giddily if her tossed-back head and the fluttering hem of an oddly demure blue tea dress against the well-formed calves of her legs were anything to go by.

It was only as Tracey looked towards them and sprang upright, and the car drove rather abruptly away just as William parked, that Sukie realised that it was Tracey Benn's car that was just nipping out of sight around the corner at the end of the road, and that therefore her friend must have lent her precious Austin Seven to somebody else, an act of generosity that would be as rare as hen's teeth. And in the brief glimpse a puzzled Sukie snatched of the back of the driver's head, she thought he looked a tad familiar but for the moment she couldn't quite place him.

But before Sukie could say anything about this, Tracey Benn clasped Sukie firmly to her bosom, and then said to her and Pattie that she hoped they had had a good time, and meanwhile there'd been a teensy-weensy change or two at the Eddy while they had been away.

And with that Tracey Benn darted up the steps to the hotel's entrance, leaving Sukie and Pattie to exchange curious looks before they indicated to the doorman that once he'd finished dealing with a gaggle of arriving guests, and as there were doings afoot to which they must attend, they would be very grateful if he could then bring their luggage inside and get it taken to their bedroom.

Tracey Benn had vanished by the time they got to the hotel foyer. But Polly spied Pattie immediately and flew to her with a squawk of pleasure (he preferred Pattie to Sukie, even though it was usually Sukie who made a fuss of him, which Sukie didn't think was particularly fair of the bird as it was she who spent an inordinate amount of time stroking him, but what could one do in that situation?).

Sukie left Pattie trying and failing to persuade the parrot to get off her wrist where he was balancing precariously, his fearsome claws clearly digging uncomfortably into the back of her hand as he dipped his head again and again in hope of a welcoming scratch, stoutly refusing to hop back on to his perch.

As Polly squawked his displeasure at Pattie's disgraceful perfunctory treatment of him, Sukie peeked into the manager's office behind reception.

Finding it empty, she trotted downstairs to see Mrs Bridge, feeling rather pleased that she had remembered to retrieve the wicker basket from William's car to return to her and was now holding it before her.

'Welcome back,' said Mrs Bridge, with a big smile as she relieved Sukie of the basket. Sukie hoped the smile was directed at her, and not at the sight of the basket and the Thermoses.

'Now,' Mrs Bridge confided, 'before her ladyship gets down here, you'd best know that John has had to move into the staff quarters. And that man has been a hero, let me tell you. An absolute hero.'

Sukie guessed that 'her ladyship' was Pattie.

'But that's not the big news, and I'm sure that Mr Bright will want to tell you that himself, and pronto,' Mrs Bridge added mysteriously. 'Now chop-chop, you run off and find him.'

Sukie went to go upstairs again. But then she stopped and turned towards the housekeeper with a questioning look, but Mrs Bridge made it clear she had said all she was going to, either about Mr Bright's news or about John (in spite of her tantalising 'let me tell you').

Decisively, the housekeeper shook her head and then she pointed towards the ceiling, and nodded at Sukie in encouragement that she go upstairs and seek out Mr Bright, prodding her departure with a 'Shoo! Vamoose!'.

Sukie frowned as she headed back up the stairs.

Why was John ensconced at the Eddy now and, more importantly, what was the 'big news'?

Mr Bright was now in his office, sitting officiously behind the desk, and – unusually – Tracey Benn was standing on sentry duty just behind his left shoulder. They both appeared to be very satisfied with themselves, and a little as if they were unlikely partners in crime. They looked extremely pleased, too, to see Sukie.

The combination of all of this was a bit strange and wrong-footing, Sukie found, and she wondered for an instant if she were dreaming.

'Ah, Miss Scott,' said Mr Bright. 'The very person. We were just about to send out a search party.'

'Good afternoon, Mr Bright, and how nice to see you looking so well. I hear there's news?' Sukie said.

'There is indeed news, and of a situation that will be a step up for you as long as you keep minding your Ps and Qs,' Mr Bright told her grandiosely. Why this might be a step up wasn't obviously clear though, as he nattered on for a minute or two in his way, which was to go around the houses and not to really say anything much. But – finally! – Mr Bright seemed to have got to the point of delivering what it was that he wanted to tell Sukie, and she breathed out slowly and realised she had become tense as she wasn't very good at waiting.

'Over the last few months Miss Benn and myself have

organised a consortium of investors, and we have just signed off on the legal paperwork on its composition and intentions,' he began. Sukie understood at this point why they had both sometimes been inexplicably absent from the Eddy. Mr Bright continued, 'And I am delighted to say that this consortium – which we have given the moniker Benn and Partners – are now the legal owners of both the Edwardes and the Capel hotels. I am a major shareholder, naturally, and I will retain my manager's role in one or other of the hotels, although I am undecided yet as to which. Miss Benn has the casting vote on the Benn and Partners board as the founder of the consortium, and as the person who raised the bulk of the investment funds, and because she is the owner of the largest number of shares. You might be interested to know that the board consists of a variety of people, from all walks of life. For instance, you will know Raymond already, of course, and Mickey from Mickey's Shelter, although obviously we didn't request that Mickey *purchase* his shares,' explained Mr Bright, a little pink on the cheeks as he mentioned the gift of the shares to Mickey, who could never have raised the capital.

Sukie was pleased about this as they all felt very invested in helping Mickey run his shelter, which had saved so many lives, and she thought it was very typical of Mr Bright to feel a little embarrassed by having made such a gesture. Then she reflected that wartime certainly made for curious bedfellows.

When else would a man who liked to wear silk evening gowns, as Raymond so obviously enjoyed in his role as maître d' of the Pink Sink (or possibly he wore this sort of attire all the time, Sukie suddenly thought), be able to rub shoulders in a business sense with somebody such as the very proper and bureaucratic Mr Bright, most definitely not an evening-gown-wearing type of gent? Or, for that matter, rub shoulders with somebody like Mickey? He delighted in being a Cockney sparrow through and through, and Sukie found him very endearing. He was also a dwarf and – wonderfully – the driving force behind a huge air-raid shelter over in the East End, which was a shelter where thousands (the press claimed it could take *10,000* people at any one time) of poor, working people could seek refuge when the bombs were dropping, or were in need of a hot meal and a blanket. Mickey was rightfully very proud that the shelter – which the press had named Mickey's Shelter in tribute to his tireless energy – operated on egalitarian lines, being 'run by the people, for the people'.

Although Mr Bright never advertised the fact, Sukie had discovered before Christmas that he had been very generous in quietly and regularly supporting the shelter and Mickey's work, and this was one of the things that told Sukie that although Mr Bright could seem a trifle tiresome at times, underneath it all he really was a very good egg. Indeed, this was why she had donated a sizeable proportion of the profits from the charitable Christmas party to the shelter as Sukie felt that Mickey's Shelter was a very just cause, and one that needed all the donations it could get.

Mr Bright continued meanwhile, 'Now that our investment money is secure – Miss Benn knowing some influential people with deep pockets having been *most* beneficial in this respect' – he turned to nod in appreciation towards Tracey Benn, who responded with a little salute of acknowledgment – 'I am delighted to say that it will be all steam ahead with getting the Capel back on its feet so that we can reopen her. Once that has been achieved, we will follow through with something of a refurbishment of the Edwardes to bring *her* up to scratch, so that we end up having two high-class hotels to run under the Benn and Partners banner.'

Sukie smiled at Mr Bright to show that he was telling her some exciting news. She tried not to let her face hint that she was just as keen to know what these changes might mean for herself as she was already starting to imagine a welter of possibilities.

She stood waiting as patiently as she could, and at last Mr Bright got to the nitty-gritty as to how it all would affect Sukie.

He looked at her, and stood up as if to emphasise what he was about to say. 'I have been impressed, *very* impressed it has to be said, by the way you have risen to the challenge of taking on more responsibility in my absence, Miss Scott, and I want to thank you for this. You have far excelled my expectations, and I want you to know that you are a *most* valued member of staff.

'I propose therefore that you continue as acting manager here at the Edwardes Hotel for the foreseeable future, sharing this office with me – we'll bring in an extra desk and chair, and install a second telephone line – as I will now also work between two and four hours a day as I am feeling strong enough for that, and hopefully I will be able to countenance a full day at my desk by the time the Capel opens and we have both hotels to run.

'However, Miss Scott...' Mr Bright paused dramatically, and he sat down again and paused as he began to run his finger down a checklist of things he wanted to say to Sukie, who was quite peeved that his writing was too tiny for her to read upside down. Mr Bright cleared his throat to indicate he was about to say something important. 'However, in addition to your hotel manager's role, you will oversee the building work on the Capel, working alongside, and reporting to, both myself and Miss Benn, as a Benn and Partners manager of the said works. Your primary responsibility will be to keep the budget in top-hole shape and to collect all the invoices and so forth, and to prepare them for payment; and you will deal with and organise the crafts-men's tenders, the decorators and so forth, and the supply of all equipment and goods they need; and then you will manage the fitting-out of the hotel once the restoration work has finished, which will also involve you finding an external foreman to liaise with who can help oversee the project. I have written out your responsibilities so that you can study them later at your leisure. Ordinarily, I would do all of this myself, of course, and I am sorry to not be more actively involved. But although I am much better in the physical sense, I think young legs are needed to nip back and forth, and up and down all those stairs to the top floor at the Capel, in order to keep the workmen on their toes, as I think it will mean lots of charging around, and I don't yet feel up to that myself, and therefore you are the obvious candidate to step forward and rise to the, er, *challenge*.'

Sukie listened intently, and then she frowned.

What Mr Bright was proposing sounded a very big role for her, a huge role, in fact. And especially so if he intended, as apparently he did, that it was to be in addition to her current responsibilities and all that she had to do every day to keep the Eddy jogging along at the standard the guests, and the Eddies themselves, expected.

Although Mr Bright felt better – and Sukie was most pleased to hear this – and despite his assurances about returning to his office on a part-time basis, she didn't hold out much hope that in practical terms he would be terribly active in the day-to-day management of the Eddy for quite some time to come, as in her experience he had always been more of a talker (well, pontificator, more accurately) than a doer, and so she pretty much expected her workload at the Eddy to remain more or less as it was currently, even if Mr Bright was going to be sitting in the hotel manager's office for the best part of a day.

Mr Bright wasn't finished with Sukie yet, though, as he said next, 'In *addition*, Miss Scott, you will also play an active role in recruiting staff for the Capel when it is ready to re-open, and in ensuring the staff in both hotels are trained to the high standard that we expect.'

Good grief, if she had thought she had been rushed off her feet in the run-up to getting everything ready for the Eddy's Christmas party, Sukie couldn't help but think, then that sense of busyness was going to pale into insignificance as to how she would be feeling if all these proposed tasks did end up at her door in the coming months.

She needed to think seriously about whether she felt up to taking all of this on, or if she even wanted to.

But then Sukie realised in a flash that she was being offered a real opportunity, one that was more or less being handed to her on a plate, and that she very much wanted to take it all on.

And then the next moment she wondered whether there was

a way she could somehow skew the situation further to her advantage.

Mr Bright helped her out on this, with his next words. 'And for your extra responsibilities, I propose that your salary rise from the current three pounds ten shillings a week to five pounds ten shillings a week, with your living-in costs not being counted as part of your wage, as at present.' He gave a wolfish smile. 'Would everything I've outlined be acceptable to you, Miss Scott?'

Sukie's eyes flicked towards Tracey Benn, who'd silently retreated a little further behind Mr Bright so as not to catch his attention. She was looking at Sukie and shaking her head, as she was raising her hand upwards.

Sukie guessed what her friend was indicating, and she knew just how to handle Mr Bright.

'How exciting all of this sounds, Mr Bright,' said Sukie in as cheerful and appreciative tone as she could muster. 'And I couldn't possibly have done what I have been able to do over the past months if I'd not been able to learn from *you*, before you were taken poorly, that is – and I know I will never be able to thank you enough for all the hotel knowhow that I managed to pick up from watching you. I certainly am very much in your debt.'

Sukie hadn't worked with Mr Bright for as long as she had not to learn the value of flattery, at least as far as the hotel manager was concerned.

In fact, the truth of it was that she hadn't learned very much else at all on the best way of doing things from Mr Bright, other than some practicalities on the ledgers and staff timesheets side. While she had been able to see that Mr Bright's brand of management worked well enough for him personally, she had found that in her day-to-day hotel life, she frequently had been able to adapt his methods to achieve more easily what she wanted. And so the skills she had picked up from him were more of the let's-not-do-that-again variety, as she felt some of his ideas were old-fashioned and fuddy-duddy.

But Sukie would rather cut her own tongue out personally than give Mr Bright any suspicion of this. She had become very fond of him, and would never want to cause him any upset, and actually she had noticed that lately he'd been watching her own way of doing things and had even softened his approach occasionally in order to bring his practices more into line with her own management style. And he had many years of experience that Sukie thought would be useful for her to draw on at times – she was relatively new to the hospitality business after all, and she understood that there must be plenty yet that she should learn.

At Sukie's praise of Mr Bright, Tracey Benn gave Sukie a discreet thumbs-up that she made sure was out of sight of the hotel manager, while he himself stroked his moustache happily at Sukie's words, and smoothed his already tidy and shinily pomaded hair. Sukie smiled encouragingly at him.

'Mr Bright, as you can imagine, you have given me plenty of food for thought. And so I am sure you will understand that I might need more time to think through all of what you have just said. But speaking off the cuff, it sounds most certainly like the dawn of a new era for the Edwardes, and the Capel too. You are building a wonderful opportunity for everyone that will work in them, while a consortium such as Benn and Partners looks to be a very sensible move forward to put both hotels on to a new and very sound financial footing.'

Her voice now turned serious.

'However, speaking solely for myself now and for any future role expected of me as you've just outlined, I'm afraid it sounds also like it would mean that a tremendous amount of extra work would be expected of me, and a very high level of responsibility.'

And then she delivered her sucker punch.

'In view of this, therefore, I'm afraid that I can't agree with you that an improvement of my weekly wage to five pounds ten shillings is anywhere near sufficient recompense for the added responsibility, or the many extra tasks that would appear to be expected on top of what I do already each day, and so I cannot accept your offer. And so while I don't want to be difficult, I'm afraid I am not willing to continue the discussions on the basis of that small improvement to my financial situation that you have just made.'

There was a silence.

When he realised what Sukie meant, Mr Bright's hand stopped dead mid-stroke of his hair, and he turned to look askance at Tracey Benn, who slowly raised an eyebrow in his direction as if to indicate 'I told you so'.

Sukie's heart was beating very quickly; it felt very bold to be speaking out in this way, and she had never attempted anything like this in her life before. To take such a firm stance could all go very wrong for her, she knew, with the end result that she might be unceremoniously cast from the Eddy for ever, and with a flea in her ear to boot.

But it was a risk worth taking. The new position *would* be demanding in the extreme, and she'd be silly for doing it for less than the market rate, Sukie told herself.

She loved the Eddy, of course she did, but not *that* much.

And if the worse came to the worst, and she was told by Mr Bright that she should sling her hook, then she felt confident she would be able very quickly to secure another job, as wartime had meant a tremendous shortage of reliable staff in the hospitality business in London. However, fingers crossed, perhaps it wouldn't come to that.

Tracey Benn smiled encouragement, and Sukie felt braver.

Mr Bright turned to glower at Sukie. He looked most put out at her temerity in digging her toes in.

He looked so wrong-footed, in fact, that Sukie guessed he had fully expected her to be very grateful, and that she would agree happily with his proposal.

She switched her gaze back to Tracey Benn, who was now mouthing something that looked like – well, actually Sukie wasn't at all sure what the word was, and so Tracey had to write it for her in the air, and then she traced a second word too.

Sukie allowed the quiet to swirl between herself and Mr

Bright. She realised there was a power in not stepping forward to fill the hush with words, at least not until she was ready.

She turned her face to him again, looking Mr Bright straight in the eye as slowly she drew herself upwards until she was as tall and straight as she could be, with what she hoped was an intelligent but hopefully not a belligerent expression on her face. She was trying very hard to look like somebody who deserved and was worthy of top dollar, rather than a petulant underling threatening a temper tantrum.

'Six pounds, perhaps? Each week,' Mr Bright suggested. His voice quavered with a slight uncertainty.

'I am sorry, Mr Bright, but that is still substantially less than the role that you have described is worth to Benn and Partners,' said Sukie quietly but insistently, and he gave a breathy squeak in reply.

To try to oil the wheels a little, Sukie added calmly, 'Would it help if I pointed out to you that if Benn and Partners has to employ a man who already has the necessary hotel manager skills to do all of what you expect, instead of me, any such man would expect – and be able to secure – at least twelve pounds a week for this level of responsibility. Therefore, if you were to offer me, say, seven pounds a week, then you, and the Edwardes and the Capel, would still be getting a bargain.'

Mr Bright blinked rapidly, as if he didn't know what to say or do.

'And if I were thinking of myself in your position and offering somebody such employment as this...' Sukie went on before Mr Bright could distract her. She had just worked out now what Tracey Benn had been writing in the air, and so Sukie was telling herself at this point that she may as well be killed for a sheep as a lamb, as probably she would never again have Mr Bright's attention with quite this level of concentration. '...Then I would, in addition, offer that person a structure of capital inducements that would be paid as incremental incentives, or bonuses, if you will, such payments to be made provided various pre-agreed timings of a schedule of works are met along the way, the monies to be paid soon after each agreed timing has been made.'

Mr Bright wheezed with astonishment at Sukie's temerity, and opened his mouth as if about to reply.

But Sukie wasn't finished yet and so she continued before he could say anything, 'Also, again if I were making somebody such an offer, I would make sure that, in a separate clause of the employment contract, that a tranche of company shares was to be awarded on completion of the project to the said employee. These shares would of course be in addition to all of the bonus payments, and awarded should the whole project be delivered on time and within the agreed budget. Or something similar. I'm sure you get my drift. As it were . . .'

As the import of Sukie's words made their point, Mr Bright's answering swallow and gurgling gulp of air were clearly audible, and Sukie noticed that he had gone a funny colour.

Tracey Benn was clearly trying not to smile, and so Sukie didn't think she had overstepped the mark totally, or at least not by too much.

'Why don't we discuss Miss Scott's points?' Tracey Benn said to Mr Bright, whose face was a picture.

Tracey Benn stepped forward to stand directly beside Mr Bright, with a hand softly laid on his shoulder, presumably so he felt they were putting on a united front, and she added, 'Although we probably don't need further clarification for the moment on your negotiating or strategising skills, Miss Scott, perhaps you will allow us to give you our decision in the morning on any improvement to the proffered terms.'

'That is acceptable to me, although I would like any subsequent offer to be made to me in writing, and if such an offer is acceptable, that the agreement is then signed via a legally drawn-up contract. If that isn't too much trouble,' said Sukie.

Mr Bright's shade deepened further, which had seemed an unlikely possibility earlier as his face had gone so dark already.

'As you have a lot to discuss, would you like me to rustle

up a cup of tea for you both?' Sukie strove that she deliver her words in a wide-eyed, innocent manner so as not to be antagonistic.

As she headed downstairs to make up a tea tray, Sukie chuckled inwardly to herself and momentarily clenched her right fist close to her hip in a little show of private celebration.

What a surprising meeting, for all sorts of reasons. Certainly, it had gone much better than she could have imagined, if she had had prior knowledge of what was going to be said to her, which of course she hadn't.

It was always annoying that men were paid so much more than a woman doing exactly the same job, but it was the way of the world, Sukie reminded herself. And a weekly wage of £7, and with no living expenses, was exceptionally good going for a young woman such as she.

Sukie felt confident that she would get her way, or nearly all of it, not least as she was certain that Tracey Benn would point out to Mr Bright the advantage of having someone in situ, as Sukie obviously was, who could crack on immediately with the work that was needed to bring the Capel up to scratch and re-opened sooner rather than later. This actually was a fact that shouldn't be underestimated, Sukie knew, as there would be a cost to the consortium if the project were delayed because of management staffing issues.

This meant that while Sukie's request was an extra weekly expense of thirty shillings on top of Mr Bright's first offer of a pecuniary increase to her wages, and although Sukie's later throwing in of extra googlies, with her suggestion of staggered bonus payments and a potential share offer, all combined to mean an additional strain on the sum that the consortium must have already set aside for the proposed budget, Sukie knew there were sound points in favour of Mr Bright and Tracey Benn giving her what she wanted.

This was because whatever way they looked at it, even with the possible shares rolled into the agreement, it was always going to be a cheaper option than either getting the consortium off on the wrong foot by a delay, as they had to find somebody else, especially as this might have the knock-on effect of risking Sukie leaving her job at the Edwardes if she felt her nose out of joint, which in itself would create another problem in the financial sense, seeing that Mr Bright wasn't yet restored enough to take full charge.

In that event, almost definitely the consortium would have to pay almost double what Sukie had proposed her new salary be for an experienced manager to come in to run the Eddy while Mr Bright regained full fitness, in part as such a person would effectively be looking after two hotels, at least for a while.

Sukie knew there weren't many young female hotel managers around with the experience that she had, and so the chance of the consortium replacing her, if she stalked off elsewhere in a huff, with a female manager who would be willing to take on the job for the weekly rate of the paltry £5 10/- that Mr Bright was keen on was exceptionally slim.

In other words, it was clearly good business to allow Sukie to have her way. She was a known quantity – employing new staff always carried with it the possibility that they might not be up to the job – and she was good with people, and if anyone could bring this project in on time, then it was likely to be Sukie.

She knew too that Mr Bright wasn't a foolhardy man when it came to pounds, shillings and pence (and especially not when he had the looming presence of Tracey Benn standing behind him as she peered over his shoulder).

Then Sukie stopped halfway down the stairs and slapped herself on the forehead.

What a duffer she was! A duffer who was an imbecile to boot.

Blindingly obvious now, thought Sukie, there were two further points that she should have raised.

Sukie almost gnashed her teeth in frustration at her own dimness.

She hadn't thought to say that if Benn and Partners was to make her an amended offer along the lines of what she had suggested, then she should also be awarded a seat on the consortium board at some point in the future if she managed to achieve everything she set out to do. She was never going to have leverage to achieve the promise of this as she had right at this very moment, and if she didn't ask for it now, she wasn't likely to be offered such a position a little further down the line, Sukie was pretty certain.

And again it wouldn't be a foolish thing for Mr Bright and Tracey Benn to agree to, Sukie believed, bearing in mind the grass-roots experience she would be about to get while refurbishing the two hotels. This would be experience that would prove invaluable in the longer term as far as the investors were concerned regarding their future financial profits, should the consortium become a success and later decide to bring in other hotels into the Benn and Partners fold that needed developing and refurbishing. Sukie could see that potentially she would have the knowhow and the contacts that would make her an indispensable member of the board.

And the other thing she felt that she should have requested was a stipulated pay review before the end of the year was out, as if she did well, they may well increase her basic wage at that point in order to keep her happy.

Damn and blast!

She wasn't as good as negotiating, after all, as Tracey Benn and Mr Bright probably believed, Sukie thought with a peevish sigh.

'Bugger,' she mumbled quietly to herself.

Sukie rarely swore, not even privately, but at this moment she felt justified in emitting almost silently a single bugger.

A few moments later, however, Sukie took herself in hand, saying that instead of getting het up about this, instead she should learn from these two omissions and consider why she had been so excited as to having an opportunity of asking for some demands that she stopped thinking about what it all might mean too soon.

Sukie told herself that she should see, as well, if she could rectify immediately the situation once more to her favour. If she didn't try to do something about this at once, she knew it would niggle away at her for months, if not years, to come, and so what had she to lose?

She returned to the manager's office, and a little awkwardly she tapped on the door.

Sukie put her head around the door, and began to speak. 'Excuse me, but two further requests occurred to me while I was on the way to make your tea that I think you should bring into your discussion before I put the kettle on...'

'Onwards and upwards,' she whispered as she went down to the kitchen a couple of minutes later, trying not to think about Mr Bright's decidedly grumpy expression on hearing these two further conditions. He hadn't looked very bright at all.

'You found him?' Mrs Bridge asked as Sukie stood waiting for the kettle to boil.

'I did,' said Sukie, not elaborating further, other than to add, 'And now I am going to take a tray with tea and a big pile of sandwiches up to Mr Bright and Tracey Benn. I don't suppose there's any Victoria sponge going begging too, is there, as I think they might be there for a while?'

'It went well then,' said Mrs Bridge with a smile, who in spite of the lack of chat had caught Sukie's drift nonetheless.

And to mark a good job well done, the housekeeper went to check what might be inside the cake tins. 'Good girl,' Sukie heard her say from somewhere deep within the pantry, and then 'A very good girl'.

To Sukie's surprise, the matter was settled before bedtime. By then Sukie had decided that it had been a surprisingly tiring day for a Monday, and she felt worn out and as if her nerves had been slightly mangled.

Still, she had been promised that a solicitor would be called to the Eddy first thing in the morning, and that every single one of her requests had been granted, other than the pay review quite as she had requested, which would now be in twelve months' time as opposed to before the end of the year. She was even going to be given the new and permanent job title of Hotel and Operations Manager.

A smiling Sukie thought it an excellent result, and that the push-back on the pay review was a fair compromise seeing that she had come out on top as regards everything else.

It was all worth grinning about, in fact very much so.

# Chapter Eighteen

Meanwhile, not long after they arrived back from Devon, Sukie had sent Pattie out to the theatre to accompany an elderly guest who wanted to see a show but didn't have anyone to go with.

The first thing Pattie did on her return from the play was bump into John on the staff stairs just as she headed up to her and Sukie's bedroom clutching her mug of bedtime cocoa.

He declared that he had moved in and was now going to sleep on the floor below her, along with the other male Eddies.

'Whose daft idea was that?' Pattie railed loudly, plumping herself down on Sukie's bed a few seconds later. 'And what was wrong with his digs, I'd like to know?'

Sukie had been sound asleep but she was quickly jolted awake. Dozy as she felt, she knew at once that Pattie was furious.

'Ssssh, Pattie,' whispered Sukie. 'You're going to wake everyone, making a song and dance like that.'

'Well, how *could* you?!'

'Pattie, it wasn't my decision, but actually I agree with it. John's shoulder is too bad now for the river ambulances, and if he is to earn a decent wage here, it's sensible that he live in if we're to increase his hours. It all blew up earlier while we were driving back from Lymbridge, but even if we had been here, my decision would have been the same as Mr Bright's. You know that John is a good worker and trained staff are murder to find.'

Pattie gave a snarly sort of groan before Sukie could explain anything else, and stalked out, slamming the door very noisily.

Sukie sighed with exasperation, and Polly flapped over to perch on her headboard in a show of solidarity. Her happy mood over her promotion was taking a bit of a battering at Pattie's exhibition of temper.

Earlier, once the dust had settled on the discussions on Sukie's new role, Sukie knew it was time that she thought through the implications of Mrs Bridge's news about John moving in.

Tracey Benn had tracked her down on one of the upper floors, and asked Sukie to come to her room to share a celebratory bottle of chilled champagne to celebrate the starting of Benn and Partners.

Sukie agreed, even though she wasn't really sure she liked the bubbly sensation of drinking champagne, although she did enjoy how giggly it made her feel. And she thought it nice to spend some time with Tracey Benn as they hadn't seen much of each other lately.

After they had clinked their glasses, Tracey Benn assumed that Sukie knew about John and a predicament, but when it was clear that she didn't, she'd quickly filled Sukie in.

Apparently, John had dislocated his shoulder once too often while on a shift on the river ambulance. Consequently, a couple of days previously he and the vessel's captain had decided mutually that he wasn't up to the job any longer, as he was going to be more of a hindrance than a help if the river ambulance crew had to spend time dealing with his shoulder when they were needed to help somebody more in need than John and his tiresome shoulder.

Understandably, he had been feeling very down in the dumps about this. As a former merchant naval seaman, he had loved his time on the River Thames, and so John made his way to the Eddy for his evening shift in a pretty sorry funk.

Tracey Benn explained that he had been just about to head down the metal steps to the basement level in order to come in through the kitchen, ready to change in the laundry room into his suit for the evening service, when, haring down the front steps right before John, shot a spivvy-looking man, who was clutching three handbags and a brown leather briefcase, all clearly having just been snatched by him.

Without a second's thought, John had given chase, followed in his pursuit by Tracey Benn, well-known for having a good turn of speed herself.

Sukie realised that this must be what Mrs Bridge had been referring to earlier when she had said that John was 'a hero'; she had been so distracted by the talk of her promotion that she had forgotten to ask Mrs Bridge later what she had meant.

'John set off like the clappers, and I went after them both. He can run, that man John, and I think he was in such a bad mood that it made him go even faster. I have a clean pair of heels myself, and I couldn't keep up,' Tracey Benn said admiringly of the impressive speed of John's pursuit. 'A hood had just come in off the street as bold as brass, who had run around the foyer snatching armfuls of handbags and the briefcase. He did it so quickly, and he held a knife, that nobody really knew what was going on or dared to stop him, and then he ran out again. He'd only been in the Eddy a few seconds, but I heard the rumpus and I was hot on his heels too as I'd been talking to Mr Bright in his office as we finalised the Benn and Partners property deals.

'But I was no match though for John, who chased the little blighter all the way along the Strand almost to Trafalgar Square, and then John tackled the robber down to the ground, paying, as far as I could see, little heed to the knife still in the robber's fist. I used my belt to tie up the man's hands, and John sat on him as he was cussing and trying to wriggle free, and then the bobby, who came to make his report after the earlier break-in here and the theft of Mrs Bridge's drawers, arrived at the scene and arrested the crook, saying there'd no more hoistings for him for a long while as the magistrate would lock him up and throw away the key.'

'That sounds as if it could all have got dangerous very quickly,' said Sukie incredulously.

'Well, John did take a nasty slash to his arm – the arm of his good shoulder, unfortunately – and he had to have stitches at St Thomas's, and a sling, and the nurse told him he was lucky an artery hadn't been nicked,' said Tracey Benn. 'And when his landlady saw the blood on his clothes and realised he was going to need help going to the lavatory and so forth because of his other tender shoulder, she said she couldn't cope with that, and so I said I'd pay for him to live here, for a while at least, and then Alan could do the necessary in the bathroom with John. So I did a deal with Mr Bright, and it's a peppercorn rent, with John doing extra hours but on light duties for now. And best of all, we retrieved all the handbags and the briefcase, and I heard Mr Bright promise each of the affected guests that they could enjoy a free night in the hotel.'

'I'm sure Mr Bright didn't want people to gossip unpleasantly about the Eddy not being safe,' said Sukie, 'and so that was sensible of him. I can't believe I'm only just getting wind of all of this. Goodness me! What a palaver!'

'I think Mr Bright wanted to sort it all out in your absence as a sign he's finding his feet more and is looking forward to returning to work,' said Tracey Benn, and they raised their glasses in a toast to Mr Bright, then John, and finally, Mrs Bridge's best drawers.

Sukie was just drifting off to sleep again when a calmer Pattie came back into the bedroom, and so she roused herself sleepily to tell Pattie what had happened.

'John's a brave man,' Pattie acknowledged once Sukie had finished telling her the story. 'I've never doubted that. But he'd better keep his distance from me while he's here. And I don't doubt that he'll soon have talked Mavis or one of the chambermaids to help him with "bathroom duties".'

'I think...' Sukie paused, and ignoring Pattie's final comment she added sternly, 'that *both* of you need to be very respectful of the other. It won't do if there's an atmosphere or words. I want you both to be polite, and professional, when dealing with one another. Pattie? Pattie, are you listening to me?'

Sukie couldn't decide if the little snore that reached from over in Pattie's bed was genuine, or merely designed to shut Sukie up.

She snuggled back under her own covers, and then remembered that the bubbles of the champagne had clean made her forget to enquire of Tracey Benn who had been driving the prized Austin Seven when Sukie had arrived back at the Eddy after her Lymbridge visit.

# Chapter Nineteen

The next evening Sukie and Simon went for a drink.

Simon was back to his urbane self, and he looked devastatingly handsome (more so than Sukie had remembered), and in fact she surprised herself by how much she enjoyed seeing him again and what a lot they had to say to each other. When she thought about how well they had got on, she found it hard to believe how tongue-tied they had been with each other when they'd been over in the horrid and dingy Camden flat.

They steered clear of mentioning what had happened at the flat, of course, and Sukie kept the conversation reasonably light, regaling Simon instead with describing the horse-ride on the moors, and how lovely it had been to catch up with Evie.

'I do miss Evie, you know. She seems to understand me so well and she talks such good sense. And I was very touched too when we drove a different way back to London than Mr Smith had taken on the way down, all the way to Bristol, where William and Pattie very kindly took me to visit Wesley's bench. It's very sturdy and in a beautiful setting, and I am incredibly grateful to them for being so thoughtful as it is likely to be the only time I will see it,' said Sukie. She didn't mention hiding the gold chain on its underside.

Sukie liked the way that Simon listened intently to what she was saying about the bench as he gently stroked the back her hand. 'That sounds a very special moment, Sukie, and as if you had the perfect weather to see it in such a beautiful setting. I'm sure that sitting on the bench will give a lot of comfort to people.'

Sukie smiled at him. Then, buoyed in part by the confidence she had discovered her new role at the Eddy had given her, suddenly she leaned across and gave him a kiss of thanks on the cheek for being so empathetic, making him look for a moment quite bashful.

And so Sukie and Simon slid back into the routine of seeing one another once more, even on a couple of occasions spending 'alone time' in Simon's bedroom at his digs, when his landlady and housemates were all out, as Sukie told him she didn't want to go to Camden again. His bedroom was much grander (and cleaner and tidier) than the poky flat, although Sukie had to resist very firmly an insistent nosy impulse to rummage around in Simon's possessions to find out a little more about him whenever he was out of the room.

Sukie was pleased that she had begun to enjoy sexual intercourse a little more, although she was still at a loss to find in the act precisely what it was that excited Pattie and Evie so. It was pleasant enough, she supposed, as a way of passing the time, although sometimes during the act she found herself making a mental tick-list of things she needed to do at work when she got back to the Eddy.

She knew, though, that she'd never be able to talk about their sex life with Simon in the frank manner that Evie had advocated. It seemed too personal, somehow, and a bit tacky, especially as she had no idea what she could suggest to up the ante a bit as far as she was concerned.

Still, they had pleasant times together in general, sometimes going to a restaurant or the movies. And when they were alone Simon was never less than very attentive and kind, and the sexual act itself seemed to work well enough for him, and so after a while Sukie didn't worry too much over her own vaguely dissatisfying feelings of take-it-or-leave-it over going to bed with him.

These days, she had plenty else to concern her, what with getting her new all-steam-ahead work responsibilities off the ground. This was what excited her, much more than when Simon laid a hand on her, she discovered.

And if Simon sometimes looked at her in a slightly questioning way, Sukie told herself that he should be happy that she wasn't one of those clingy, demanding girlfriends, the sort who were constantly angling for commitment and marriage and kiddies. They were happy enough as they were, and so why should either of them rock the boat by wanting more?

Several weeks jogged along happily enough in this way. It was quite a nice period as the mini Blitz seemed to have lessened – or at least the devastation in Central London halted – and it wasn't long before normal life seemed to be reasserting itself as the days lengthened. Sukie's stints with the mobile canteen were cut to one a week, although she remained on call for the other.

It was quiet too below stairs at the Eddy. Things seemed to have stalled between John and Mavis, with neither being particularly upset. Sukie was pleased about this, although more pleased that Pattie and John remained politely distant with each other, and gradually Sukie relaxed about them working and living under the same roof together.

In fact, there hadn't been a whole lot of opportunity for any friction or name-calling as Pattie was rarely at the Eddy these days unless she was working. She spent every free moment she could wrest away from the hotel either doing her voluntary work at William's office or else going over to his house to spend time with him and the little ones.

Fortunately, John seemed not to expect this to be any other way.

It was all systems go over at the Capel, meanwhile, and Sukie spent most of her days darting backwards and forward between the two hotels. As she had anticipated, Sukie found she worked well with Tracey Benn as they spent hours together discussing budgets and the schedule of works.

But, somewhat to her surprise, Sukie discovered that she liked even more dealing with all the builders and the roofers and the plumbers as she put the work out to tender, as although quite often challenging in terms of organisation and project management, it was also usually incredibly good-natured and even fun.

Sukie found she loved standing in the empty rooms at the Capel, planning how they would be, or wandering down the corridors with her feet ringing on the floorboards now the carpets had been lifted, the sunlight shafting through the sooty windows, as the dust motes swirled in the air around her. Sukie's mind raced with plans and ideas, and she would always head back to the Eddy with a renewed sense of peace and purpose. She saw herself as a person that was ambitious now, and serious both about herself and about doing well. Sukie rather liked this new version of herself.

Tracey Benn would stroll around the Capel whenever the whim took her, and Sukie would always try to walk with her unless she was very busy.

'I'm very pleased with how the work is progressing, as the timings and the figures are looking good,' said Tracey Benn one day, as she gently nudged a bit of new plaster work above a skirting board. 'You do know that this is very largely down to your pleasant and professional manner of dealing with the workmen, don't you? I like the way you make everyone feel as if they were all playing for the same team.'

'I tend not to let them see you kicking the plasterwork to see if it shoddy,' joked Sukie, 'as I find this goes a long way in keeping up morale of the builders.'

Tracey Benn laughed, and then Sukie pointed out how they were improving on the ancient plumbing system.

Lying in bed later that night, Sukie thought about her friend's assessment of the situation, and she realised that she did indeed have the knack of being a firm but fair forewoman, and of lightening the odd tense moment with humour.

She had meetings every two days with a man called Padraig O'Reilly, who owned the firm of builders to whom she'd awarded the contract for replacing the Capel's roof, and then subsequently Sukie gave his firm the contract for the rest of the Capel's refurbishment. Padraig O'Reilly's family was from Ireland originally, but he was second-generation and had been in London for such a long time that an occasional Irish lilt, presumably picked up from his parents, could only be heard on certain words, although Sukie had to smile each time he used the word 'jakes' to describe a WC.

Mr O'Reilly's firm hadn't been the cheapest of tenderers for the roofing job, but Sukie had thought his careful itemised description of the proposed work, and the many measurements he had taken when he had come to look at what needed to be done, were impressive, as was the way he urged her to keep back twenty per cent of the total fee until the whole job had been completed to her satisfaction. And he had a good reference from the Savoy, where his firm had recently carried out some damp-proofing work on the lower levels, and so all of that combined to sway the tender in his favour.

But what really swung it was that Sukie recognised him – she didn't think he recalled her as he didn't say anything – as being the man who would often lead the teams of rubble clearers when the mini Blitz was at its height earlier in the year, and who she had taken to making sure he had a large mug of tea. She'd been impressed back then with the quiet and efficient way he had worked, and the respect accorded him by those he worked with clearing the rubble and making things safe, and so she hoped that this meant she was making a good choice in awarding him the contract.

She wasn't wrong, as the care Mr O'Reilly's firm took with the re-roofing, the polite nature of the workforce and the way they cleaned up after themselves at the end of every day sub-sequently made Sukie confident in agreeing to use them on the bedroom levels.

Mr O'Reilly was very patient in answering Sukie's questions, and he commended her for wanting to understand all about struts and joists and weight-bearing walls, and the complexities of bathroom and central-heating fitting.

Within a week they had become Padraig and Sukie to one another, and Sukie discovered the intricacies of how a building was put together to be endlessly fascinating.

Padraig's army of employees had among the male chippies and sparks – Sukie was gratified to see – a substantial number of women doing quite important jobs. Sukie particularly liked it that Padraig's chief electrician, Sarah, who was beautiful but efficient-looking in her heavy-duty boiler-suit and with her russet hair covered by a knotted headscarf, was probably no older than Pattie.

Soon, Sukie made sure that each morning a huge catering urn was filled up with tea and placed in the hall of the Capel so that those working on the refurbishment could have a hot drink whenever they wanted.

'I do apologise about the state of the crockery, Padraig. I know nearly all of it is chipped, but I can't use any of it in the hotel but it still seems serviceable,' Sukie told him on the first morning the urn was in position.

He held a cup up to the light, before lifting a second, and then he frowned and shook his head as if in dismay.

Sukie's heart gave a little jump and quickly went to apologise again, but he stopped her by holding up a hand. She noticed the twinkle in his eyes when he said, 'I'm only messing with you, Sukie! That bunch of eejits will be so made up at bottomless cups of tea, they'd drink it from anything. I thank you on behalf of us all.'

This certainly seemed to be the case, and it wasn't long before early each Friday morning Sukie was asking Chef to make up a huge batch of Cornish pasties, which she placed still warm on large metal serving trays close to the urn. The pasties' filling was little meat and lots of swede and potato, but Chef did wonders with seasoning to make each shiny egg-brushed pasty a delicious treat, and every morsel would be snaffled within fifteen minutes of Sukie sending the trays over.

Unfortunately the roofing work was more complicated than it had at first seemed. It had been nearly eight months since the Capel had lost its roof by the time the builders moved in to begin the refurbishment, and this meant that the top floors of the hotel had been left open to the elements over the harshest months of the year.

When she first inspected the state of the hotel Sukie was horrified at the terrible state of most of the furniture and fittings on the lower floors, as rain and snow had leaked down through the building and down at least three storeys, causing a lot of damage as it did so. Everything was in a worse state than she had expected, and there were now unpleasant infestations of pigeons at the top level, and mice on the lower levels.

Sukie made John her assistant, as she wanted to give him more responsibility, although she asked that he still man the hotel bar on three evenings a week, which he was happy to do. And so, once the building had been made structurally safe, they spent a long time going through each room, making endless lists of what could be salvaged and what couldn't, and they prepared a careful note of things they could sell on.

Everything that Sukie and John felt could be re-used in one way or another was then lugged about by two of the strongest men in Padraig's employ. The poor chaps huffed and puffed sweatily as they pulled furniture and boxes along corridors and down the stairs so that everything could be itemised and then stacked together in the Capel's largest function room.

Things to be sold on were placed in another room, and Sukie called in an auctioneer to discuss the sale of these items. Auctioneers were doing well out of the war, as many people had to refurnish new accommodation and quickly.

And anything left that seemed serviceable but which didn't have a financial value in terms of selling on was sent over to Mickey's shelter as Sukie knew he would be able to find a use for just about everything that was no longer useful for her.

Once the bulk of the guest accommodation was empty and

they could let the dog see the rabbit, Sukie employed an architect. He and Padraig then consulted with Sukie as to the precise re-design of the bedrooms and bathrooms and, correspondingly, the hotel's plumbing and electricity, in order to bring it all up to modern standards.

Sukie contacted the managers of several London hotels nearby to discuss if they had any ideas of how she might buy hotel furniture at a competitive rate (she was keen to get as much of it matching as possible, but furniture makers had massively scaled down their output from pre-war levels to provide furniture and goods needed by the Forces, and so this wasn't as easy a question to answer as it once would have been). She was lucky that one of the managers she spoke to told her of two establishments that were getting ready to cease trading, having found the fifth year of the war and the resulting tightened financial income to be the straw that was breaking the camel's back in terms of their viability.

Sukie then went to these two hotels in person and spent some time with each manager, who were both very glad to sell a sympathetic Sukie furniture, kitchenware, linen and so forth as job lots after she and John had inspected everything thoroughly, all of which was subsequently piled up in the restaurant, and listed carefully before being covered with the prerequisite tarpaulins in order to keep out the building dust.

Padraig heard a whisper on the grapevine to do with a vast number of unused rolls of wallpaper going begging at a warehouse, and when he and Sukie went to see it, she was thrilled to find it was of excellent quality and that she could buy it all as a job lot and at a knockdown price, once Padraig had bargained the price per roll lower as he pulled in a favour from the warehouse man, that was.

As she had hoped, John turned out to be a reliable deputy, and so Sukie allocated him the task of daily quality control, and this meant that each morning he carried out a thorough inspection of what the builders had done the day before, and alerted Sukie to anything that was giving cause for concern.

Sukie had noticed John's thoroughness and attention to detail when she had watched him at work behind the bar of the Eddy, and so she didn't think much would slip past him, an assumption that was quickly proved correct.

Once the Capel had been made weather-tight, the remodelling of the floors and each bedroom began in earnest. The sixty-one previous bedrooms it had had were now being remodelled into forty-eight (with the pokiest of bedrooms being got rid off, and nearly all of the bedrooms remaining now having their own lavatories and hand-basins).

Sukie had thought that while in theory it was sensible to have more rooms for rental each night, if private facilities were installed in as many rooms as possible, then they could market the Capel to a different clientele, one who would be happy to pay significantly more for modern conveniences such as what would be on offer.

Business at the Eddy was doing well too, and of course Sukie was still continuing with her voluntary stints driving the mobile canteen, although she tried to keep it to only two afternoons a week.

Although Sukie found her days were packed and flashed past her in what felt like only an hour or two from when she got up to when she went to bed, each night she fell into bed tired but with a satisfyingly big tick-list nearly always achieved.

And if she squeezed in some time with Simon as well, she would be extra tired when she climbed what would feel like then to be a long way up to her and Pattie's bedroom on her return.

But she was young, Sukie told herself, and this pressure of work wouldn't be for ever.

And so she would look forward to the start of the next day, when she would nip not long after the break of dawn over to the Capel to see what was what before Padraig's workforce, or John, arrived and everyone got stuck into the technicalities of getting the hotel ready for its grand re-opening.

*

At the start of June, Sukie looked around and decided that she was very happy with everyone's work, and the general progress that had been made on the project so far. She thought that they deserved a little fun as a reward for their hard work.

Then the announcement came of thousands of Allied troops arriving on the coast of Normandy, a new strategy that seemed in all likelihood to be good news, and Sukie decided the boat must really be pushed out as a mark of respect of these brave men.

London was caught in the grip of a heat-wave that showed no signs of ending any time soon and so, she thought, what would be nicer than if all the Eddies and their families, and Padraig and his workers, all came on an outing one afternoon, and enjoyed a picnic and some games? The guests could come too, if they wanted. It could be a happy shindig for a huge number of people, funded by Benn and Partners as a thank you for everyone's efforts.

Before she said anything of this idea to her fellow Eddies, Sukie planned to bring it up with Mr Bright and Tracey Benn at one of their weekly catch-up meetings, point out that a treat like this might be just the ticket for encouraging everyone to work harder afterwards.

When early one evening she was lolling in a precious two inches of bathwater with an almost untold luxury of – thank the heavens above! – a new bar of soap (and one that was even perfumed to boot), Sukie practised different ways of raising the idea of a summer party with Mr Bright and Tracey Benn, and what her various responses should be if her ideas weren't well received.

In the event, Sukie needn't have worried.

Although initially Mr Bright looked – as Sukie knew he would – very dubious about the whole idea, thinking primarily of the expenditure involved, he promptly changed his mind and started to nod his approval of the plan the minute Tracey Benn indicated to him the Benn and Partners' party line on this with her reply, 'How wonderful, Sukie. It will cost us a bit, clearly, but the returns will far out-strip this long-term. Goodwill is very valuable, and I – and I'm sure Mr Bright, too – shall see this as an excellent way of building this. What a novel idea, and so thank you very much.'

Sukie couldn't help grinning widely, and she promised that neither of them would have to lift a finger as regards the arrangements, and they could leave everything to her.

'I know someone who can help with this,' said John. 'We could all cram on his river boat and we could go down to Greenwich Park, and we can easily walk there from the river. Depending on how many people we have, he could do it all in one trip, or maybe two, or even three if necessary.'

Sukie looked at the map. It wasn't a bad idea at all.

The Eddy and the Capel had the advantage of being only a stone's throw from the river, and Greenwich wasn't too far down the Thames from them, although it was on the other side of the river, with the park only a hop, skip and a jump away from where a boat could dock.

The newspapers, meanwhile, remained full of the news of the huge movement of British and American troops to France.

It seemed as if a new stage of the war had begun, and Sukie and Simon discussed the growing feelings of confidence they discerned around them that the war was – at long last – starting to turn in their favour. Simon confided that well in excess of 100,000 Allied servicemen were involved, and maybe as many as 150,000.

'And we don't put our neck out like this if we feel it's going to go wrong,' he said. 'I think this might be the start of the liberation of Europe.'

Sukie thought Simon probably wasn't exaggerating. He worked in Whitehall and had dealings at the War Office. And certainly people seemed more optimistic than a few months previously. The Baby Blitz hadn't dented morale, as far as she could tell, and for the first time Sukie detected an optimism on the streets that felt new to her.

She wanted to echo this positive feeling. She headed to the printer that had made her the Christmas party posters, and asked for a full-colour poster to advertise the day out, with happy-looking cartoons of Spitfires pulling a banner that set out the pertinent details of the day out, while the Edwardes and the Capel hotels themselves would be portrayed as cartoons walking off to a green park with the Greenwich Observatory shown.

When the posters arrived they were more than a trifle naughtier than Sukie had expected, as the artist had taken the liberty at the bottom of the poster of adding six pin-up girls, à la the saucy minxes that were regularly painted on to the noses of American bomber planes as morale boosters, followed by two toddlers – one standing and one crawling – wearing stripy romper suits and waving rattles so that the day out didn't appear as if it was an adult-only affair.

These cheeky ladies were depicted (thankfully, in Sukie's opinion) as on their way to the picnic, as they were carrying huge picnic baskets with gingham tablecloths spilling over the sides, and they were blowing kisses from their smiling, heavily lipsticked mouths. The very similar-looking and immensely popular pin-ups that adorned the US bombers were often painted in their underwear and lying in very come-hither poses, which wouldn't have been at all appropriate, but these girls looked happy and purposeful in – Sukie hoped – a slightly more Sunday-school attitude.

Tracey Benn walked into the office as Sukie studied the posters. 'Nice legs on those gals! Very eye-catching, I must say. Well done, Sukie, you've just made sure everyone will want to be there for this outing!'

Pattie snuck in from reception to peer over Tracey Benn's shoulder. She gave what Sukie could only describe as a guffaw and then she said, 'Very demure, and I'm sure Mr Bright will think so too.'

At that moment Mrs Bridge bustled in to talk to Sukie about

one of the chambermaids. She caught sight of the minxes and silently froze in her tracks with a look of shock on her face, and Sukie had to do some very animated talking to divert the housekeeper's attention away from the bawdy nature of the ladies and on to how jolly the background scene looked, pointing out firmly how the toddlers seemed to be looking forward to their feast, and how gaily the flags pennanted in the breeze.

'Yes, those romper suits look just the ticket,' Tracey Benn deadpanned, 'seeing as how much *romping* around there's likely to be, inspired by these well-proportioned lasses at the, erm, *bottom* of the posters.'

Sukie stared at her friend with widened eyes in an attempt to urge her to say no more in front of a prudish Mrs Bridge.

Tracey Benn took the hint, although she couldn't resist adding before she left the office, 'Top drawer, Sukie, top *drawer*, if I may say,' in what Sukie knew instantly was a veiled reference to the theft of Mrs Bridge's best smalls, although fortunately Mrs Bridge was still transfixed by what was before her on the posters and so she didn't seem to have heard Tracey Benn. Or noticed that Sukie and Pattie were doing their utmost not to laugh out loud. Still, Sukie wasn't totally sure she approved of the posters herself as the girls were all wearing *very* short shorts and skirts, as they strutted along on provocatively high heels.

But when she saw how much talk – and jokey laughter – the posters generated when she put them up around the hotel, she relaxed as they were certainly doing their job of promoting the bash as a fun day out. She even caught Mr Bright admiring them on more than one occasion, muttering, 'Capital,' as he stared intently at one part of the poster or another.

In fact, so many people signed up to attend the jamboree, that Sukie had Chef cook up a batch of biscuits that she took over to the printer as a thank you for them making the day such a talking point with their playfully naughty interpretation of Sukie's instructions.

# Chapter Twenty

The day of the E&C Jamboree, as Sukie had named it on the posters, dawned bright and sunny.

Sukie was relieved that at least it wasn't raining, as she was feeling quite tetchy first thing and she knew that heatwaves were often interspersed with thundery hot rain.

Her downbeat mood was because the jamboree's preparations had taken a bit more work – well, a lot more, actually – than Sukie had anticipated, and she was feeling tired and a bit on edge, as the deeper she had got into the arrangements, the more she realised that a lot could go wrong, especially if the weather turned and it poured.

She walked down to the river at seven o'clock, but the brackish, oily calm of the River Thames and a cloudless sky promised a day that looked to be set fair, and so she relaxed a little. The warm weather had made the river smell like slightly over-ripe cabbages, and even though it was early, Sukie could see small swarms of furiously flapping flying creatures dipping and diving about on the surface of the water.

The Capel had work suspended on it for the whole day, while only the merest skeleton staff was left on duty at the Eddy, with no bar service or hot meals available, and only a cold buffet for lunch and dinner. Sukie told the guests that anyone who was staying there but who chose not to accompany them to Greenwich could have a reduction on the daily rate.

Nobody was being charged for the day out, but Sukie wanted everyone to feel spoiled and so Chef and his team had been busy for nearly a week making lots of food and gallons of ginger beer and zesty lemonade, while Sukie planned there'd also be hot tea and a range of alcoholic beverages too.

She arranged with John and Pattie – both under strict instructions to be nice to each other, and if they couldn't manage that, then they should at least be professional – that they would be in charge of the first two out of the three boat journeys that would be taking everyone down-river to Greenwich.

John would go in the first boat, along with a contingent of Padraig's men – the unmarried ones. Their job was to set everything up, and so they would haul over the blankets, deck-chairs, sun umbrellas, cricket and rounders and soccer gear, some folding tables, and the food and water, napkins and tablecloths, cutlery and plates, and the first aid kit (although Sukie very much hoped this last item wouldn't be called upon).

Once they had found a good spot on flat ground to set up, with lots of shade from nearby trees, the captain of the boat would head back to pick up Pattie, who was going to be in charge of escorting over all the guests, and the staff of the Eddy and Capel hotels who were bringing their families. Once the boat's captain had given Pattie directions to where John and the others were, she would make sure that all of her charges found their way over to the picnic area and got themselves sorted out.

Sukie had hired a string quartet who would accompany the picnic at lunchtime, along with a livelier band who did dance tunes and reels for later in the day, as well as a Punch and Judy show. Then there was a friend of Simon's who knew about bugs and butterflies, and who was going to organise a nature walk and a nature table, for which there would be prizes for the children who collected the highest number of leaves from the widest variety of plants, and for those who caught the most butterflies with the special nets he provided.

Entertainment for the adults included an artist who would offer sketching lessons, and a music hall comedian who could tell jokes and lead a sing-along. There was going to be bingo, a crossword competition and a limerick-writing prize. And many of the staff were looking forward to a Ludo championship between the Eddies and Padraig's men that Sukie was sure would be hotly contested. Cards would be taken too (both ordinary decks and Happy Families for the children), and a selection of dominoes and board games.

Sukie had worked out a timetable for all the various events, and had made sure that John was going to organise setting everything out roughly according to zones, so that there was a card and board games area, a children's entertainment area, seating and blankets for those who wanted to be near to the music, a food and drink area more or less in the middle of everything, and a quiet, comfy area with lots of cushions and blankets to lie on for those who simply wanted to nap. Nearby would be the cricket and rounders, and if anyone still had any energy left, soccer.

She wanted the day to be relaxed and fun, but for there always to be an activity just about to start for those who felt energetic.

'Padraig, I want to ask your advice,' Sukie had said a day or two earlier. 'Do you think it might be an idea if several of the tougher-looking chaps were unofficial watchers, just in case there's any funny business? We'll have the free food and alcohol, so I'm worried people in the park might try to gate-crash our party.'

'You probably should be more worried about my workers letting loose on the scran,' Padraig joked, but when he saw how concerned Sukie was looking, he assured her that she could leave it with him and she wasn't to worry, that everything would run like clockwork, he was certain.

Tracey Benn had driven Sukie and John down to Greenwich Park a couple of days previously so that they could decide on various options of where they'd like to place everything. Sukie had been keen to locate the bulk of everything close, but not too near, to the public conveniences as she wanted to avoid any jokes about 'inconveniences', while also avoiding any unwholesome smells if the heat made it all a bit whiffy.

John seemed very on top of everything he had to do. He had drawn a rough plan of how it all should be, which he had run past Sukie, and he had her meticulously planned timetable.

He had contributed his own idea for an event, and had blushed when Sukie said she thought it sounded really fun. It was for an 'E&C Olympics' with teams and events marked off on a large scoreboard. This was to be aimed at the families, and John had listed various races like a three-legged race, a wheelbarrow race, an egg-and-spoon race, a mothers' race and – of course – a fathers' race. There was tossing-a-shuttlecock, and a triple jump of three forward jumps from a standing start.

Sukie had unearthed a huge bag of rosettes when she had been looking for Christmas decorations back in December. When she had seen the folds of silk and the ribbon tails, and the cardboard discs with their gold lettering, she had been taken right back to the pre-war horse shows where she'd been a determined competitor in the show-jumping classes, and she had wondered what on earth had been the event at the Eddy that the handfuls of gaily coloured rosettes had been used for. Still, now they would be ideal as prizes.

A guest was staying with them at the Eddy who had with him a St Bernard dog called Bernie, and so Bernie was going to come too, and there was going to be a Guess Bernie's Weight competition. Sukie knew that some of the children on the day out would be scared of Bernie, as they wouldn't be used to dogs as so many families had decided to put their beloved dogs and cats to sleep at the start of the war as the government had advised, but Bernie was such an old softie that Sukie thought he would win them over.

Mickey was going to bring a group of children who had lost their parents in the earlier Blitz. He'd warned Sukie that one of the children – a little chap called Philip – was very ill with complications following polio as a baby, and was probably really too poorly to be there, but Sukie said that as long as she

194

was given instructions as to how they should make Philip as comfortable as possible for the day, he should come as it would be just horrid for him to know his friends were having a treat and he couldn't go.

'He's a nice little lad, is Philip,' said Mickey, 'and he's not had much luck in life as he were right poorly as a baby, and now lives with his granny in a damp old room as he's lost his parents and they don't have two pennies to rub together.'

'That settles it,' said Sukie, 'he must definitely come and spend a few hours being a little boy who's at a party. It will be lovely to have him with us, even if somebody has to take him home early if he gets tired.'

Mickey suggested that Sukie speak to someone he knew who had a milk cart, and when Sukie talked to the owner of the cart, he said that as it would be two ponies pulling the cart rather than one large horse, he was happy to bring some shorter reins and a couple of saddles, and then the kiddies could have pony rides, as long as Sukie could arrange for a couple of sensible lads to lead the ponies as he didn't think his feet were up to it.

Once the second tranche of people were on their way to the party, there'd be a massive clear-up of the breakfast things back at the Eddy, and so Sukie and Mr Bright, and the Eddies involved in this clear-up, would come on the third boat, along with any stragglers who hadn't made the previous boats.

Simon told Sukie that he was going to come over, he hoped, about lunchtime, and William and his children would be there too, while Tracey Benn was going to drive down.

The events for the smallest children would end about three-thirty in the afternoon, so that anyone wanting to step in before their little ones became fractious could get them home in good time for an early night. And then a boat back to Covent Garden would leave at roughly hourly intervals until dusk, although anyone who wanted to come home in the dark would have to make their own way back. And, Sukie reminded everyone, if they were out late then they still had to make sure they were up in time for work the next day if they were on an early shift.

It was midsummer's night, the longest day of the year, and so the sun wouldn't be setting until very late, and Sukie expected that there would be some weary, but hopefully happy, Eddies and guests on the morrow.

# Chapter Twenty-one

Everything ran surprisingly smoothly, at least for a while.

Mr Bright gave a short speech and then declared the jamboree open. A huge cheer went up from everyone gathered around.

Alan proved surprisingly nifty with an egg and spoon, although when Sukie saw how clumsy many of the runners and riders were, she was glad she had agreed to Chef's idea that the precious eggs be hard-boiled first. Then Mrs Bridge and Chef teamed up for the three-legged race, and very much to Sukie's amazement managed to see off all comers.

'They are quite a team – who'd have thought Chef would have had such a clean pair of heels. I wonder if they can be persuaded to go in for the wheelbarrow race?' mused Pattie naughtily as she stood with Sukie as they watched John pin a red rosette for first prize on each of their chests.

'Don't you dare, Pattie! Imagine if they did and then they took a tumble and injured themselves. We'd have no food, and as for what mischief the chambermaids would get in to without Mrs Bridge on their tails chasing them along, I can't bear to think about it.' Sukie couldn't prevent herself giving a tangible shudder at the mere thought.

John turned out to be a natural at teaching the children to play rounders, and then lots of people got roped in too, both men and women, and so it proved to be a strongly fought match and a lively start to the day's team games, especially as Mr

Bright provided a surprisingly witty commentary on a loud speaker.

Sukie looked around. Everyone seemed settled in and as if they were set for a lovely day, and she began to relax a bit.

Poor Bernie the St Bernard found the heat a bit much, though, and was panting furiously, and Sukie was just about to send him back to the cool of the Eddy when a kindly park keeper wandered over and whispered to Sukie about a secret tap that was hidden in the undergrowth. After asking Padraig for a surreptitious hand, Sukie begged Philip to help her cool Bernie down as she wanted the little boy to feel he had an important job to do. Working as a team, and with Padraig very gently helping Philip move about, they doused Bernie's thick fur with cold water, which made him much happier as he lay in the shade afterwards and snoozily allowed children to pet him and stroke his velvety ears, while their parents tried to guess how much he weighed (twelve stone six pounds, Sukie knew, as she had taken him the day before to the weighbridge where her mobile canteen was garaged at night). Philip squealed with joy when Bernie rolled on to his back so that he could pour some cold water through the long hair on his tummy.

'Well done, Philip – you've made Bernie the happiest dog in the park, don't you think?' Sukie said to him, and was rewarded with a huge grin and him clapping his hands. Padraig lifted Philip so that he could stroke Bernie, and it was obviously making the small lad so happy that the two grown-ups shared a look that mixed sympathy for poor Philip with pleasure at how happy he was just at that moment.

The look went on for a second longer than Sukie felt quite comfortable with, and so she broke it by turning to point out to Philip the ponies that had pulled the trap and who were now giving pony rides to some very excited children would also be very glad of a cool drink every now and again, and so might Philip be able to remind Padraig when they needed a drink?

Sukie was admiring Bernie's black, tan and pristine white fur, and pointing out to Philip the gentle and solemn manner in which he would 'shake hands', if he could be persuaded to sit up first, when Tracey Benn strolled towards her, making Sukie do a double-take in sheer surprise.

Well, the surprise wasn't that Tracey Benn was heading her way, as of course Sukie knew she was coming. Tracey Benn loved a do, and a chance to dress up, which meant it was inconceivable that she would miss this out, especially given Benn and Partners' role in funding it.

The surprise was that Tracey Benn, usually notoriously evasive about her personal life (other than when she was trying to shock Sukie with a small salacious snippet about something exceedingly risqué), was walking hand in hand with a much shorter and rather gingerish-looking chap who was dressed in clothing that was far too warm for the day.

Sukie realised that she had never seen her friend with a beau. But because of the finger tattoo of the intricately inked snake, and Tracey Benn's often androgynous dressing (of the type that Marlene Dietrich had made famous in *Morocco*) and her tales of gay abandon that had once caused Sukie to say to her 'so you won't die wondering!', Sukie had assumed that Tracey Benn would necessarily be attracted to someone as flamboyant as she was herself.

Apparently, this was not the case. Or at least, not just now.

Sukie couldn't help but stare as they seemed such an ill-suited couple, especially as Tracey Benn had to be a good four to six inches taller than her tweed-suited companion, who was pink of cheek and looked to be sweltering in the heat, especially as he was wearing a neatly buttoned waistcoat as well.

Tracey Benn caught Sukie's eye and smiled happily, and then she leaned across and boldly planted a kiss on the very top of the head of the man beside her, and as he smiled and put an arm around Tracey Benn's waist as he gazed up at her, Sukie suddenly realised who it was.

It was only Mr Watson, the rather officious jobsworth who had tested Sukie's driving on that frosty morning at the start of the year, and had then so irritated Tracey Benn by demanding that the Austin Seven be used for official purposes.

Goodness. What a turn up for the books!

'Miss Scott, allow me to introduce Mr Albert Watson,' said Tracey Benn, a definite twinkle in her eye.

'Charmed, I'm sure, Miss Scott. You might remember me from the depot when you had to drive the old ambulance,' Albert said to Sukie, shaking her hand a little too firmly. His voice had still its slightly squeaky edge about it.

'I remember you very well, Mr Watson, and how are you? How nice to have you here with us for our jamboree, although our Tracey Benn has been playing her cards very close to her chest as regards you,' said Sukie carefully, not daring to look at Tracey Benn. 'Might I interest you in a nice cold glass of lemonade or ginger beer, Mr Watson?'

As Albert softly repeated the word 'chest' in a manner that suggested he was remembering something very pleasant, he turned to head off towards the drinks table on Sukie's direction.

Watching him go, Tracey Benn leaned towards Sukie, and said in a stage whisper from the side of her mouth, 'He's a tiger, let me tell you. A hot-blooded tiger! He might be short and only weigh one hundred and fifty pounds, but let me tell you that one hundred and forty pounds of that is all—'

'I think you'd better stop right there!' Sukie interrupted.

Tracey Benn lifted her left hand to give Sukie a quick glimpse at her middle finger between the first and second joints. This was the opposite middle finger to where the tattooed coiled snake sat so delicately, and as she leaned forward for a closer look Sukie saw there was the recent addition of a tiny head of a roaring tiger that had just been inked on. And on the corresponding bone of her little finger was a paw print.

'I've just had them done, within the last hour,' confirmed Tracey Benn proudly, emphasising her words with a too-casual wave of her hand, 'as we didn't get much sleep last night as we played many a tiger game between the sheets!'

With a playful 'grrr' in Sukie's direction, accompanied by a clawing motion of the hand with the new tattoos, Tracey Benn turned to follow Albert, who was now standing beside the drinks table where he was holding up a glass of ginger beer in her direction.

Words failed Sukie, and so she shook her head, but only with very small shake, as if to herself.

But not Padraig, who made Sukie jump when he broke her train of introspective thought when he announced, 'Hmmm, nice *tíogair*. Did you ever enquire of yon *cara* quite what it was that the person who inspired the snake tattoo had to do to be honoured previously?'

Sukie hadn't realised he'd been standing so close. Normally she was very alert to this sort of thing, but she guessed she'd been spending so much time recently with Padraig that she'd got used to having him nearby.

He had told her previously that *cara* was Irish for friend, and it wasn't much of a stretch for Sukie to make out that *tíogair* must mean tiger.

Sukie turned to Padraig, and asked him with a serious look on her face, 'Did I ever ask you this very important question?' She raised an eyebrow in query, which she had been practising since she had seen Tracey Benn do it and had liked the effect it had. 'Why did the tiger lose at poker?'

Padraig shook his head, so that Sukie could then give him the punchline. 'Because he was playing with a cheetah.'

They laughed. It was a feeble and very old joke, but it felt funny as they stood side by side in the sunshine.

'I wish I still had my mouth organ as I could have gone wa-wa-wa-wa ... But that got lost on a site over in Whitechapel. In fact, I think I lost the dratted thing on the first day I saw you out with the mobile canteen, standing there with your large teapot. Instead, shall I nip over to let the comedian know you can take over from him?' Padraig replied.

Playfully, Sukie hit him on the arm. Then she felt a quiver of pleasure that, after all, Padraig had remembered her from when they had first met, even though he hadn't said anything until now. She decided that she was fond of the mouth organ and that she wished she knew how to play one.

And then Simon said a simple, 'Hello,' beside her, and the happy moment dissolved into a *pfft* of nothingness.

Sukie hadn't noticed Simon approach, and although she hadn't been doing anything to be ashamed of, all the same she felt a little uncomfortable.

To try and disguise this, quickly Sukie introduced Simon and Padraig to each other. 'Simon! Say hello to Padraig. I think I might have told you, but in case I didn't, Padraig and I are working on the Capel's renovation, and it's all going very well even though there is a lot of work to do still, what with Padraig's firm being very busy and him having some very good ideas how we can, er, update the plumbing and the, er, central heating that have meant some walls coming down...' Sukie knew she was rambling on in a little too much detail to Simon as to how she and Padraig were acquainted, but she couldn't seem to stop herself.

Simon stared at Sukie with a look that was a trifle more intent than was normal.

Padraig seemed oblivious to any awkwardness between them as he enquired in his easy manner whether Simon would be up for some cricket in a little while.

To Sukie's surprise, rather than coming to sit in a deck-chair alongside her as she suggested, Simon opted instead to head over alongside Padraig to where there was a group of men, some in cricket whites and all in shirt sleeves, including a couple of chaps who were buckling on leg guards and others who were putting up wickets, and a few more swinging their arms about and flexing their shoulders as if getting ready to bat.

Sukie felt a trifle vexed, although she couldn't put her finger on precisely why.

Certainly Simon had pressed on her his jacket and tie he'd removed for her to look after while he went to play in what Sukie felt was a slightly cavalier way, and he had appeared to be a bit too ready to make his way over to the cricketers. But this wasn't the crime of the century, and he hadn't said or done anything that was wrong as such, and she normally wasn't sensitive over this sort of thing. Perhaps he was making a point that he hadn't liked her larking about with Padraig, but then she bristled slightly as she reminded herself it had all been very innocent and Simon should trust her as she wasn't the flighty or the flirty sort.

But then Sukie thought she was reading too much into it, and perhaps Simon had really just fancied a chance to bowl a few overs, or whatever it was that cricketers did, and so Padraig's offer that Simon join them seemed too good to pass up.

Sukie told herself that she needed to snap out of it. She didn't want to become a shrewish sort of person and so any behaviour like this on her part needed nipping in the bud. That would have been her advice to Pattie, at any rate, should Pattie have come to her with a similar dilemma.

Sukie fetched a glass of water and a bun, and went to sit on a deck-chair, carefully arranging Simon's jacket and tie on the back of it so that it wouldn't crease.

She sat down and immediately wished she had brought a sun hat with her, as the glare of the sun was bright. She shaded her eyes with her fingers, and found herself watching Pattie with William and Dot and the twins. It was fascinating.

They looked incredibly relaxed with one another, as Pattie was noisily playing snakes and ladders with Dot, clearly letting Dot win, while the twins were piling cushions and blankets on top of William as he lay in the grass. Sukie could hear the laughter of the children, and William's pretend cries of 'no, no, I can't stand it!' that were rising to a crescendo as if the twins were causing him agonising pain, which made the children laugh even harder. Then they all – Pattie and William included – played 'Sleeping Lions' and then 'What's the Time, Mr Wolf', after which Pattie bet all three children that they couldn't run to a marker before she caught them, which made the whole trio of children squeal with joy when a bare-footed Pattie gave chase across the grass.

Sukie couldn't tear her eyes away. To her it seemed unusual, but very nice all the same, that a family – and they did look like a family, even though Pattie and William weren't married – could play together in this unabashed manner.

Sukie noticed too the way that every minute or so, either William or Pattie would catch the other's eye and give a small smile or nod of encouragement to the other, and how genuinely and naturally Pattie seemed to enjoy playing with the children. They were all very tactile with one another, and several times they lay in a big heap together.

It seemed so very wholesome, Sukie thought. To anyone who didn't know, Pattie looked like a young mother who loved every moment spent with her children. They all seemed so comfortable together that it looked as if Pattie and William had been in each other's lives for years, if not decades, instead of just a few short months.

Sukie watched then as Tracey Benn escorted Albert over to Pattie and introduced him, and immediately William and Pattie made them welcome, shuffling over and shaking out a spare picnic rug for Tracey Benn and Albert to sit on, not that this lasted long as soon there was a new game of Mr Wolf underway that included the newcomers.

Sukie sighed and inspected her hands. They were a bit rough, with some dry skin and ragged cuticles. Normally Sukie would be proud of the work she did with the mobile canteen and all the washing up that had resulted from this as it was such a good cause, but now she felt miserable.

It was a poor show on her part that she hadn't been anywhere near as welcoming to Albert as Pattie and William had, and nor did she ever look at Simon with anything like the frank cheerfulness with which Pattie stared at William, and he mirrored back to her.

It was as if Pattie and William knew all the best – and the worst – of each other, and that none of that really mattered to them. All that was important was that they were together, and that they all wanted everyone else to feel happy.

As if to rub it in a bit more, Mickey and Philip went over

to the group, and immediately Mickey was given a couple of cushions to sit on while Dot immediately began bossing Philip around, which he enjoyed if his belly laughs were anything to go by.

Sukie wasn't sure what she was feeling, other than that it wasn't very pleasant. She examined her feelings for a while, and decided that jealousy was the most apt description. Some people seemed much better at pulling others into the family fold than she was, that was all there was to it. But it did hurt that she wasn't more skilled in this department as it left her as something of an outsider, she decided.

More broadly, she didn't understand what attracted Pattie to the older William, nor Tracey Benn to the very dull-looking Albert. She couldn't imagine being in their shoes and finding either man the slightest bit attractive. But the ready smiles and quick glances of both Pattie and Tracey Benn at their beaux revealed that each woman was fascinated with the object of her affection.

But maybe attraction was like that – a chemical reaction that was there, or it wasn't, and there were no in-betweens. Certainly, Sukie had always thought that the colour of Wesley's skin, so shocking to many people when they had seen them together, had always been the least interesting thing about him.

She tried to remember exactly how she had felt when she had been with him, and was sad to discover that she couldn't *feel* it anymore when she thought back. She could recall more the belief and memory that being by Wesley's side had made her feel alive and vital, but sadly no longer what it had actually felt like, or the surge in her tummy and chest when he was near. All she could remember for certain was that she had had those feelings, once upon a time, back when she and Wesley seemed to have their whole lives before them. But that feeling seemed a very long time ago now, and Sukie felt she had crossed some sort of Rubicon to a place where she could no longer clearly recall in exquisite detail every plane and curve of Wesley's face.

Sukie looked towards Simon, away in the distance. He was

getting ready to bat in the cricket match, and she saw him drink some cider and then walk to the wicket. Although he was a fair way away, Sukie could tell he was enjoying himself.

There was no denying what a handsome man Simon was. He was tall and athletic, and he walked with a real grace. His good looks were easy on the eye, and his fair hair shone golden in the sunlight.

But the sight of him did not make her catch her breath, or her heart beat even a tinier bit faster.

She turned to stare at the other young women around her, as distractedly she bit off one of her scratchy hangnail pieces of skin.

Nearly all of these women, and quite a few of the older women too, were gawking at Simon with what looked to Sukie to be very much like lust. Any one of them looked as if they wouldn't need much persuading to walk right up to him and slip their arm through his.

Sukie knew that the majority of these women would think her peculiar for not being keener on him than she was.

She remembered the last time they had had sexual intercourse to see if that would ignite a tickle of desire for him in her belly. It didn't. Or rather she remembered looking up at him as he energetically moved above her, and then how she had given a low groan, not of her own excitement but more as a means of hurrying things along to their inevitable end. That hadn't been very fair of her, she knew.

She stared towards William again, and this time saw him slowly running a finger up the back of Pattie's arm from her elbow up to the sleeve of her blouse, and Pattie's slight but (to Sukie) still discernible leaning towards him in response. Pattie simply yearned for William in the physical sense, any fool could see that, Sukie decided.

She sighed again; yes, she was envious of Tracey Benn's tiger games and of the obvious depth of Pattie's commitment, in part as she couldn't imagine herself ever feeling like that about a man again.

Sukie reached for her handbag and drew out her pad of Basildon Bond writing paper. She would divert herself by writing to Evie.

*Dearest Evie,*

*I am writing you this from the midst of our midsummer picnic in Greenwich Park. There are lots of people here, and everyone seems to be having fun.*

*Well, actually I feel a little blue, but I think that may be because I've been working hard getting all of this celebration sorted and I very probably need a nap.*

*I remembered though as I was walking across the park earlier today, those summer revels you organised in Lymbridge all that time ago, when the piglet escaped, and you and Peter had a secret kiss! That was a fun day, wasn't it? Although when I look back on it, we all seem very young! What a lot has happened since then.*

*Nothing so exciting for me here this afternoon as a secret kiss, and so I think I might risk a second lemonade so that I don't feel as if I am too much of a stick in the mud.*

*I have been watching Pattie and William very closely, who also have the children here, and I must say they do seem very happy together, and so I am wondering if they might not be extremely well-suited after all—*

Sukie didn't get a chance to write anything further as, without warning, a clearly tipsy John literally growled at her side.

He must have read the final sentence over Sukie's shoulder as, with a sudden lurch forward and a grunt of temper, he ripped the pad from her hand, tore off the top sheet and then rent the letter to a spray of confetti fragments.

Sukie was horrified, and she glanced quickly around to see if Mr Bright was anywhere near (he wasn't, thankfully, as he was just about to bowl to Simon), while Tracey Benn seemed only to have eyes for Albert, and Pattie and William were teaching the children how to play cat's cradle, with Philip looking like he was picking up the general idea very quickly.

Sukie absolutely didn't want anyone to notice the state John was in, as she felt the fact she had promoted him to work with her directly might be seen as a black mark against her, and her not very exacting skills of reading a person's character, if he was about to wreck the fun of the afternoon.

She stood up and furiously pulled him along with her as she marched away, past the tree under which Mickey was sitting in the shade, along with Raymond from the Pink Sink (who was wearing a very conservative pair of slacks and a shirt), with Polly in his cage beside them, and up towards the observatory a long way above them, right at the top of the hill.

'Whatever has got into you, John?' Sukie snapped when she couldn't see anyone she knew nearby, unable to hide her crossness for a second longer.

'Whaddya mean, Susie, um, Sukie?' John slurred as they panted up the hill, as the incline was steep and he was staggering rather than walking.

Ignoring for the moment the belligerent tone of his words, Sukie dragged him behind some trees so that they were absolutely out of sight of everyone.

'You're drunk, and that is disgraceful,' admonished Sukie, wagging a finger at him. 'This is a family day out and nobody needs to see you acting like a twerp. And that was a *private* letter you had no business reading...'

John hung his head, but it was to no avail for Sukie continued in this vein for quite some time.

'It's time you let bygones be bygones and accepted that Pattie can't forgive you,' said Sukie. 'She's found somebody else, and I'm sure she'd love it if you did too.'

And then John said surprisingly softly, 'It's just too much seeing her playing happy families with that old git, and rubbing my nose in it.'

'John, William's not a git and I don't believe that is what Pattie is doing, and I think deep down you know it isn't true,'

Sukie said, moderating her own voice to match John's. 'You had your chance with Pattie, and you hurt her badly, you must see that. She's had the good fortune to meet somebody else, but even if William wasn't around, do you think that *you* having too much to drink and behaving in this way would be in any way appealing to her, as I really don't. You have to chalk this all up to experience, and let Pattie be, whether you are hurting inside or not. And you have to sober up. Right now.'

John dolefully nodded his head, in what Sukie hoped was agreement.

Then he looked at Sukie and attempted to focus his eyes. 'There was that moment in the Haywain when I thought we might be destined for something, and I thought you felt it too. I don't suppose that now you and I would make a good—'

'Certainly not,' said Sukie briskly. 'I've no idea what time you are thinking of in the Haywain. But in any case we'd be terrible together, and if you still want to go on working at the Eddy, I suggest you button your lip once and for all about any such daft ideas. I do have a young man of my own, remember.'

John opened his mouth and looked around as if to see where Simon was. Then he raised his hands as if to signify, 'I hear what you say but he's not here, is he?'

'Not. Another. Word,' said Sukie, and she scowled at John to show how irritated she was by the whole affair.

Then she surprised herself by slapping the top of his arm in temper, almost as if she wanted to punish John for how her own day felt increasingly tainted with dissatisfaction and frustration. The slap was nothing like the playful tap she had given Padraig earlier, Sukie realised when she felt John quail a little under her hand.

'I'm sorry, John – I think that was a bit more than what I meant it to be,' she said.

John gave a hangdog shrug that seemed to suggest that he felt he had been so out of order that she was within her rights to treat him in this way.

She felt as if she had let herself down, as she really didn't approve of corporal punishment in any form, or any strong-arm tactics, no matter what the circumstances, and certainly not in the workplace. Her fingers tingled slightly with the strength of her blow.

She apologised again, but still John didn't admonish her.

She knew that she would have come down like a ton of bricks on any Eddy she caught acting as she just had. And so, as a form of penance, Sukie then marched John up and down the steep hill for what had to have been an hour, until he had sobered up quite considerably and Sukie had stomped off some of her own bad temper.

She hoped it would look to any of the Eddies, if they noticed what she and John were doing (which she really hoped they didn't), as if they were deep in conversation about something to do with the refurbishment of the Capel.

Whenever Sukie glanced towards those at the jamboree, it didn't seem that anyone thought it odd that she and John were tramping about as they were, and she didn't notice anyone obviously staring at them. She knew she should feel relieved but still she felt irked and out of sorts.

When at last they re-joined the others, and after Sukie had apologised again to John, who seemed to care about the slap much less than she did, she sought out Alan.

As he seemed pretty much sober, thankfully, Sukie said she was sorry for possibly spoiling Alan's day (was she going to spend her whole afternoon apologising to somebody or other? she wondered grumpily), but would he, as a special favour to her, keep an eye on John and make sure he didn't have anything else alcoholic to drink? Alan nodded that he would.

'Buck up, mate, it might never happen,' Sukie heard Alan say to John, and John reply peevishly, 'It already has, pal,' as she headed back to her deck-chair.

Sukie slumped back down again. William and Pattie had disappeared with the children, and Tracey Benn and Albert were nowhere to be seen either. She heard Polly screech happily from somewhere over her shoulder, and so she guessed Polly was having a good time.

Well, at least someone was, thought Sukie.

She looked about her once more, and her spirits rose a little when she saw just what a roaring success the jamboree seemed to be. At any rate she could see lots of smiling faces, and the sound of laughter and happy yells as people played various games.

Over in the distance Sukie could see that Simon was still playing cricket, and she rather thought that he hadn't even noticed her absence.

Sukie blew out a breath through her mouth and thought that as far as she was concerned the afternoon was something of a write-off in terms of how much she was enjoying it, and then she wondered how soon she could make her escape and return to the Eddy. The sun was still high in the sky, and so Sukie knew it would be very bad form if she disappeared quite yet.

There was nothing for it. She moved from the deck-chair to lay down on a rug and closed her eyes, her legs crossed neatly at the ankle. Within a minute she was asleep.

# Chapter Twenty-two

A nap worked wonders and when Sukie roused fifteen minutes later she felt her normal sense of equilibrium restored.

She got up and began to mingle, and after a while she was enjoying herself.

Everything progressed as Sukie had hoped over the rest of the day and at last the shadows began to lengthen. Gradually the big gaggle of jamboree-goers started to thin, and Sukie watched as the various Eddies started to tidy everything away in preparation for the homeward journey.

She felt exhausted, but in a nice way, and as if she had no inclination to join in with the going-home preparations, and so she closed her eyes and catnapped.

Eventually Simon found Sukie. He leaned down and kissed her cheek a tad sloppily, and so Sukie thought he might have been enjoying the keg of cider perhaps a little too much.

'That was a long game,' Sukie said.

'Wasn't it?' Simon agreed. 'A belter, in fact, and good averages. And luckily no beamers. A nice cut from Padraig, though.'

It was like Simon was speaking a different language and so Sukie smiled at him to show she was listening but she didn't have a comeback.

He was clutching a paper bag, a bottle of wine stoppered by a cork that had been removed and then pushed back in a little, and two glasses. 'Bring a blanket and let's climb to the top of the hill, Sukie. You're not going to believe how marvellous the view is from up there.'

Sukie didn't have the heart to tell Simon that she had already climbed to the top of that particular hill at least ten times that day, when she had been strong-arming John about in order to sober him up.

Meekly, she folded a blanket that she placed over her arm, and lifted up her handbag and cardie, and Simon's jacket, and they set off up the hill as those still left at the jamboree began tidying things away in the lengthening shadows and getting ready to go home.

It felt a longer way up now than it had done earlier in the day, but at last they got high enough that Simon was happy, and they chose a spot that would allow them to watch the dipping sun, and carefully Sukie spread out the blanket on the ground.

They sat down side by side. Simon ripped open the paper bag to reveal reconstituted egg and cress sandwiches and two rock cakes.

'This is a feast and I'm starving,' Simon announced.

'All that cricket, I expect.'

He laughed and pulled the cork from the bottle, pouring her a glass of wine, and then he filled one for himself.

'To us, Sukie,' he said, and touched his glass to hers.

Sukie's heart stuttered.

The view before them was lovely and the low sunlight almost orange. It was romantic and perfect. But she didn't really want to be there, and she didn't really want to be with Simon in the wider sense, she knew now after a day when she hadn't been able to think of much else.

She'd never been in this position before and she felt put on the spot. To buy some time before she began the difficult conversation she knew was coming, she touched her glass to his, and asked, 'How do you think today has gone, the picnic and activities, I mean, and not the cricket?'

For a while they ate the food as they chatted more normally than Sukie thought they would, talking about all the activities that had been going on around them and how much everyone seemed to have enjoyed themselves.

'The cricket match was top hole, Sukie, and very hotly contested,' Simon said. 'Did you see my innings?'

'Well, probably with not enough attention, I confess,' she told him. 'In fact, while you were at the crease I had a bit of a situation to deal with concerning John, who had a bit too much to drink and then he came over all maudlin at seeing Pattie and William together. It was very sad. They have both hurt each other, and it must be difficult for him now seeing Pattie with somebody else.'

Sukie fell silent.

Simon took a chug of wine and put his arms around his knees as he stared at the view. He lit a cigarette and inhaled deeply. Sukie thought how dashing he looked at that moment.

'Simon?' Sukie said after a while. 'I think you are a wonderful, handsome, amazing man, and that any girl would be proud to have you on their arm.'

He turned to look at her.

'I've tried, I really have, Simon, but I'm just not sure we are terribly well-suited to each other. I enjoy seeing you, but when I look around, I'm not sure I enjoy seeing you in the way that I should. And I think you feel the same way,' said Sukie. 'We could easily go on as we are, and then we'll slip into marriage and children, and in five years we'll be making each other unhappy, and wouldn't we be feeling then we settled for something we shouldn't have?'

Simon poured some wine into Sukie's glass. 'You are so beautiful,' he said, and briefly stroked her cheek, 'and I don't think I deserve you.'

Maybe it was the wine, or the effect of spending hours in the sunshine, but then they spent an hour talking honestly and openly about their feelings, and their hopes and fears, during which time Sukie skirted around the fact that the sexual act between them hadn't quite been all that she expected.

'Sukie, I do want you to know that I have very much enjoyed

making love with you,' Simon told her, and she flushed at him being so forthright. 'But I think there has been something about you and me that has shown me that perhaps I am a bit more inclined towards the Pink Sink side of things than I allowed myself to acknowledge, even privately. I know I'd never act on it, but it has made me think.'

'I thought that was probably the case, but it hasn't made me feel any differently about you, probably as I always felt, I think now, that we were never totally right for each other,' Sukie told him.

Simon filled up their glasses again and they sat by each other in oddly companionable silence.

The sun began to set and they finished the last of the wine. And then Simon pulled out a hip flask and poured them each a generous tot of whisky.

Simon put his arm around her. 'You can do much better than me, Sukie.'

She laughed. 'I doubt that. But it would be mean of me to keep you for myself, when we could perhaps both be happier with someone else.'

In the last rays of daylight Simon looked at Sukie. 'You are beautiful, Sukie, you truly are.'

'And you are too, Simon.'

It was true; to Sukie it looked in that moment as if she had an Adonis beside her. An Adonis she felt totally comfortable with, but one she could easily leave without regret.

Tipsy now, Sukie laid her forehead against Simon's. Then, slowly and deliciously deliberately, they were reaching for each other, the last moments of sunlight reflected in their eyes.

The emotion of talking so honestly together felt overwhelming, and they fell backwards, for the first time having a real passion to their kisses, and Sukie reached for the fly of Simon's trousers and he softly lifted up her skirt and pulled her cami-knickers to one side.

And as they lay companionably together afterwards, Sukie for the first time having begun to understand what it was about sexual congress that drove Pattie and Evie wild, they looked up to the heavens. High above them were a series of shooting stars that lit one after another across the starry sky.

'Let's make a wish,' said Sukie, and Simon agreed.

She wished for Simon to be happy and to follow his true inclinations. And then she made her own wish that she be brave enough to follow her own romantic urges, or at the very least be a bit more grown-up about them.

She noticed Simon's face was serious as he made his own wish.

They didn't ask each other what their wishes were, but they smiled at each other as they finished the whisky.

Then, as if sealing an unspoken pact, they kissed again and then they did it a second time, slowly and with a seriousness about it that felt vital and special. And as what felt at first like a series of tiny electric shocks brought her skin alive, before sparking though her whole body, at last Sukie completely understood what she had been missing previously. As she opened her eyes while her body trembled, the shooting stars continued to fire high in the shroud of darkness that domed above them, and Sukie felt blessed that she had experienced this with Simon.

They weren't to be for ever, or even until tomorrow. Yet it was a perfect moment. She was glad she had Simon beside her at that moment, and she felt very safe in his arms.

As they walked down the hill to find the car that Simon had borrowed, Sukie said, 'That was lovely, but I don't want you to think it changes how I feel.'

He kissed her brow. 'It was one of the best feelings I've had. But you're right, that was the last time,' Simon told her.

Sukie stopped walking, and kissed him properly.

It had been a wonderful experience, and already she could hardly believe that she, Sukie Scott, had been so overtaken by desire that at the time she hadn't cared a jot if anyone had caught her and Simon. Well, maybe if that person was Mr Bright, but only him.

Best of all, she understood that the whole evening had been a complicated way of her and Simon saying farewell to each other, and that there had been something so final about the whole experience that had certainly told them both that it would be the final time they would lie together like that.

Sukie smiled into the darkness as she sat beside Simon as he turned the car around.

He reached for her hand and brought it to his lips, and Sukie smiled again.

She felt as if her wish for womanhood was happening, slowly unfurling around her. And, more thrillingly, as if she was truly ready for the next chapter of her life.

# Chapter Twenty-three

The next morning Sukie felt surprisingly cheerful. This was in spite of her embarrassment that she had been so overtaken by lust that she had behaved in such a wanton manner with Simon out in the open air high on the hill in Greenwich Park.

But actually the more she thought about it, the more she realised that she didn't feel *that* embarrassed. Sukie assured herself that it had been a once-in-a-lifetime experience and that she would never dare to do such a thing again, and so she should just put it behind her and chalk it up to experience.

Pattie was getting dressed when Sukie sat up in bed.

'Simon and I ended things between us last night,' she told her friend.

Pattie stopped with one shoe on and the other only half on, her hair flopping comically across her face. 'Gracious! What brought that on? You seemed so good together that I thought it might be for keeps with you two. You don't look it, I must say, but *are* you feeling upset?'

'No, I'm not upset at all, although I probably should be. I feel relieved, actually, as I think I'd been worrying about it, but without knowing that I was, if you know what I mean, although I hadn't felt as if I was thinking about Simon and me much. If you want to know, I think seeing you and William together yesterday was the clinching factor, as when I watched how all the while you and he were playing with the little ones you kept smiling at each other, it made up my mind for me. That's the kind of relationship I want to have, and I realised that I was never going to get that with Simon. We do like each other quite a lot but we just don't have what you and William have,' said Sukie.

'I found it a difficult subject to raise with him at first, especially as the sunset was incredibly lovely and of course Simon looked very handsome and manly, and I almost felt a fool for being such a dolt when he seems so perfect. Oddly – or maybe not – once I took the plunge and we began opening up to each other, Simon agreed he felt the same not-quite-sure way about me, which gave me a pang, but only a tiny one – I think it was more that my pride was dented rather than anything much to do with him!

'And the fact we were then talking to each other in a way we hadn't before seemed to loosen something between us, and so we had a nice time finishing a bottle of wine and then drinking some whisky. And after that we had a cuddle and then one thing led to another at the top of the hill, and, um, you can guess what happened next.'

Pattie gasped, her eyes round with shock, as ordinarily Sukie was so well-behaved.

Sukie took no notice. 'And for me it was the first time I'd, well, you *know* ... I think the fact I knew we weren't going to do it ever again rather broke down my inhibitions, which was a surprise to me, although I'm not sure Simon noticed anything different particularly.'

Pattie kicked off her shoes and climbed into bed with Sukie. 'Let them wait downstairs for five minutes for me to go on duty. This is much more exciting! Really, the very first time for you? Now, go through it all again. Slowly, mind.'

And so Sukie did.

As she talked to Pattie, Sukie realised that she would always feel grateful towards Simon.

'When I look back on this time from the future, Pattie, I think I'll be glad that I met Simon. We weren't right for each other,

220

but I suppose he was pretty perfect as a bridge between Wesley and – if I'm lucky – another man I can really love,' said Sukie.

'You will meet somebody, Sukie, of that I'm sure,' Pattie said. 'And Simon had a lot going for him – he's kind and considerate, and I think he was a very safe option, for a while at least.'

'I don't know why Simon and me didn't work better together. If I were to write down everything about him that I liked, he would seem damn nigh on perfect,' sighed Sukie. 'It was just that I was never excited at the idea of seeing him, although I almost always had a pleasant enough time when I did. And, taking last night out of the equation, when we went to bed I always felt somewhat take-it-or-leave-it.'

Pattie laid her head on Sukie's shoulder. 'Well, "pleasant" isn't a ringing endorsement, is it? Or take-it-or-leave-it, come to that. You're very lovely and hardly an old maid, Sukie, and you deserve to feel the collywobbles at the mere thought of your lover. When I met William, he gave me the heebie-jeebies – it wasn't always nice as I was terrified and full of the jitters that he wouldn't feel the same about me, but then when I got used to him, I saw that even if everyone told me I was making a huge mistake, I wouldn't listen for a moment. I felt alive with William at my side in a way that made me want to be with him, come hell or high water.'

Sukie laughed and said, 'It's lucky for you then that he's not a wrong 'un.'

'So last night was pretty special then?' said Pattie with a naughty look in her eye, and she had to duck very quickly when a laughing Sukie threw Polly's paper bag of peanuts in their shells at her.

Sukie had a remarkably similar conversation with Tracey Benn later that morning, with Tracey Benn adding that it was a shame as Simon was so eligible, but that once Sukie had realised exactly how she felt, which sounded at best lukewarm, it was best to nip it all in the bud, as it was easy to slip into a routine that wasn't really right but which would be much harder to escape from later down the road.

'Now that I've got your attention,' Sukie changed the subject, 'I think you've been very sly about you and Albert... How long has that been going on?'

'A lady never tells!'

Sukie laughed at the uncharacteristically prim tone in Tracey Benn's voice, before adding, 'Just as well you're not a lady then!'

'Suffice to say, a man who knows his way around the engine of an Austin Seven in the way that Albert does, is not to be trifled with. He knows even more about a woman's body than he does about engines,' Tracey Benn said playfully after a while.

Unable to drive the image of the stuffy-looking Albert from her mind, Sukie found that a difficult statement to believe. But Tracey Benn's glowing skin, bright eyes and shiny hair all pointed towards a woman who was currently very happy with her body and whatever her lover might be doing with it.

And the more Tracey Benn spoke about Albert, the more she warmed to her subject, to the point that she appeared poised to give Sukie some very salacious details as to precisely what her and Albert's tiger games might be, making Sukie imagine some things to do with Albert that she thought she might find immensely hard to unimagine.

Thankfully, at that moment Sukie was called away by Padraig to make a decision about something to do with the hand-basin taps in the second-best bedrooms at the Capel.

This was a relief to be sure, as Sukie definitely did not want to know too much more about how the tiger had been let out of his cage in the first place, she told herself a trifle prudishly as she stared at the taps Padraig was showing her.

She was pleased at how many of the old taps from the Capel were perfectly serviceable for their purposes, and that Padraig was going to make sure that the others would be donated to deserving people who were rebuilding their homes after being hit by bombs.

She needed a bit more time to get used to Tracey Benn being

attracted to such an ordinary man, she supposed, but she doubted she'd ever quite understand what it was about the other one in that particular pairing that had drawn them together.

'You're very distracted today,' said Padraig. 'Unusually so for you, I'd say.'

'Do you think so?' Sukie felt a little flattered that he noticed how she was ordinarily. 'In fact, you saved me from hearing in a bit *too* much details about Tracey Benn's tiger games with Albert.'

Sukie felt herself blushing, and the more she tried to stop it, the hotter and pinker she got, causing her to wave a hand furiously in front of her face. Padraig laughed, and again Sukie noticed the way his eyes wrinkled pleasantly at the sides when he did this.

'That would do it. Make you distracted, I mean,' said Padraig, and Sukie had to hoot at the jokily grim timbre of his words and the funny way he'd raised his eyebrows at her.

It was perhaps a little step into the too-familiar for the both of them, and so immediately they had become serious again, the taps seemed to demand a bit more of their concentration after that than they had previously. The result was that it was several minutes later before Sukie dared to venture, 'I was a bit surprised to see that you didn't bring your wife or your young lady yesterday, Padraig.'

'Me?' Padraig sounded deliberately casual. 'Oh, I'm married to my work, and so don't have anyone. And of course I wanted to make sure my reprobate crew remained in order, so I knew I'd be busy.'

Sukie knew this wasn't at all the case as Padraig's workers were all very sober and sensible.

He kneeled on the ground and checked the tightness of a couple of what Sukie thought might be valves on the pipes with his wrench. 'I saw you, though, with your young man. You make a very handsome couple,' Sukie thought she heard Padraig mumble from somewhere beneath the hand basin.

'Oh, did we?' Sukie felt caught on the hop rather. And then

she said in a voice that matched Padraig's casualness, 'It was nothing serious, more friends than anything. In fact, Simon and I decided to end things last night.'

'Ah.'

Sukie's ears throbbed with the intensity of the ensuing silence, and then when Padraig told her there should be a delivery of copper piping later in the morning, she threw herself into being very interested in the delivery arrival and the best place to store the pipes.

'Sukie, I don't have the words to say how sorry I am over yesterday, and I'm sure you were furious with me. If it helps, I've a bruise on my arm and my legs ache from being marched up and down that damned hill like one of the Duke of York's ten thousand men.'

John was clearly most contrite over his drunken antics of the day before when Sukie finally caught up with him later in the morning, but by then she felt even more in a breezy good humour, and so at first she brushed aside his words of apology with 'another day, another dollar'.

John and Sukie stared at each other, John with a slightly bemused look on his face, as he had obviously expected the dressing-down of his life, and then solemnly they shook hands on not talking about it again on the understanding no similar incident happened in the future.

She was struck by how subdued and ashamed of his behaviour he looked, and so Sukie really hoped he'd stick to their bargain as she liked him and didn't want to give him the push from working with her.

'I'm only going to say this once, but you know we absolutely cannot carry a dead weight or someone who is unpredictable and risks upsetting everyone, don't you, John?' John nodded grimly. Sukie went on, 'So you have had the one chance you can get in this respect, and if anything similar happens again, it would be a shame but you will have to go immediately. Do you understand?'

'I would expect no less,' he said. 'I'm a fool, but hopefully a wiser one now. I'm going to give the grog a rest for a while, and I'm going to try to wish Pattie well.'

'I think both of those decisions are sensible,' said Sukie, and with that she very noticeably changed the subject. 'Now, where are we with the wallpapering on the third floor?'

And John looked a little less hangdog as he replied with his usual efficiency, 'It's all in hand and they are doing a good job, and not needing in general that extra roll of paper we allocated per room.'

Sukie was relieved that none of the other Eddies seemed to have noticed John's bad behaviour, and Alan was a discreet chap so she didn't think he would breathe a word.

And as she had proved to herself with Simon, one couldn't make oneself have feelings if they weren't there, and if Pattie didn't want to be with John, then that had to be the end of the matter. Sukie was sure that John would get over Pattie in time, although she very much hoped that this would happen in the very near future.

Sukie couldn't dwell on John for too long, though, as she had other Eddies to think about.

Aside from some sunburn and the odd hangover from the younger contingent, Sukie noticed that both Mrs Bridge and Mr Bright were plain tuckered out after the exertions of the previous day, and so Sukie made sure they could have the afternoon off to recuperate.

Even Polly was weary, and spent most of the day with his eyes firmly shut and his beak tucked over the top of a wing so that he didn't have to hold his head up.

Bernie the St Bernard was equally done in, and so his owner allowed him to curl up on a square of carpet beneath Polly's perch, and the pair of them snoozed the day away beside Pattie on reception at the Eddy, Polly's high-pitched snores punctuating the rumble of Bernie's deeper ones, much to the amusement of the guests who were checking in and out.

*

At teatime, there was a tap on the office door, and Mickey walked in. He had a favour to ask of Sukie.

On the way home Philip had whispered to Mickey that he had something he longed to do. It was to see the sea, which he had never done.

Mickey was wondering if Sukie might be able to help.

'I wouldn't ask but 'e's a grand wee chap, an' 'e deserves summat nice,' said Mickey.

'He certainly is a grand wee chap. Leave it with me,' said Sukie, and she picked up the telephone receiver to get things moving.

# Chapter Twenty-four

As usual, Tracey Benn was the obvious place to start as she was always full of ideas, and so once she had answered Sukie's summons to the office, Tracey Benn then had a word with Albert, and soon the cronkiest of the converted ambulances was offered to Sukie for a trip to the seaside.

It was used to teach volunteers to drive in, and was heavy to manhandle and temperamental to change gears in. But it had a huge advantage as it was big enough to take a wheelchair for Philip, as well as several other people travelling in the back, and Sukie thought it the perfect solution.

She and Tracey Benn studied old maps that belonged to the Eddy of both Kent and Essex, and they decided on Whitstable as the best bet. It wasn't too far – which was a strong factor in its favour in terms of petrol consumption, and also because Sukie felt nervous about contemplating a very long drive – and the Old Kent Road meant there was an easy and straightforward route out of London, while the terrain of the town itself was very flat. Tracey Benn knew it quite well, and promised that although the beach wasn't sandy it would be a perfect place for Philip to go into the sea as the water was nearly always calm, and the distance from where the beach started to where the waves lapped at it wasn't too great.

Padraig offered to come too so that he could map-read. And, he said, if they went for a walk, if Sukie were tired after hauling the heavy old ambulance around (she insisted that she should drive, even though Padraig offered), and Mickey didn't quite feel up to pushing the very sturdy wheelchair far, then at least Padraig could make sure that Philip had a good blow in the sea air.

It wasn't long before Alan admitted that he had never been to the seaside either, and so Sukie said he could come along too on the jaunt. And for politeness' sake, she asked Mr Bright if he fancied it as well, and although she had assumed that he would decline, he replied that it was a topping idea and he'd very much like to accept Sukie's kind offer.

'You'll come, won't you, Pattie, and William and the kiddies? There'll be a picnic and lots of towels and cushions. And I've got to have someone sane to help me keep Alan and Mr Bright in order, and help with Mickey and Philip to make sure that they get a good view of the water, as it might not be easy with Philip so immobile and with Mickey having such little legs,' said Sukie.

Pattie roared. 'Trust you to try and please everyone, Sukie. A small boy wants to see the sea, and suddenly it's shaping up for a rum do, with a motley crew of waifs and strays. I'd have thought that Padraig was pretty sound in the keeping-everyone-in-line department though...'

'He's going to be far too busy reading the map.' Sukie then quickly changed the subject by declaring that she had itchy feet for the seaside too, and Pattie nodded her agreement.

Lymbridge wasn't too far from the coast and everyone who lived there had very happy memories of spending days swimming in the sea and messing around in rock pools. Before the war, obviously.

Sukie and Pattie were quiet for a moment as they remembered the many sunny hours they had spent on the beach. 'Happy days,' they said in unison.

The next day, Pattie told Sukie that William liked the idea of bringing the children along and joining Sukie and 'the gang' down in Whitstable, if that was all right with Sukie, although if Sukie agreed, then she and William would make their own way there.

Then Tracey Benn said to Sukie that she and Albert would drive the Austin Seven down to Whitstable as well, 'just in case you need some help'.

Privately Sukie thought it was all getting out of hand, and that it was a huge waste of petrol. She didn't mind Alan and Padraig coming, or Mickey, and of course she had asked Pattie, but she could do without everyone else, and in fact she was having second thoughts about Pattie and her entourage.

She suggested that perhaps the petrol rations couldn't be stretched, and was ignored in this by both Tracey Benn and Pattie, who said that everyone had been so good for so long in not using the cars for anything non-essential that the world wasn't going to end if they had a little run out for a day.

Sukie knew when she was beaten and so in mild retaliation Sukie asked Mrs Bridge if she would come too, and told her that Tracey Benn and Albert would love it if she travelled with them in the Austin Seven. She doubted that having the housekeeper with them would be Tracey Benn and Albert's ideal manner of driving down to the coast, but they had invited themselves along and there was no such thing as a free picnic, after all.

John opened his mouth as if to see if he was invited too, but before he could say anything, he was given a long list of things to look after in Sukie's absence. Sukie had prepared the list to circumvent a repeat performance of his drunkenness at the jamboree. As Sukie reiterated, work at the Capel was progressing well, and it wouldn't be too long until the carpets would be put down, and the furniture arranged in all the rooms, and so they were about to be moving into the next stage of the development.

He closed his mouth without saying anything, and read diligently through the list, a small crease between his brows deepening when he saw the many tasks he had been given.

*

The motley group of people set off two days after this, as Sukie dared not leave it much later. She knew that Mickey felt increasingly concerned about how Philip was faring, which wasn't very well by all accounts; and for herself she wanted to crack on with recruiting staff for the Capel, but she wanted to get this out of the way first.

Increasingly, she felt irritated with herself that she had agreed to a whole day out of the Eddy at such a busy time. She'd forgotten her words to Pattie about missing the seaside.

But when Sukie saw how thin and pale little Philip had become and how excited he was by the thought of seeing the sea, she was determined to give him the very best day out, as even to her inexperienced eyes he looked as if he had gone downhill since the hot day in Greenwich Park. And to spend a few hours giving a little boy a time to remember seemed suddenly a very small thing to do, but one that was much more important than scheduling in a load of staff interviews for the various posts that needed filling at the revamped hotel.

She put on a cheerful voice and said, 'Hello Philip! What a brilliant idea of yours about going to the seaside – we are all very much looking forward to it.'

'I'm lookin' forward to it too.'

Sukie had to lean down to hear Philip's faint reply, and she hoped that the quietness of his voice was more to do with feeling shy than not very well.

'Poor little mite, my heart goes out to him,' she said to Mickey in a whisper when she stood up, making sure Philip couldn't hear, and then before they set off she sent Mickey out to see if he could find at the newsagents a new *Hotspur* that the little chap hadn't read.

Bernie seemed to have taken up residence near to Polly, and so while they waited for Mickey to get back, Sukie brought Philip over to the dog so that he could stroke his ears and remind himself how soft they were, which he did with enthusiasm while Pattie and Sukie looked at each other and then smiled sadly as they turned to watch Philip laughing in glee as Polly asked him the inevitable 'Where's the rum?'.

It proved to be a lovely day out for all of them, although Sukie didn't properly relax the whole time they made their way to Whitstable.

She had never driven an ambulance on anything other than short hops across the city, and once they left the bustle of the busy roads in London she was worried about driving jerkily as she didn't want to cause Philip any discomfort. She also fretted about the logistics of what they would do if they broke down, or they couldn't find any public conveniences.

As he was installing Philip and the wheelchair safely in the ambulance, Padraig noticed Sukie's anxious face.

'Don't you worry,' he said. 'I'm sure it will all be fine and run like clockwork. We have a huge picnic that Mrs Bridge has prepared, I'm good with a spanner and engines, and I've checked the spare tyre is serviceable, and Mr Bright knows somebody in Whitstable who says we can use his jakes if we aren't near a public convenience.'

Sukie loosened the tension in her shoulders, but only very slightly at Padraig's reassuring words, and as she drove she found that she began to listen to Mr Bright, who was travelling in the back of the ambulance along with Philip, Mickey and Padraig.

'There once was a little boy called Philip,' Mr Bright began jauntily, 'and he went to the seaside with his very good friend Mickey. And a goldfish.'

The next line was, 'There once was a little boy called Philip and he went to the seaside with his very good friend Mickey. And a goldfish and a ghost!' The third line ended, 'And a goldfish and a ghost and a gumdrop!'

Philip very quickly got the idea that the whole line had to be repeated, and a new word added to the end that began with a 'G'. Soon everyone in the ambulance was shouting out the line and taking it in turns to add a new word. It was quite hard thinking of new words begining with 'G', Sukie thought as they crested Blackheath Common, so perhaps Mr Bright had chosen the best letter.

But everyone else seemed more imaginative than her, and soon there were gates, goats, gibbons, ginger, garlic, Grumpy (from *Snow White and the Seven Dwarfs*), gin, gable, and so on.

Sukie didn't think she had ever heard a child so happy as Philip was as they drove deep into the Kent countryside. Mr Bright sounded very jolly too, and Sukie realised this was a side of the hotel manager she had never seen. He would have made a wonderful father or school teacher, she thought fondly.

Padraig hardly needed to guide her at all, as Sukie had memorised the map so thoroughly, and well before she expected to, they crested a hill and drove down towards the sea.

When they arrived in Whitstable, the Austin Seven was there already, and Sukie could see that Albert and Mrs Bridge were getting on like a house on fire as Tracey Benn looked on with a slightly bemused expression on her face.

William and Pattie were there already too, waiting patiently with the excited children for the highpoint of Philip arriving.

It took a while to get everyone organised and undeniably it was a strange procession that made its way to the sea, first gingerly crossing the foreshore on which rows of unfurled barbed wire had been curled between wooden struts.

Originally this barbed wire had been aimed at slowing Jerry down in the event of an invasion, and was a common feature of virtually all the waterfront locations around the country wherever it was conceivable that a craft might land.

But this deep into the war nobody believed any longer that invasion was imminent, and so it wasn't long before Sukie noticed the occasional strut where local people would lift the wire off its nail so that they could step over and then make their way across the stony shingle to the water's edge.

Sukie and Pattie sat beside each other on the pebbly beach once they had all safely navigated the wire and they watched as everyone else went down to the water for a paddle, Padraig carefully carrying a happily whooping Philip while Dot and the twins trotted alongside him.

Sukie and Pattie were used to the golden sands and the dramatic surf of the South Devon beaches, and so they felt that the North Kent coast didn't compare, although when they saw the way everyone was soon larking about in the gentle waves as they paddled and splashed each other, and the gales of laughter emanating from their very peculiarly composed group of friends, they supposed that if one hadn't grown up near the spectacular beaches that they had, then what was before them was a very good substitute indeed.

The sky was a deep blue and the clear water almost as flat as a millpond, and so it was easy to see why everyone was enjoying themselves in the sunshine.

'I know Kent's had a hard time in the war as Jerry flew over it so often and made free with the bombs, but sitting here on the beach, it's almost as if the war has never been,' said Pattie, and Sukie agreed.

Then Sukie added, 'I suppose that's what being at war does to us all. It all comes to seem normal after a while. I know that these days I hardly see the empty places where houses used to be when I'm driving the mobile canteen. I think I've got used to the piles of rubble, although the other day I saw a wall fall down from a bombed-out house, and then a number of rats ran through the dust and went charging down the road, and that did seem unusual. It was as if the Pied Piper had come to Stepney, when I saw all those little brown things scurrying over one another in their panic.'

'Ugh,' said Pattie. 'Don't think about it, Sukie. This is a perfect summer's day, and so enjoy it as it won't be that long until it's autumn and then winter.'

'Ugh,' echoed Sukie. 'Don't remind me, Pattie.' She wasn't a fan of the cold weather.

The pals lay back and lifted their skirts to just above their knees to catch a little sun, as they listened to the noisy seagulls and enjoyed the feeling of the sun hot on their bodies, with the salty tang of the sea fresh in their noses.

Sukie quickly fell asleep as hauling the heavy and stiff steering of the ambulance this way and that had rather tuckered her out. The faithful old ambulance had shuddered on the hills, both up and down, and there had been some moments when it had taken several attempts for Sukie to get it into gear.

When she awoke it was a while later, and the sun had moved quite a way across the sky. Sukie realised that she must have been in a very deep sleep as now everyone was dotted on picnic rugs alongside her, and Mrs Bridge had propped an open umbrella, its handle weighted down with a couple of large stones, in a way so that Sukie's face was in the shade.

Padraig and Albert had lugged the picnic hampers down from the ambulance, and Sukie thought that the salted hard-boiled egg and a slice of bread and butter that was soon passed to her had never tasted so good.

She was pleased to note that the fresh air had perked little Philip up no end, and he was clearly enjoying playing with William's children.

Sukie looked around.

Mr Bright and Alan had large white cotton hankies over their heads, each corner neatly knotted, and their feet were bare and their trousers were still rolled up to the knee, as they were intently studying the racing form together. Padraig had Philip leaning against him so that Philip could sit up easily alongside Dot and the twins and play with them on their level. And with the children thus occupied, it meant that William and Pattie could have a little rest, and so they were lying on their backs with their eyes closed. And Mrs Bridge and Albert and Tracey Benn were still chatting away happily, with Mickey sitting with them.

When he saw her looking at him, Mickey smiled and tipped the brim of the ancient Panama hat he was wearing in Sukie's direction as a thank you.

Sukie gave a tiny wave of acknowledgment back, and after

a second boiled egg and a slice of Victoria sponge, and a glass of Mrs Bridge's special elderflower cordial, she lay back down in the sun again.

Right at that moment, all was good with the world, the upturned corners of her mouth seemed to say.

# Chapter Twenty-five

As work at the Capel neared completion Sukie became busier than ever, and over the coming weeks she spent hours with John as they checked and then re-checked everything at the Capel had been finished to her satisfaction.

Sukie took nearly a whole week supervising the placement of each and every stick of furniture in each freshly decorated and carpeted bedroom, and then she oversaw the stocking of the linen cupboards.

Pattie had been a chambermaid at the Eddy as her first job, and so to save Mrs Bridge's legs, Mavis was installed behind reception at the Eddy, which left Pattie free to be brought over to the Capel to supervise the washing of all the crockery and cutlery, and to check that all the bed linen and towels, and the tablecloths and napkins, passed muster. Sukie told Pattie too that after she interviewed the new chambermaids, of the ones that Sukie liked, Pattie was to give each one a test bedroom to clean and make up, in order to check that they knew what they were about.

Once all the upper floors had been completed, and the kitchen refurbishment too, it was time for the dining room and the function room to be redecorated and re-carpeted, and the bar totally made over from scratch. At this point Mrs Bridge and Chef came in to supervise how the kitchen equipment should be placed on shelves and in cupboards.

It was a lot of very hard work, and Sukie grew sick and tired of traipsing up and down the stairs, as until all the redecoration was finished the lift was out of bounds, with all its mechanisms carefully covered to make sure that no dust got into its rather temperamental workings, and so there was nothing for it but to run up and down the many staircases.

Padraig proved a boon in this period. He was calm, and pretty much always jovial, and Sukie realised that she always felt more cheerful after she had seen him.

She took to thinking up things she could talk to him about, once even deliberately avoiding him all day so that when she did allow him to find her late in the afternoon, she was able to suggest they share a glass of beer in the kitchen. Handily, she had stashed a couple of bottles of Mackeson there earlier, hidden in a wooden tea chest.

'Would you mind if we ran over the schedule once more?' Sukie asked as she leaned down to pick a bit of lint from her skirt, as the sounds of his workmen packing up and them troop-ing out of the door gradually began to quieten. 'Perhaps we can do it in the quiet downstairs.'

'Oh.' He sounded a bit more surprised than Sukie would have hoped for, especially as the room they were currently standing in was utterly silent, but he followed her down to the kitchen obligingly enough, and then looked at her with an appraising glance as she went over timings and figures they had already discussed earlier in the week.

'Sukie, was there something else you wanted to—' His words were interrupted by his foreman shouting down the stairs, 'Boss. Boss! There's a second delivery of those khazis for the staff floor that 'ave arrived an' yer needed ter sign, or send 'em...'

Padraig gulped the last of his stout, put the glass in the sink and, with an apologetic look at Sukie, went upstairs to check why they had had a second delivery of the toilet bowls they had already received.

Sukie lost her nerve, poured her own drink down the sink and snuck out of the kitchen the back way.

She wasn't certain why she felt more than a little miffed at her and Padraig being interrupted, but later in bed she had to laugh to herself when she thought of it being the staff lavatories that had been the culprit that had broken into their tête-à-tête.

A day or two later, Sukie was called into Mr Bright's office.

'Miss Scott, I hope you are going to be as pleased about this as Miss Benn and myself are,' said Mr Bright.

But before Sukie could enquire what he meant, Tracey Benn pushed across the desk towards Sukie a new name badge. 'Director of Hotel Operations' it announced proudly.

'We needed to promote somebody at the consortium,' said Tracey Benn with a straight face, 'and we racked our brains as to who that might be. In the end, we thought we'd have to make do with you!'

Sukie gave a little frown as she absorbed her friend's words.

'Really? Are you serious? Me? A promotion?' squeaked Sukie as she finally understood the gist of what was being said and Tracey Benn nudged some paperwork towards her.

Sukie's heart surged with pleasure.

'I'm so excited, I can't see where to sign,' she said.

'On the dotted line, right alongside where it says: "Sukie Scott, Junior Partner at Benn and Partners",' said Tracey Benn.

The three of them toasted Sukie's promotion with a small tot of brandy each, and it made every fibre of her body glow with satisfaction and happiness.

But this heady feeling lasted only briefly as Sukie reminded herself to keep her feet on the ground and that she must show Mr Bright and Tracey Benn that their confidence in her was not misplaced. There was still an awful lot to be done with both hotels, and once the hotels were ready for business following their upgrades, then the really hard work would begin. Such as making sure that both hotels had near full occupancy. And were each turning a healthy profit.

This final stage was going to be very taxing indeed, Sukie knew, but as she pinned on her new title badge, she was ready for the challenge.

One night not long afterwards, just as she wearily climbed the Eddy's stairs to the staff floor on her way for a longed-for early night, Sukie realised that it felt as if the jamboree and the Whitstable outing had been years ago, rather than a matter of weeks, or might it even be a couple of months now?

Her legs and shoulders ached, her hair badly needed a trim and she felt very tired.

She was in need of an overhaul herself, Sukie thought. She had clothing coupons saved, and she had been meaning for months to treat herself to a new utility suit for work. When she had time to leave the hotels, and go shopping, of course – which didn't look as if it were likely to be any time soon.

Sukie stopped to look out of a window that was at the stair return that led to their floor, and the dusky long shadows announced the nights were drawing in.

This could only mean one thing: autumn was just around the corner.

For an instant Sukie fancied she could smell the distinctive scent of fallen leaves being burned and chestnuts roasting.

She breathed in again, but it had vanished.

'Sukie,' she heard Pattie cry from somewhere below her. 'Sukie? SUKIE!'

'Shh, Pattie,' hissed Sukie, a little grumpily as she knew this, whatever it was, would mean a delay for her being able to fall into bed. 'Why ever are you making such a racket?'

'Come to the kitchen, *please*. I have news.'

Absolutely the last thing Sukie felt like doing at that moment was to head back down to the kitchen again. She'd spent all day dealing with people and had been looking forward to an hour or two of blissful quiet as she snuggled in bed with a good book.

She looked wistfully towards her and Pattie's bedroom door, but at the sound of another insistent 'Sukie!' from Pattie, reluctantly she then turned around to plod back to the kitchen again.

There she found quite a group standing around the kitchen table, on which was a tray of champagne saucers and two bottles of chilled champagne, so cold that Sukie could see the condensation on the sides of the dark, thick glass of the bottles.

Among those there were Mr Bright, and Mrs Bridge, and Alan, and Mavis, and several chambermaids and waitresses. Tracey Benn was opening one of the bottles of champagne in a very professional manner, as William and Pattie stood hand in hand beside her with matching broad, slightly coy grins on their faces.

Sukie realised at once what must have happened, but she let Pattie break the news as a filled champagne saucer was pressed into her hand.

'You'll never guess, Sukie!' squeaked Pattie. 'William has asked me to marry him, and I've said yes. But before he did that, William telephoned Father to ask for my hand, and Father gave his blessing!'

'Congratulations and well done!' said Sukie, and raised her glass to toast the happy couple.

She doubted that William would have been welcomed into the Yeo family fold with quite the enthusiasm Pattie was suggesting, but she was pleased for them all the same as although initially she had had some doubts, after what she had seen at the jamboree she was increasingly certain that they were well-suited.

Sukie peeked at the kitchen clock, and decided that as it was only eight-thirty it wasn't too late for her to telephone Evie. She wanted very much to see what her friend thought about the whole shebang, and to find out how the news had gone down at Bluebells.

Unobtrusively Sukie slid her unfinished champagne back on to the kitchen table, and blowing Pattie a kiss and then miming sleepiness by putting her palms flat together and lifting them to her cheek, she slipped out of the kitchen as excitedly Pattie turned to speak to the other Eddies.

As Sukie headed to the office she passed John on the stairs, and she was just about to fill him in on what had happened when he said, 'It's okay. Alan's told me. I'm on my best behaviour and so I'm just going to go and wish them well. And that's all I'm going to say to them, so don't you go worrying.'

Sukie patted his arm, and then watched with a slight frown as John went down the stairs away from her, as she tried to gauge his mood.

But he hadn't sounded upset, and as far as Sukie could tell from the set of his retreating shoulders he didn't look angry and so she didn't think he would make a scene. She hoped he wouldn't, anyway. And frankly, if he did, she felt too tired to police it; she would let someone else have the pleasure.

The telephone in the office was ringing as Sukie went in, and when she picked it up, it was to find Evie on the other end on the line.

'Evie Rose, I was about to call *you*!' said Sukie. 'I can guess what you are ringing about. In fact, I've just this second raised a glass of champagne to toast the happy couple. The celebrations are continuing downstairs as we speak. Pattie and William seem very made up.'

'That's more than Father then.' Evie's voice had a morose undertone.

'Ah. I wondered about that. Pattie made it all sound peachy, of course. How has Susan taken it?'

'Oh, I think she'd bowed to the inevitable, and more or less bossed Father into giving his permission.'

'Well,' said Sukie, 'if it is any comfort, as I know Robert and Susan would in an ideal world have chosen someone more Pattie's age, Pattie and William do seem very happy together. The more I watch them, the happier I think they are. Anyone can see that William is absolutely besotted with her, and the kiddies love her too. And William himself seems a very solid sort of chap and so I'm sure he'll try hard to make Pattie content.'

'I think Mother feels that Pattie could be bringing up three children of somebody else's if anything happens to William. And if they have children themselves, he'll be an old man by the time those children get to marrying age,' said Evie in a sombre voice.

'She's right on both counts,' agreed Sukie. 'But Pattie is very joyful and maybe joy is best grabbed with both hands, no matter where it comes from. I think the war has taught us all that.'

Evie said she supposed Sukie was right. 'And of course William has the huge advantage of not being Leonard Bassett,' added Evie in a more reconciled voice. She and Sukie laughed, as they had never understood what Julia, Pattie and Evie's other sister, had seen in the dull-as-ditch-water Leonard.

Still smiling, Sukie then had an idea. 'Evie, what about if we organise Pattie's wedding party as the event that officially opens the Capel? You and Peter, and Robert and Susan, and everyone else, of course, come up here, and we can put you all up – as our guests, of course – at the Capel. I'll have to check with everyone, of course – by this I mean Tracey Benn and Mr Bright, as there will be a financial implication – and not least the blissful couple, but I can't see anyone saying no. What do you think about that? Would you all come to London if we work out a way of getting you all here? Do say yes, Evie, as that would be a lovely way of giving them a send-off, and also properly marking the next stage of the Capel's reincarnation.'

And so the friends fell to planning and scheming, and once Sukie had replaced the receiver on top of the telephone base, she nipped downstairs again, this time with much more energy. She was keen to run her idea as soon as possible past Tracey Benn and Mr Bright, who agreed instantly, casually waiving aside Sukie's offer that she should pay herself for all the Yeos to stay at the Capel, which on the way downstairs Sukie decided that she could spring for herself, and this was how she presented the idea to her fellow Benn and Partners directors.

She had now saved quite a bit of money through having her higher wages, and already having been paid two of her bonuses for hitting her agreed targets in the hotel refurbishment, and she would have been happy to spend her savings in this way, although she was pleased when it was obvious that a financial sacrifice on her part wouldn't be required.

Pattie and William were delighted with Sukie's proposal when she raised it with them just before William headed home to relieve the neighbour looking after the children, and actually as she spoke, Sukie realised there was a practical benefit in having the Yeos stay at Benn and Partners' expense.

The Yeos, and also some of the more easy-going and amenable of the long-term guests at the Eddy, could be moved into the Capel, the long-term guests at a vastly reduced daily rate, in order that the staff who would have been recently recruited could practise their new roles in a real-life situation.

It would enable the inevitable teething troubles any new establishment faced to be ironed out, but as the Yeos wouldn't be paying, and the other hotel guests would be getting such a good deal, it was very unlikely these guests would complain about anything.

In fact, Sukie thought they would be thrilled to have such a special role, and she decided that she would tell them all to order odd things on room service and at strange times, and to generally put the staff through their paces in any number of ways they could think of.

Sukie's plan going forward was that after this dummy run of hotel operation, gradually the Capel would be filled up by those currently at the Eddy. The Capel was a larger hotel, and so after the Eddy's guests were installed, then slowly they would start taking in new guests at the proper rate, but only once Sukie and Benn and Partners were confident that everything was as it should be.

Meanwhile, a slightly less extravagant refurbishment would start over back at the Eddy, again with Padraig at the helm of the workmen, with the plan that all that needed doing there would be finished in time for Easter the following year.

This had all been carefully budgeted for in the financial accounts that Tracey Benn and Sukie spent a lot of time looking over and totting up the expenditure. Sukie and Padraig had worked very hard at bringing the project in up until then at high quality but under budget and, so far at least, Sukie was pleased with the way things had gone, especially as they had managed to achieve all of this in a shorter time than Padraig had originally suggested the work would take.

This had given Sukie a little breathing space in terms of time, and it meant she could turn her attention now towards organising what would almost inevitably turn out to be the Wedding of the Year.

# Chapter Twenty-six

Sukie had only been to one wedding before – Evie and Peter's – and so was woefully uncertain as to what the protocol should be, especially as William was a widower. She thought it best not to remind Pattie of this.

But then Pattie said they would be getting married in Islington registry office, and so only a modest reception would be required.

William's sister and her children would be there, naturally, and William's children. And there would be the whole Devon contingent on Pattie's side (so Robert and Susan, Evie and her family, Julia and Leonard Bassett, and James and his girlfriend Jane Cornish), plus Mr and Mrs Smith, and Timmy and Tricia and their children, and Linda and her family. There'd be quite a lot of Eddies, of course, and some of William's colleagues. But that would be it. Oh, and Mickey and Philip. And Padraig and whoever he wanted to bring. Not forgetting Tracey Benn and Albert.

John was not invited, however.

Sukie totted up the numbers and realised that would mean somewhere between forty and fifty people at the reception, and if everyone who needed to be put up at the hotel took up their invitations, then probably about thirty of those would be guests at the Capel.

Sukie wondered if she should have a word with Pattie as to the meaning of the word modest. But then she thought that once there were more than twenty people going to anything, it wasn't that much more difficult to arrange for a turnout of fifty, and meanwhile a substantial number of guests like this would be a pretty good way to test how the Capel was going to handle guests and functions in its new incarnation.

Albert told Sukie he could organise a bus that would take everyone from the Capel to the registry office and back again, and so that was one thing less to worry about.

And when Sukie said she'd arrange for a wedding cake that would be an ordinary sponge, but – as was usual these days – it would be topped by a removable cardboard cover decorated with icing so that it looked like a traditional iced wedding cake, with the cover taken away when the cake was sliced for the guests, Mrs Bridge and Chef almost screamed in horror.

'As if we'd let that happen,' gasped Mrs Bridge. 'Pattie deserves the best we can do.'

'I've a favour or two owing from a couple of my pals,' said Chef, 'who were very pleased over the turkeys at Christmas, and so I might be able to get some icing sugar and marzipan.'

'Not on the black market, I hope,' said Sukie.

Chef and Mrs Bridge knew what Sukie felt about sticking by the rules.

There was a long silence.

'Ask us no questions and we'll tell you no lies,' Chef said eventually.

'And it is for Pattie, after all,' Mrs Bridge added.

It was a strong argument that she couldn't really fault, Sukie consoled herself by thinking later, even if it did flout her belief in not having anything to do with the black market.

She diverted herself by arranging the music with the chaps who had been in Wesley's band, who promised some nice afternoon tunes for everyone to shimmy about to.

Sukie managed to cut a very good deal with a photographer, saying that if he took some lovely pictures and was very reasonably priced, then he would be first in the queue when she needed to get some professional photographs done for events at the

Eddy and the Capel. He said she would have him out on the streets at the price she was offering, but there was a twinkle in his eye and so Sukie decided he was joking.

And Mr Smith pulled a string or two in Whitehall – what an advantage it was that he had a job of influence at the War Office – and this meant that everyone from Devon could travel up and back in a convoy of military vehicles, even though this was technically strictly against the rules, but a blind eye would be turned.

It wouldn't be terribly comfy and they would probably have to rough it on the journey with some serviceman, but the vehicles would be coming to London anyway and returning to the West Country as Plymouth was a strategic part of the country's naval operations, while army personnel were often trained on the rugged terrain of Dartmoor, both of which meant that heavy vehicles were always moving military personnel about. It helped too that dear Mr Smith offered to arrange everything and at no cost to anyone coming up from Lymbridge for the wedding, and so everyone from Lymbridge decided it would be a huge adventure to travel in this way, with Mr and Mrs Smith joining them in the lorries, even though Mr Smith was allocated a petrol ration for coming to London.

Sukie was sure that Mr Smith would have promised something nice for those involved with the vehicles as recompense, but it was good that he had as Robert and Susan, and Linda and her family, certainly didn't have much money for this sort of travel.

'I wonder if I might be permitted to provide the champagne for the wedding breakfast?' Mr Smith added. 'I brought a lot of it before the war – some of it very good – and it is still in the cellar in my London house. I don't want to step on anyone's toes, but it would be my pleasure to have some bottles sent over.'

'I think that might be very acceptable,' said Sukie, 'but first let me check with the happy couple.'

Pattie literally almost fainted with happiness when told of Mr Smith's generous offer.

'I take it that's a yes then?' said Sukie.

Evie and Peter, with Nellie, of course, were the first to arrive, as Sukie had wanted them to make a proper holiday of it, although while in town Peter would be attending some meetings to do with his work.

Mrs Bridge stepped in to look after Nellie one afternoon so that Pattie, Evie and Sukie could go and use some coupons to buy outfits for the big day, and get their hair done.

At a clothing and shoe shop that Tracey Benn recommended, Sukie chose a teal-coloured utility suit that made her feel both smart and business-like.

Tracey Benn had told her that the next time she and Mr Bright went to see the bank manager to discuss the finances of Benn and Partners, Sukie should come too, and so her choice of outfit had to be appropriate for both Pattie's wedding and the visit to the bank manager.

Actually, the suit hadn't been Sukie's first choice, as she had initially picked out a less fashionably cut outfit in a muddy brown.

But before Sukie could hand over her clothing coupons, Tracey Benn breezed into the ladies' outfitters, grabbed the suit from Sukie's hands and held it up for inspection, before declaring, 'Well, if you are trying to look sixty-five and totally washed out, Sukie, then this is perfect.'

Sukie tried to snatch it back, with a slightly grumpy, 'It's very practical. And in a colour that won't show every mark.'

'It's at least two sizes too big and it will swamp you, and the colour is like a swamp too, which is handy if you're going to be rolling around in the mud, but not so much otherwise,' insisted Tracey Benn.

Sukie looked towards Pattie and Evie to back her up, but they were both nodding agreement at Tracey Benn's words.

'You are all infuriating,' announced Sukie, and stalked over to the rail of suits. 'I like clothes with a bit of roomy give in them.'

'As I remember from seeing you trying to climb up into the cab on that day at the Peckham depot when you had your driving assessment. That skirt was particularly loose, if I remember,' said Tracey Benn, and then nimbly reached around Sukie and lifted off the rail an outfit in a bright teal with a very nipped-in waist and tight skirt. 'Give this one a go,' she urged.

Waspishly, Sukie took it, but when she put it on, she admitted that Tracey Benn was right. It fitted snugly, very much so, in fact, and showed off her figure, while its bluey-green made her eyes look of aquamarine hue and deep and mysterious.

When Evie and Pattie saw how wonderful Sukie looked, they begged Tracey Benn to work her magic with them, to which she replied, 'Now you're talking my language, ladies!'

While there were rafts of giggles emanating from the changing room as Evie and Pattie tried on the clothes Tracey Benn picked out for them, Sukie treated herself also to a smart pair of green suede lace-up shoes, with a small heel, that she'd seen on display in the shop window. The soles were wooden but divided across the ball of the foot by something that looked like rubber so that the sole could bend as Sukie walked, but they looked fashionable while still managing to be hardily sturdy.

As she looked at the suit and the shoes, Sukie realised that they were the first clothes she had chosen for herself since coming to London getting on for two years previously, as her clothing coupons had been put towards essentials such as stockings or underwear, and the cardie for Mrs Bridge that Sukie had given to her at Christmas using her own precious clothing coupons to get it.

Sure enough, Tracey Benn helped Evie and Pattie find much more fashionable outfits than they had first been tempted by, and as the three friends stood in line by the cash desk, Tracey Benn dusted her hands together and made herself scarce.

'My job here is done,' was the last thing Sukie heard before the door closed behind her friend with a sharp tinkle of the bell attached to it.

'I've never met anyone like her,' said Evie weakly.

'Nor me,' agreed Sukie.

After they had been to a West End hairdresser, Sukie treated the three of them to afternoon tea at the Ritz.

'Pattie, my wedding present to you,' said Sukie, as they sipped cups of Earl Grey, 'is for Padraig's men to decorate a room of your choice at William's house, or they can do the paintwork outside, whatever you want. It's been difficult to know what to get you, Pattie, when William has a home already that you can just move into' – Evie gave a heartfelt nod of agreement at Sukie's words – 'and so I wondered if perhaps you might want to get a nursery ready? Obviously if you think William would be offended at this idea, and think I was interfering – which is the last thing on my mind – then I can go back to the drawing board as to what your wedding present should be. But I thought it might be nice if you started your married life with something in his house that felt very much as if you had been involved in how it looks. And Padraig and I had a long talk about it, and so he will do whatever you both want.'

'Gracious, that is a big present, and I really hadn't expected anything, as you putting all the work into making sure the day itself runs without a hitch is really more than enough to give us a wonderful send-off,' said Pattie, and then she leaned forward to give Sukie a hug. 'Let me have a word with William about which room to do. I might need to get Dot's approval too, as she has an opinion about everything!'

'I bet Dot does,' said Evie, as she and Sukie exchanged looks as they had talked earlier together about potential problems Pattie might face once she was actually living in William's home with the children. 'While we're on this subject, and please don't be offended, but my advice would be to ease yourself into the family extremely gently, Pattie, to give the children time to get used to you being there all the time. I know they love you and are used to seeing you there, but when they see you every single morning it will be a reminder that their mummy isn't coming back. And they are so very little that it could take a while before they think of you as their new mummy.'

'William says I just need to be myself,' said Pattie. 'But I am under no illusion that it will all be plain sailing.'

'Shall we have a glass of bubbly to celebrate these nuptials?' said Sukie, as she didn't want the happy mood to plunge into something darker. 'Raymond, downstairs in the Pink Sink, suggested we pop down to see him.'

'How exciting,' said Evie. 'I've heard so much about him.'

'You won't be disappointed!' Sukie and Pattie cried as one.

# Chapter Twenty-seven

All the other guests at the Capel seemed to settle in well upon their arrival, and the hotel's staff worked hard to give everybody precisely what they needed at the moment they needed it.

At the first supper that had everyone gathered in the dining room, Sukie, Tracey Benn and Mr Bright stood before them.

Every table had been given a bottle of house champagne, and Sukie had put candles on each table that she had rubbed with pine oil. The scented candles were just in case anyone noticed the tiniest trace of lingering new paint smell, although Mr Bright and Tracey Benn assured her that it was only there if one sniffed really hard, and anyway, after a few nights of the guests smoking their cigarettes, cigars and pipes, any such whiff would be totally erased.

Sukie tapped a teaspoon on a wine glass so that there could be a moment's hush, and then once everyone was quiet she said, 'If you will indulge us, hotel manager Mr Bright would like to interrupt your meal very briefly to say a few words.'

Mr Bright stroked his moustache as he stood up straight.

'It is very good to welcome you here with us tonight so that we can all celebrate this new chapter in the life of the Capel Hotel. And for those of you here from the West Country ready to celebrate Miss Yeo's and Mr Jones's forthcoming wedding celebration and their life together, we especially welcome you to London,' said Mr Bright. 'Let us raise our glasses to phoenixes rising from the ashes, by which I mean the Capel (and certainly not Miss Yeo and Mr Jones in any way), and to new beginnings and happy marriages.'

'New beginnings and happy marriages,' everyone toasted back.

Sukie whispered to Evie a few minutes later, 'I don't know what has come over Mr Bright these days. He's getting to be quite a good public speaker, which nobody could have described him as before.'

'Must be somebody's influence,' Evie whispered back. 'Can't think who, though.'

The only fly in the ointment was that Polly was definitely out of sorts.

Sukie had noticed the odd feather had been pulled out from his chest, and he was off his tucker.

On the morning of the wedding he was nowhere to be found, and Sukie had the icky feeling of apprehension in her stomach that one gets if something goes wrong. It would be a horrible start to Pattie's married life if her wedding day was marked by the end of Polly.

Sukie wondered if Bernie, now a permanent resident in the foyer of the Eddy, might have eaten the parrot.

'Don't be daft,' Padraig told her. 'That lazy lummox would never do that, not when all the guests are saving crusts from the restaurant to slip to him.'

Nellie was climbing all over Bernie at that moment, and he was placidly sitting there, looking very much as if he was trying hard not to nod off. Sukie was inclined to agree with Padraig that Bernie didn't look a likely culprit for causing Polly to go missing.

She and Padraig made a systematic search of the Eddy, and Sukie asked every member of staff to keep an eye out for him, but not to let Pattie know that the parrot was missing, if Pattie were to hove into view.

Sukie didn't think that Pattie coming back to the Eddy was

likely as she had told Evie to make sure Pattie was occupied over in the wedding suite at the Capel, where Pattie had slept, and where Evie was currently acting as her maid of honour, with Susan as wing-woman. Pattie and William would sleep there tonight, with his sister looking after the children back at his house.

But Sukie thought if she didn't tell everyone at the Eddy to keep schtum, then somebody would be bound to unintentionally make Pattie feel sad by mentioning Polly's absence.

The ceremony at the registry office was short but sweet, after which everyone came back to the Capel.

The reception was lovely, and managed to be low-key enough as was appropriate for it being William's second wedding, but cheerful too as it was Pattie's first.

Robert stood up to give a short speech.

'I feel proud to have us all gathered together here. My three daughters – Evie, Julia and, of course, Pattie – are all with us, as is their brother James, and with assorted partners and husbands. I welcome William and his three children into our family fold – and if they are half as happy as Susan and I have been, then they will be very happy indeed. Let's raise a glass to the bride and groom.'

'The bride and groom,' said the room.

And then there was a deafening screech of 'Where's the rum, Mr Bright?' which made everyone hoot with laughter.

Polly swooped across the room and landed on Pattie's shoulder, and then rubbed his head against her cheek.

'That bird's jealous,' Padraig said to Sukie.

'How on earth did he get here?' she wondered out loud but in a very relieved way. 'There're no windows open at the Eddy and there are double doors to reception. And how on earth did Polly know where to go?'

'I suppose that's love for you, as it will always find a way,' said Padraig. 'Polly is going to take it hard when Pattie stops work.'

'He will,' Sukie agreed. 'I'd rather hoped that she would want to stay on. But she's going to leave in the New Year, and then she'll work with William and his charity, and I think she'll have her hands full with those kiddies too.'

'That she will,' said Padraig.

'Hello Sukie,' said a familiar voice.

It was Simon!

She felt flustered. She hadn't been doing anything amiss, but she certainly hadn't expected to see Simon. It was reminiscent of how he had arrived at the jamboree, and she felt wrong-footed as it all felt a bit clumsy that she was discovered by Simon chatting to Padraig for a second time.

'Fancy a beer, mate?' said Padraig in his pleasant way. 'Here, have this seat while I sort one out for you.'

Simon sat down in Padraig's chair, although not before Sukie had noticed him shooting rather a shirty look towards Padraig's back as he headed to the bar, and then a more appreciative look at her smart teal suit that accented all her curves and dips in the right places. Then before Sukie could say anything, Simon glanced at Padraig again before firmly turning his back on the bar as he said to her that Raymond had told him about Pattie getting married, and he'd only dropped in to wish them the best and he wasn't going to stay.

'How are you, Sukie?' he asked then.

'A bit tired, if I'm honest, but very well, thank you,' said Sukie. 'You?'

Simon took a breath as if he was going to ask Sukie something, but Padraig chose that moment to plunk down a tankard of beer in front of him. And then, although Padraig promptly headed off to talk to Mr Bright, it seemed to Sukie a little as if Simon's unexpected arrival had taken the wind out of Padraig's sails rather as he didn't seem to be walking with quite the normal spring in his step.

Simon likewise seemed suddenly to have rather a thwarted air about him, with the result that he and Sukie chatted for a few minutes about this and that, although nothing very much really, and it was only as Sukie watched Simon smile a slightly sad but resolute smile, a little as if he was gracefully acknowledging a soft sense of defeat, and then head over to William and Pattie to offer his congratulations, that she wondered if perhaps a little bit of the reason that he was there was in fact for him to judge whether or not she was missing him. She was pretty certain she hadn't given him that impression.

'Very easy on the eye, I must say,' Evie said in a low voice to Sukie as she slipped into the seat that Simon had just vacated.

Who was Evie talking about? Sukie wondered. But when she followed Evie's eyeline, it was obvious she meant Simon.

'Isn't he?' agreed Sukie, as she watched how readily Simon smiled when he was talking to the newlyweds, and how perfect his white teeth were. 'I think I probably need my head examined as I'll never meet anyone with his good looks. But, although he's never dull, and we enjoy talking to each other, he just doesn't make my heart beat faster.'

'Hmmm,' said Evie. 'Might there be another reason for that?'

Sukie looked at Evie in puzzlement. She had no idea what her friend was talking about.

Evie's 'Sukes, you are hopeless,' didn't help much.

# Chapter Twenty-eight

The next month was another that passed in a blur of activity.

There was a point where both hotels were running with not quite complete staff, which wasn't helped by Pattie and William being on honeymoon with the children in St Leonard's on the South Coast, as Pattie's absence told Sukie how much she had come to rely on her friend. She was going to miss Pattie when she left, although she did rather like having a bedroom to herself for the first time in nearly two years.

Polly was definitely missing sitting beside Pattie on reception at the Eddy as he hardly ever asked where the rum was these days, and so when she went to bed, Sukie took to taking Polly up with her, and then everywhere she went, he being quite happy sitting on her shoulder as she moved about. After a few days she was pleased to see his appetite improve, and that he stopped yanking out his feathers, which was a relief as he'd been getting to look quite moth-eaten.

Pattie and William returned from honeymoon, and so although Sukie had been going to put Pattie on reception at the Capel, for Polly's sake she put Pattie back on the desk at the Eddy as he seemed more settled there, and she used new members of staff over at the Capel's reception.

Sukie designed a questionnaire for guests at the Capel aimed at finding out what they could do better, and she was gratified that very little came up, other than when tea was ordered from the rooms on the uppermost floors, it wasn't always piping hot.

Padraig came up with the solution to this, which was that a large walk-in cupboard on one of those floors be converted to a small kitchenette so that hot beverages could be prepared by the staff much closer to where they needed to go.

He also suggested that Sukie got the firm who had installed the lift to come back and slightly alter how it answered the press of a button from the top floor when a guest summoned it. It was only a small matter, but it made the lift arrive significantly quicker, which Sukie liked.

All in all, Sukie was pleased with how things were going at the Capel, and so she suggested that Mr Bright decamp over there with his office, and then she could crack on properly with the refurbishment at the Eddy.

Her optimistic mood was tempered, though, by two things. The first, and most important, was disturbing news from Mickey. Philip's health had taken a dip, and he was going to have to be sent away permanently if suitable accommodation couldn't be found for him in London. The room he and his grandmother lived in was running with damp and they had to share a bathroom with four other families.

Sukie had become very fond of the little boy, as Mickey brought him over quite often to see Bernie and Polly. So was Mr Bright, who had taken to spending an afternoon a week with him and Padraig (who was needed for carrying purposes as so many places had steps that made hefting the wheelchair about nigh on impossible if it were a day when Philip was in pain and he needed the chair), and the two men enjoyed taking Philip perhaps to the pictures or for an outing to one of the sights of London.

Sukie wondered that Padraig never suggested that she accompany him and Philip on these outings, but he never said anything and so neither did she. In fact, she realised that generally Padraig wasn't talking to her with the same enthusiasm that he had done back in the summer, and she felt a little saddened by this, but she supposed it was inevitable now that they were moving on to the final snagging at the Capel as they simply didn't have so much work-related stuff to discuss.

Pattie was going to stay working until Christmas, it had been decided, and she told Sukie that William collected Philip quite often too, so that he could have an afternoon playing with Dot and the children. 'And Padraig brought Philip over yesterday, and all he could do was play tea parties with Dot, he was so worn out, even though the twins tried to jolly him along. Dot got a bit teary and this upset the twins and Philip too, I think, and then Padraig cheered them all up by reading them a story, but they couldn't stay long as it was obvious that Philip needed an early night.'

'That was nice of Dot and the twins,' said Sukie.

'Isn't it?' Pattie replied.

Philip struggled to rally.

'The poor mite isn't good, isn't good at all,' Pattie said to Sukie one morning a couple of days later. The tone of Pattie's voice told Sukie immediately that it was Philip she was speaking of.

Pattie added, 'William saw him yesterday with the children, and he and I were talking about it this morning, and we wondered if we should do a small early Christmas party for Philip at our house. Padraig was telling us that Mickey said to him that it's looking likely he'll have to go into some sort of nursing home but they'll almost definitely send him to one out of London, that's if they can find one who will take him for free, and I hate the thought of him not having any friends around him or anyone he knows.'

Sukie remembered that a lot of the festive decorations from the Christmas party of the previous year were still in place in the basement of the Eddy. It would be an ideal venue for a children's party, as there had been pictures of Rudolph the Reindeer, and all his friends, and Father Christmas painted on the walls, and it wouldn't matter how much mess was made as Sukie was going to refurb the space anyway once the upper levels had been sorted.

'I know!' Sukie cried. 'Let's do it as a surprise party for Philip, and we can hold it where we had the Christmas party at the Eddy. It's Guy Fawkes next week, and so we could get sparklers to mark that for the other children as nobody can have a bonfire or fireworks in the blackout. But we can make it as much like Christmas as we can for Philip, and I'm sure Mickey will be able to rustle up a number of deserving youngsters from his shelter, and there'll be your three too. And so it will be sort of two children's parties for the price of one! I think we've got some tiny reindeer and Father Christmases that must have been ordered in years ago for some event or other, but never used, and I'm sure we can find a use for those.'

Sukie thought for a moment, before adding, 'I suppose I'd better have a word with Mickey and Padraig as to whether they think this a good idea or not, as I really don't want to make Philip's health worse or do anything he wouldn't enjoy.'

It was also Sukie's way of addressing the second issue, which was that Padraig seemed keen still to keep their conversations on a business-like footing. She was missing their jokey banter.

'I'm sure Philip would love it.' Padraig smiled when Sukie broached the subject. 'Who doesn't love a party, after all?'

It was the first time they had talked about anything not work-related in a while and it felt nice, Sukie thought. 'I'll have a word with Mickey and, provided he thinks it's a good idea, we'll have to put our thinking caps on.'

Mickey did indeed agree that it would cheer Philip up, and so they decided the early Christmas party should be on what had previously been Fireworks Night pre-blackout, in early November, just in case an early placement came up at a nursing home and Philip had to move away.

# Chapter Twenty-nine

Sukie got quite tired of hearing Mr Bright practising his 'Ho ho hos' in the run-up to the party. He was going to be Father Christmas, and had gone to town on his costume, having borrowed it from a theatre in Drury Lane.

Then she remembered Mr Bright at the previous Christmas party. He had only come out of hospital on that day following his head injury when he had been hit by a drunk who had wandered into the foyer of the Eddy from off the street. Although clearly delighted to be ensconced once more in his beloved Eddy, back then poor Mr Bright hadn't been able to do anything other than sit in the bar and drink copious amounts of whisky with Raymond and Mickey, seemingly oblivious to Raymond's shiny silk halterneck evening gown. Sukie remembered laughing when she had seen this. To see a much heartier Mr Bright now, obviously very excited about being Father Christmas, was very heartening.

He'd thrown himself into asking local traders for donations of presents to give to the children, and the Savoy and all the other hotels and hostelries, and had got such a tremendous haul of donated gifts that every evening Sukie would spend quite some time wrapping them up in brown paper, with a coloured dot on the back, to denote whether the gift was suitable for a girl or a boy, and what the rough age of recipient should be.

Mr Bright kept getting the coding wrong, and so Tracey Benn

stepped in to say she would pass him the appropriate presents, as the thought of a ten-year-old boy with a knitted toy in pink wool, or a tiny girl with a 500-piece jigsaw of a train, wasn't to be contemplated.

'Although actually, I think this is what children probably should be given,' Tracey Benn said with a slight challenge in her voice, 'as why shouldn't girls be encouraged to like trains or small boys pink knitted toys?'

She saw Sukie's concerned face as Sukie was imagining immediately the ensuing tears and tantrums. 'But I doubt this is the event to get on that particular soap box,' added Tracey Benn in a conciliatory way, and Sukie gave her a grateful look and mimed wiping her brow.

Padraig built a grotto for Mr Bright – sorry, Father Christmas – to sit in, with Mickey and Tracey Benn being sent off to the costume department of the Drury Lane theatre to be dressed as elves. Pattie was going to organise the queuing for the presents, and so she went to the theatre with Mickey and Tracey Benn, and came back clutching her costume of the Sugar Plum Fairy.

'It's very pink,' said Sukie.

'Pink is Dot's favourite colour,' said Pattie. 'Personally I feel like a pink blancmange in it, but I think she'll be made up.'

'Let's hope so,' said Sukie.

Padraig also made a beautiful sleigh for Philip to sit in and some cut-outs of the reindeer to pull it. The sleigh was a lovely forest green, and Padraig had had one of the more arty of his decorators paint the reindeer. All the reindeer had their names on large luggage labels strung on ribbon around their neck, but Rudolph's name was struck through, and the name Philip written underneath.

'Oh Padraig, that *is* a work of art. It's lovely.' Sukie felt very emotional at the thought of all of the hard work that had gone into the sleigh, and she leaned over to touch the woodwork. She tried to say thank you, but found she couldn't quite get the words out, her throat felt so choked.

'My pleasure,' said Padraig. There was a silence as they both stared at the sleigh.

Then Padraig said, 'Will you be asking your young man to the party?' at exactly the same time as Sukie asked, 'Will you be dressing up?'

'I don't have ...' Sukie blurted out, as Padraig spoke over her with 'A candle is what I'm thinking I'll be!'

'No confusion there then,' mumbled Tracey Benn, who happened to be passing.

Pattie went to town on organising Christmas party games for the children, and all the Eddies practised singing carols. The trusty band of Wesley's friends were coming back to play festive tunes. Sukie had said to them that the party would only be for two hours tops, and it would start at two o'clock in the afternoon, but they said that she wasn't to worry as they were happy to play for as long as they were needed.

The party food was of the jam sandwiches variety, and mince pies. There'd be cocoa or hot milk to drink, and Chef was going to make marshmallows to go on top of the drinks.

Tracey Benn walked into Sukie's office, her arms around a huge teddy bear. 'Don't ask where he came from,' Tracey Benn said, as she jauntily adjusted the bow tie around the bear's neck. 'This is for Philip – I thought it could be a present from all of us. And if he's not well enough to come, then we can have a competition among the children to win it.'

'If we get to having to have a competition,' said Sukie, 'you are organising and running that. It will be mayhem.'

'Ho ho ho,' said Tracey Benn, clearly thinking it would be easy to do.

'Hold that thought,' replied Sukie with a straight face. She knew better what it would mean.

# Chapter Thirty

On the morning of the party, Sukie stood and looked about. It had taken about a week of grabbing a spare hour here and there to get the basement ready for the children's party. It was going to be quite a large affair as any kiddies staying in the hotel had been invited, as well as many Mickey knew from the huge bomb shelter he ran.

Sukie gazed up at the stars hanging from the ceiling alongside reams of tinsel, and the fake Christmas trees, all from the previous year, were rearranged to give more of a sense of it being a festive grotto. It all looked lovely, although more Christmassy than a bonfire night celebration ordinarily would.

Padraig had tirelessly constructed Wendy houses and wigwams, and small tables and chairs. He even made a little train engine for children to take turns playing on, and somehow he had managed to find some unbreakable snow globes for the children to shake so that they could see the snow falling through the water. He'd also placed buckets of sand unobtrusively in a corner, just in case the sparklers got out of hand, and Sukie had strict instructions that they were only to be lit well away from the tinsel and paper chains.

Meanwhile, Sukie had two presents that she wanted to give personally later in the day. One was a child's mouth organ for Philip, and the other was an adult mouth organ for Padraig, as a small thank you for everything that he had done – she remembered him telling her how he had lost his on the very day they had first set eyes on each other. Padraig really had gone above the call of duty to make Philip's party as special as possible, and Sukie thought that if Philip were feeling poorly then Padraig could play for him and maybe teach him a tune or two.

Pattie and Sukie had all the children downstairs in the basement and were walking around with their fingers to their lips to let everyone know they mustn't speak.

'Right,' said Pattie. 'When I give the signal of waving this Union Jack, you must all – quietly! – crouch down on the floor, so that you can all jump up and say, "surprise". Shall we have a practice?'

It took several dummy runs but eventually everyone got the hang of what they must do when Pattie waved the small flag.

'I'm in awe,' joked Sukie. 'But I hope Philip arrives soon, as I can see those jam sandwiches being eyed-up very hungrily.'

'You go and stand guard over the food, and I'll stay here,' said Pattie. Then she said loudly, 'I'm going to give a prize of an extra iced bun to the child I see being stillest and quietest from now...'

This ensured everyone was as quiet as mice, even the little ones, as Padraig carried Philip down the stairs, with William going before them and clumping down the stairs very noisily as he talked in a really loud voice about something to do with Bernie the dog that he needed Philip to help him with in the basement.

Sukie knew that this was to cover up any noise from the children below, but also to give Philip a reason for them to be taking him downstairs.

They turned the corner into the room where everyone was, and there was a huge roar of 'surprise!' and everyone began to clap.

Philip beamed, and Sukie breathed a sigh of relief. She'd been concerned that he'd be overwhelmed by all the fuss. But when he saw the sleigh that Padraig had made him to sit in, he kept making Padraig carry him around it again and again, he was so thrilled to have such a throne. Gently Padraig sat him down on the wooden seat, and then passed Philip the ribbon reins of all the reindeer.

Sukie didn't think she'd ever seen a little boy look so happy.

Pattie seemed to feel likewise, and the friends rested their arms around each other's waists and smiled as they looked on.

'Sukie, William and I have decided something,' said Pattie quietly, and Sukie had to listen very intently against the rising chatter of excited children. 'We're going to offer Philip a home with us, if he wants it. William has talked to Philip's granny, and she agrees it would be good for the little mite as he's too much for her, really, as her own health is failing. And William has seen Philip's doctor, and spoken with Mickey, and this morning we got the okay that everything is suitable. We're going to talk to Philip tomorrow, when all this fuss has died down, and see whether he'd like to come and live with us.'

'Pattie, have you both really thought this through?' Sukie sounded very concerned. 'You know he might not have long, and in that event, it would be very sad for everyone to see, for you and the children, and William too, of course.'

'You're right,' said Pattie. 'But wouldn't it be sadder if we knew that we could help him have a family life, and we didn't do this? Dot and the twins love Philip, and if he were to die, of course they will be sad and very sorry. But William and I have talked about it, and we think that if we tell them that every day we have Philip with us is something wonderful to treasure and that we are all very fortunate that we are in a position to help him, then perhaps this can be a gift to them that will help each of William's children grow into adults who will always want to help those more unfortunate than themselves.'

Sukie was thunderstruck at the selflessness of her friend and her new husband. Tears welled and her throat ached with a huge lump of emotion. She didn't want to cry when there were so many children around. But she was perilously close.

Pattie laughed at Sukie. 'Philip might not want to come,

though. But if he does, can his room be the room you have decorated as our wedding present? We'd thought we'd put him in the parlour so that he can be at the centre of everything, and he can choose exactly how he wants it.'

Sukie hugged Pattie close. 'Of course he'll want to come. And it will be my pleasure to have Padraig get his bedroom ready as soon as he possibly can, and in whatever way Philip decides.'

And then Sukie definitely had to reach for her hanky to wipe her eyes, after which she had to pass it to Pattie because, as usual, Pattie was without her own, just when she needed to sort herself out.

The party was a lively and very noisy affair, and all the Eddies who weren't busy came to help, as did most of the taxi drivers who had ferried the children over from the streets around Mickey's shelter.

A raucous round of carol singing went down a storm, as did the running about the children did to the music of the band.

Everyone ate their fill of jam sandwiches and mince pies, and had their cocoa.

And then with many a 'ho ho ho', the children lined up to go into Santa's Grotto for their presents.

Sukie laughed to see how firmly a very pink Sugar Plum Fairy controlled the queuing children, tapping any impatient ones gently on the hand with her silver wand that had a large star at its tip, saying, 'Santa knows who's naughty, you know. And I don't think you want him to know you are being naughty, do you? If you are very good from now until you get into the grotto, I think he might have forgotten about any naughtiness in the queue.'

Sukie went and sat beside Philip on the sleigh, and said to him, 'I think Santa's got a special present for you, once everyone else has their presents, but to keep you going, I have something from me to you. Don't show it to Padraig yet, though, do you promise, Philip?'

Gravely, Philip promised, and then he took an age to open his present, looking at it from all angles before he undid the twist of paper that was tied around the newspaper wrapping.

He went all bashful when he saw what Sukie had bought him. 'Thank you,' he whispered at last, and he clutched the mouth organ to his chest with both hands and looked up to Sukie with shining eyes as he thanked her a second time.

She had the impression that he hadn't had many presents in his short life, and she pulled him close in a cuddle, and he nuzzled himself against her.

'Happy Christmas, Philip, even if it is a little early. We all love you very much – you do know that, don't you?' Sukie was rewarded by Philip nestling into her a little more closely.

Mr Bright came over after a while and presented Philip with his giant teddy bear from Santa. Sukie stood up so that the teddy could have her seat.

Mr Bright drew up a chair close to Philip and asked him if he wanted to hear a story about when Father Christmas was a little boy. Philip nodded, still clutching the mouth organ in one hand, while with the other he held the arm of the teddy.

'Well, what very few people know is that when Father Christmas was growing up he wasn't called that at all. Can you think what he might have been called?' said Mr Bright.

He craned downwards so that Philip could whisper in his ear.

'No, he wasn't called Reginald, although that would have been a very good name.' Mr Bright and Sukie smiled at each other at the thought of Santa really being called Reginald. Goodness knows where Philip had got that from.

'Rudolf – yes, Rudolf himself (and so we have it on very good authority and we can pretty much be certain it is true) – told me Father Christmas was called Philip when he was young,' said Mr Bright, and Philip laughed. 'And he had a teddy that helped him – who I think might have been called Reginald, now you come to mention it. But the elves, when they saw that there was a teddy in Lapland helping Santa put the presents in the sacks for all the children all over the world instead of themselves, went on strike and refused to get to work brushing the reindeer because they were so upset... It was Christmas Eve and so whatever was going to happen?'

Philip grabbed Mr Bright's hand. He clearly had an idea what Father Christmas should do about the striking elves. Sukie left them at this point, and went to stand at the back of the room.

Tracey Benn had rustled up a lot of sparklers, as she knew how much children loved them, and especially so when they wouldn't have celebrated bonfire night with outside fireworks in a long time.

As Mickey doled out the sparklers, Tracey Benn said, 'Right, anyone who has heard the name Guy Fawkes, put your hand up.' There was a good show of hands. 'It's in memory of a foiled plot to blow up the Houses of Parliament hundreds of years ago. There would have been a huge noise if the plot had worked. Who can yell "bang!" the loudest? Once we have decided that, we can turn the lights off so that the sparklers look very sparkly.'

The shouted bangs were very loud, and Sukie thought she might have a headache later, although a glance towards Philip showed that he wasn't at all disturbed by the din.

Then the lights were dimmed and the sparklers lit, the innocence of the children's excited faces giving Sukie huge hope for the future.

It was such a perfect moment, especially as the band was singing 'Rudolph the Red-Nosed Reindeer', except, of course, their version was 'Philip the Red-Nosed Reindeer'.

The sight of Tracey Benn, dressed as an elf, with the diminutive Mickey at her side in his matching garb and coming up to no higher than Tracey Benn's elbow, as the children clustered around them, should have been comical, but it was too sweet a view for that.

And in the enchanting soft light of the sparklers, Sukie saw Philip in the sleigh cradling the mouth organ and with the huge teddy leaning against him, and a sugar-plum Pattie and William standing alongside, with Dot and the twins standing in a line on the other side of the sleigh, and suddenly Sukie was reminded of the nativity scene.

She felt the lump in her throat again, but she wouldn't give in to it, as she thought if she let out a single tear, it might really open the floodgates.

She noticed Padraig standing nearby watching the children with the sparklers, and so to distract herself, she went over to him, saying, 'I've got something for you, Padraig. It's a small thank you present. You have worked *so* hard and I want you to know how much you, I mean your, er, work, has been appreciated by me, by us all.'

She passed him the carefully wrapped – even if it was only newspaper – gift she had chosen for him.

He said thank you and slowly unwrapped it, opening the paper delicately so that it could be used again.

Padraig stared at the mouth organ, and then looked at Sukie with a strange expression.

He reached a hand into his own pocket and pulled out a neatly wrapped present.

Sukie saw the label said, 'For Sukie, the brightest star guiding us all to our heart's desires.'

Padraig gravely passed it to her.

Sukie couldn't take her eyes off his face. She wasn't used to seeing Padraig look serious like this. He always seemed to have a ready smile, with the skin around his eyes wrinkly in good humour, but right now there was no crinkling going on in the skin around his eyes and his mouth was, uncharacteristically, in a straight line.

Their fingers touched, and Sukie experienced a tiny electric shock.

She realised she had never touched Padraig before.

She felt a shift of something urgent deep within her. For a moment it reminded her of how she had felt when lying on the grass up near the Greenwich observatory after she given in to her own lust and had felt a burst of passion shoot through her as bright and vital as the shooting stars high in the heavens above her on that midsummer's eve. And on this November afternoon she felt an insistent but even more delicious quiver than she had experienced that summer night sweep right through her.

Rattled, she looked down at the present, hoping that Padraig hadn't noticed the tremble of her very fibre.

She unwrapped his gift, taking as much care as he had.

Sukie stood staring at what was in her hand. It was exactly the same mouth organ she had just given Padraig.

'Jinx,' he said.

'Jinx,' Sukie echoed, but in a more quavery voice.

And suddenly she realised what Evie had been driving at at Pattie and William's wedding reception.

Perhaps what – or more precisely, who – she had been waiting for had been under her nose all the time. And now he was standing right before her.

'I forgot to say thank you for the present,' she said after quite a long silence.

It was a lame thing to say, she felt, but right at that moment it was the best she could come up with.

Padraig took a step closer to her.

He leaned forward and whispered softly right into Sukie's ear, 'There might be a forfeit for that.' She noticed his eyes were glittery, with a distinct crinkle about the soft skin at the edges of them.

Sukie put her own mouth near to his ear. 'I'm rather hoping there will be,' she said in a voice so low that he had to stand very close to her in order to be able to make out her words.

They stepped back and stared at each other. It rather seemed as if they had just made a transaction.

Sukie wasn't quite sure of what the transaction might be. It felt something adult and alluring, and Sukie thought back quickly to the wishes made in the bar of the Eddy all those months earlier, on Twelfth Night. The Sukie of back then felt very young and innocent compared to the Sukie of now.

She looked at Padraig. He looked very manly, not in the first flush of youth, certainly, but somebody who hadn't run from the ups and downs of life. There was a certain worldliness about both of them, she felt, and she was grateful for everything 1944 had thrown at her, both good and not so good.

Sukie touched Padraig briefly on the arm, and received the same jolt as previously. He didn't flinch or back away – indeed, he seemed to lean towards her – and this made Sukie think they had just definitely agreed to *something*, and as she started to smile, and Padraig smiled back at her, she realised she was eager to find out what that something might be.

'I think we need to make a wish on our jinx,' one of them said, and the other nodded. And then they linked their little fingers, and it felt to Sukie as if a circle had been completed. It felt as if she was coming home.

And in the flickering light of the sparklers and with her nerve ends across her body popping and fizzing, Sukie hoped very, very much that they were both making exactly the same wish.

# Credits

Kitty Danton and Orion Fiction would like to thank everyone at Orion who worked on the publication of *A Wartime Wish* in the UK, and also agent Cathryn Summerhayes at Curtis Brown.

**Editorial**
Victoria Oundjian
Olivia Barber

**Copy editor**
Laura Gerrard

**Proof reader**
Natalie Braine

**Audio**
Paul Stark
Amber Bates

**Contracts**
Anne Goddard
Paul Bulos
Jake Alderson

**Design**
Rabab Adams
Tomas Almeida
Joanna Ridley

**Editorial Management**
Charlie Panayiotou
Jane Hughes
Alice Davis

**Finance**
Jasdip Nandra
Afeera Ahmed
Elizabeth Beaumont
Sue Baker

**Marketing**
Tanjiah Islam

**Production**
Ruth Sharvell

**Publicity**
Alex Layt

**Sales**
Jen Wilson
Esther Waters

Victoria Laws
Rachael Hum
Ellie Kyrke-Smith
Frances Doyle
Georgina Cutler

**Operations**
Jo Jacobs
Sharon Willis
Lisa Pryde
Lucy Brem